Published in the United States by Feral Cherry Press LLC.

Library of Congress Control Number: 2026905473

ISBNs: 979-8-9947181-2-4 (trade paperback), 979-8-9947181-0-0 (eBook)

Interior art design by Rebekka DeReu, 2026.

Cover art design and illustration by Rebekka DeReu, 2026.

Never Duel a Damsel

The School for Scandalous Women Book One

Rebekka DeReu

Note

The author and the other people who helped bring this novel into existence **did not** use Artificial Intelligence (AI) at any stage in the process.

Content Guidance

Sexual content between consenting individuals. Fatphobia. Foul language. Parental manipulation and gaslighting. Light kidnapping. Brief, non-descriptive mention of retching. Injury without detail.

Dedication

For those who had to be their own rescuers.

And for my husband, the person who helped me realize I could demand more from life.

Prologue

June 7th, 1806

S carlett Halloway, put the sword down! Do you hear me? Your parents will have me dismissed when they hear of this."

"It's a sabre, Miss Melanie, not a sword." A hysterical giggle bubbled from Scarlett's mouth as she sprinted across the lawn in the park.

The wind dragged across the sabre in her hands, making each footfall like slopping in mud. When peering behind her, the strands of her hair freed from their braid whipped across her face.

The boys of the fencing class shouted while running after her, struggling to shake their fists while wrapped in their protective jackets. One, Fitzhenry Neels, tore off his gloves, threw them at her, and slipped on one as he ran over them. His booted feet flew through the air before he hit the ground with an "*oof*!"

Scarlett's governess and the fencing master lagged behind the boys, stopping to apologize to every passerby. Luckily for her, their adult sensibilities were incapable of making a scene out of her theft and subsequent flee.

"Someone stop the girl." Her governess, Miss Melanie, bent over her knees and panted from her strawberry-red freckled face.

For once, Miss Melanie might have been right on matters of decorum. Ladies perhaps should not run for she looked positively dreadful.

Luckily for Scarlett, she was no lady. Not yet, anyway.

A group of gentlemen and young misses down the walkway formed a half circle and marched towards Scarlett. Her slippers raked through the grass as she skidded to a halt. Clutching the sabre in her arms, she whirled around to find a gap between the furious boys, their master, Miss Melanie, the gentlemen in their pristine riding garb, and the ladies in their intricately stitched spencers. There was no opening.

Bending her knees and sliding into a lunge, she pointed the sabre at anyone who dared to take a step towards her.

The fencing master held his empty hands in the air and crept forward. "What is your plan, child? How old are you, ten? It's unsafe for someone of your stature to be running around with a weapon."

"I am eleven."

And he need not remind her of such. She had cried on her birthday that February morning when Miss Melanie wished her felicitations. Why celebrate? It only meant she was one year closer to ladyhood and all of the unwritten rules which came with it.

"Fine," the fencing master conceded. "You are eleven, but you still cannot fence."

"Whyever not?"

"Well, because you are . . . You know what you are." He waved her off, his moustache twitching in time with his fingers.

"A girl?" she offered.

Indignation sparked to life in her puffed chest. *That is the weakest excuse.*

"Precisely. You cannot learn because you are a young lady."

"And you never will because fencing is for men like us." The Langley boy, who was a few years older than Scarlett and much larger, stuck his tongue out and glared at her.

The fencing master's wispy mustache sagged as he scowled. "You can't take lessons, so give Fitzhenry his sabre back."

A pout pasted to his face, the Neels boy stomped his feet and crossed his arms.

Scarlett lunged towards the fencing master. "I know what I'm doing. I've been watching your lessons for weeks now. I've practiced at home with a butter knife."

A gentleman removed his top hat and kneeled before Scarlett's poised weapon. "If you give me the sword, I will buy you a sweet."

"I don't want a sweet, or a glacé, or a new dolly. I want to fence." In a sweeping swipe, Scarlett swatted the hat out of his grasp with the sabre. "If you want the sword, you must fight me for it."

"I don't have time for this. These young men's parents are paying me to teach them to fence, not to chase a silly girl around the park." The instructor stomped towards Scarlett with outstretched arms.

Silly girl? She was not silly. Was she? Her intentions were entirely serious, including when she had issued the challenge to fight anyone for the sabre. If he did not wish to chase, then they must duel. It was the only natural way to resolve this dispute.

Charging at him with her eyes shut, Scarlett wailed and plunged the sabre into his tailcoat fabric.

"She tried to stab me!" The man yanked at his clothing, poking a finger through the new tear.

Scarlett rolled her eyes. *And they say ladies are prone to the dramatics.*

"Come now, a young lady does not act this way. Give us the sword, and we shall invite you for tea." One miss tiptoed from the edges of the circle.

Another followed at her heels, pulling her back by the elbow. "Ava, be careful. She's a wild child."

Wild child? Silly girl? Scarlett's mind raced too quickly to push these names aside. Why should she be considered more ridiculous than the boys who had equally as unrefined skills in the sport? A question better left to be pondered another time when she wasn't surrounded by adversaries.

The miss named Ava shook off her friend. "No, she's harmless. She's no more wild than I was at her age."

As the two ladies stepped Scarlett's way, Miss Melanie crept behind her. Digging the toe of one slipper into the lawn, Scarlett twirled in place, slashing all three women's skirt fabrics in one swift swing. The whites of the petticoats shone under the beating afternoon sun.

As Scarlett turned back around, Miss Melanie caught her by the arm, her fingers squeezing so tight the sabre fell to the ground. Fitzhenry scrambled to pick it up and scurried back to the gaggle of grumbling boys.

Miss Melanie yanked Scarlett to her side. "Apologize to all these people you have terrorized."

Scarlett mumbled her regret to the sky. Her only true regret was not getting a single good blow in. Slashed fabrics weren't worth the ceremonial salute at the end of a fencing match.

"Now let us return home and teach you the manners of a proper young lady. Again." Miss Melanie's voice was laced with irritation.

Tripping over the back of Miss Melanie's ruined skirt every three steps, Scarlett tugged her arm to free it from the woman's grasp as they stumbled through the park. Her jailor refused to release her.

One couple strolling down the flagstone path shook their heads as they passed.

The woman's bonnet shaded her sulking visage. "How

unfair. The girl was only trying to have a spot of fun."

The man tamped the butt of his walking cane into the ground. "What she did was unsafe, May. This is why women are not meant to fence. Your lot is much too emotional for the sport."

Turbulent tears rushed down Scarlett's cheeks and warmed against her skin in the heat of the summer breeze. She swiped at them with the back of her free hand. They would only serve to prove the man right.

Upon return to Halloway House, Miss Melanie led Scarlett into the library. "Sit quietly in here while I inform your parents of your antics before someone else does." She slammed the door shut.

Thunderous shouting echoed through the house. Scarlett winced as the sound of stomping shook down the hall and passed by the closed library door.

My parents can't be so mad if they find me here peacefully reading, can they? It was a suitable act of penance.

Picking through the shelves, Scarlett pushed aside a book on arithmetic. *Dull.* Then a collection of Shakespeare's works. *Wouldn't want to become more dramatic, now would I?* And next a historical description of the Crusades. *Too many swords involved for the moment.* Finally, she flipped through a crisp-paged, cloth-covered book written by someone with a droll name.

"Plato."

As she skimmed the pages of *The Republic*, she mouthed

along to its words, eventually stumbling across a particularly intriguing line.

"So justice, hm?" She hummed to herself. "It is how one does good by friends and *right* by enemies."

Tucking the book under her arm, she floated down onto the settee. The cushions flattened with a *pffft*. She cracked the book open on her lap and flipped to page one.

"If I will not be allowed to wield a sharp sword, then I will wield a sharp wit."

Chapter One

April 1816

Scarlett hurried from her bedchamber, tiptoeing down the stairs into the main hall. One hand grazed the weathered oak railing, and the other tucked a copy of Aristotle's works behind the small of her back.

She managed to shove the book into a drawer of the hall table just as her mother exited the study and clicked the door closed, shutting her father's grumbling voice inside.

"Scarlett, dear, you have made us late. Why did it take you so long to dress? Your hair does not even appear to be styled." She approached Scarlett with outstretched hands, poking and stabbing her scalp with hair pins. "And remind me to take you to the dressmaker's for some new styles for the season. Your wardrobe is much too outdated. You don't know how beautiful you are, and neither will anyone else in these old frocks."

"No, mother, I know exactly how beautiful I am. I'm never allowed to forget so, and I don't think old dresses will hide this fact."

Trust me. I've tried. Scarlett swatted her mother's meddling hands away from her face.

"We had to rush to finish my coiffure because I lost track of time in the library," she explained.

Their shared lady's maid had actually begun dressing Scarlett's hair in the library because she'd been too absorbed in her reading. *But mother does not need to know that. She would only take away the books for a week to remind me of the usual pastimes for an unwed lady: shopping, batting one's eyelashes, and fanning one's decolletage.*

"Remember, Scarlett, a proper lady must deny her beauty. A man will find your lack of humility distasteful," her mother chastised as she studied her own reflection in the hall mirror and fussed with the mousy-blonde mass of curls atop her head.

"The man I someday marry will not find forced humility a virtue."

If she someday married. Considering the choice of men in Mayfair during the 1814 and 1815 seasons, 1816 didn't offer much hope of providing a suitable man with a large enough brain with which Scarlett could carry on a single conversation, let alone an entire marriage.

"Pride is a fault, dear."

"No. It's a strength and one that, frankly, people should stop hiding under the guise of being 'virtuous.' It's dishonest. That is what I find to be a fault." Scarlett's chin slowly rose as her sentence came to a close. Although, it was not as if she was entirely faultless.

"Is that more of your philosophical chatter?" Her mother's voice muffled from her scrunched neck as she spoke into her own bosom. She hitched up the front of her gown. "Honestly, you fill your head with too much nonsense. Be grateful you still have your looks. Otherwise, the Ton would never forgive your wild ways. In my day—"

A racket of barking interrupted the lecture. Scarlett's Irish setter raced down the hall and scrambled over the rug, rumpling it under his paws.

"Brissot! How are you, my boy?" Scarlett ruffled the silky red fur on his chest.

In his excitement, he ran in circles around her, only stopping for a moment to break wind.

"Ugh! Will you ever train this beast?" her mother shrieked.

Scarlett clutched her sides, gasping from laughter. "He's a dog, mother. He needn't subscribe to the same set of manners we do."

Brissot pounced at Lady Halloway's heels and weaved around her legs, nearly knocking her over. She teetered on one foot.

Their ancient butler Forbush trotted towards them in his best attempt at a run. He panted heavily between his words. "I'm sorry. My lady. He has just. Finished his dinner. And is. Unmanageably. Energetic."

Forbush shooed Brissot away, then took up his position by the front door. Scarlett mouthed an apology, which the man accepted with a wrinkled smile.

Scarlett's mother smoothed her skirts in a huff. "It's fine, Forbush. Now inform the footmen that Scarlett is finally done flattering her vanity and we are ready to leave."

Forbush stood still, staring at the wall beside the front doors. Last Scarlett heard, this had been his post since before her father's birth, maybe before her grandfather's as well. There may even have been permanent scuff marks from the man's shoes in the exact spot he stood for the last handful of decades.

Except for that one particular afternoon when she was a child. He'd stood firmly between where she sat on the settee holding her Plato and where her father stood shaking with rage.

"Forbush!" Gold bracelets jingled on her mother's wrist as she waved her hand in front of his face.

Startled, Forbush jumped to attention. The thin hairs which were combed over the top of his liver-spotted head trailed slightly behind him. "Yes, my lady?"

"We are ready to leave for the Grovington's. His lordship has decided he is staying in tonight."

With visible effort, Forbush bowed. His bones cracked with each inch of movement. He rushed out the hall, yelling for the footmen to ready the carriage.

The drive to the Grovington's was short in distance but long in sighing silences. Scarlett and her mother never had enough in common to fill a whole carriage ride with conversation.

"As your father has declared, this is the season in which you must marry . . . " Lady Halloway trailed off. "Scarlett, are you listening?"

"Yes, mother. I can listen and look at the square out the window at the same time."

Cast by moonlight and lampposts, the shadows dancing along the stone paths beneath the trees were particularly diverting. It did not, however, take much to divert Scarlett's attention from her mother.

"Don't be impertinent. As I was saying, this is your third season out. The whole Ton is aware this is by choice. You have had plenty of offers both years prior and declined all. Your father and I worry if you don't marry this season, the whole Ton will believe you to be a flighty partier only interested in dancing and wine. Or worse, a spinster in the making." Her mother's ear baubles shivered in fright.

Scarlett rolled her eyes. *Would that truly be so bad?* Yes, if it meant never leaving her parent's chaperonage.

"Don't roll your eyes. It's not ladylike."

"I don't care about always being ladylike. And I will marry when I please and to whom I wish." Scarlett punctuated her words with a waving fist.

"You are incorrigible. The man you marry will still hope to find you as a *lady*, not a wild creature." A sneer curled Lady Halloway's upper lip and transformed into a smile when Scarlett sat up straighter at the word *wild*. "So shape up quickly. You will need to marry this season simply for the sake of your father's sanity. He has been fretting over the expenses since we delayed your debut. We did not expect our daughter to take so many seasons to find a match. It has been costly."

Throughout the years, their estate had consolidated down to a butler, a housekeeper, one lady's maid, a cook, one groom, and two footmen who acted as coachmen when needed. Her father had dismissed his valet the year prior.

Scarlett kept quiet. She fussed with her moss green gown. Her mother had picked this fabric to match her eyes. When they'd purchased it her debut year, they'd spared no expense. When her father, the Viscount Halloway, had later received the bill, his howling voice had been heard throughout the whole house. It had shaken everything down to the candlesticks.

"Need I remind you we are fortunate enough the Ton seems to have forgotten the scandal you caused in the park?" Lady Halloway twisted the bracelets around her wrists.

"That was so long ago, mother."

"Yes, so don't push that luck with another season full of your antics, diatribes, and rejections of perfectly fine gentlemen."

"Perfect in your opinion, not mine," Scarlett mumbled.

Her mother continued, "You don't need to love him. You need only find a suitable gentleman who will care for you. Do you understand?"

"It's difficult enough for me to tolerate London men. You needn't worry about me expecting love."

Scarlett glanced at her mother who was fiddling with her wedding ring and sighed. It was not as if she was against the concept of marriage. It was that she was against the idea of marriage to a man who would not treat her as herself but rather as what he believed to be a typical female who must surely love ribbons, puppies, embroidery, and singing. Well, she did love Brissot, but that was as far as that related.

Love in a marriage, however, now that was a charade. An impossibility. And she certainly did not believe in love at first sight like what occurred in the novels her lady's maid blathered on about. All she asked for was a marriage built on mutual respect. Which would be better than what her parents endured.

There was, however, one benefit the right kind of marriage could afford her: freedom. An escape from under her parents' thumbs. An excuse to no longer attend these shallow society events. A chance to read her books in peace every day without the need to hide them in drawers and under seat cushions. Maybe even an opportunity to take up real fencing as a hobby in place of her covert butter-knife fencing lessons she continued to give herself in her bedchamber.

But, as her previous season demonstrated, a husband who would allow, perhaps even encourage, her to conduct herself thusly would be impossible to find at such events. Her only hope was to endure and find one who fulfilled half of her expectations for her future. A man who had interests of his own to occupy him and could suffer her, for marriage to her would surely be a wild ride. That was all she could ask.

With a whinny of the horses, her thoughts and the carriage both rolled to a stop in the lane bustling with people pouring into the first ball of the season.

Chapter Two

T he stagecoach ride was bumpy from Portsmouth to London, and Tate was having an awful time sketching on his drafting paper. Charcoal smudged all over the heel of his palm. It didn't help that his stomach was still upset from the sail out of Belgium. A gurgle rose from his belly, up his throat, and into his mouth, reminding him why he'd accepted a commission for the British Army and not the Royal Navy.

He knocked on the roof of the coach. "Slower, please. I'm in no rush to return."

After another rumble ripped through his gut, he set his sketchbook and pencil aside. The bridge he was designing would have to wait until he had a solid desk to work on again. He shut his eyes and leaned his head against the seatback.

"We are almost there, sir," the driver yelled from outside. "I see you are in uniform, are you on leave or have you finished serving?"

"I finished. It's actually been four years since I have been home."

"Goodness! Didn't they give you leave? Four years is a long go at it. I'm sure you're plum excited to see your family again. And maybe even a chit?" The driver leaned over the side of the bench, peering into the coach and grinning. A gap where two front teeth should have been revealed itself.

With a pinched, tight-lipped smile, Tate inched further from the window. "No, it's just my brother and I. There was no point in returning to London to see only him. Besides, he's the one who bought me the commission in the first place. I can't very well waste money to see him when he so obviously wanted me gone."

"He must want you back now on accounts of he did not renew it."

Tate shrugged and picked at a loose thread in the binding of the coach's bench seat to keep his mind from wandering to his stomach.

Father had tried so hard to fix his motion-related malady, to train it out of him. Every family trip to Bath, every season's travel to town, even every jaunt over to their neighbor's for dinner, Tate had been forced to sit backwards, the worst seat in any carriage, with the hopes of perfecting himself. It'd never worked. Every time, his father had said perhaps his sickness was for the best, for it might keep him from eating. Then, when father died, his brother had continued the torture until Tate had a horse of his own to ride.

The driver interrupted Tate's brooding, "Still, I'm sure you can't wait to see all of the pretty ladies dressed in their fancy gowns at them famous London balls. What I would give . . . "

Throat cracking as he forced a laugh, Tate picked up his charcoal pencil and pad of paper. "I should return to my work." The only reason he chose to suffer a move back to London. An architect could not build a career from the countryside.

With a huff, the driver scowled and scooted upright on the bench.

Tate tapped the end of his pencil against his knee. Streaks of black smeared into the fabric of his trousers. *My stomach is unsteady enough already. I do not appreciate the reminder of how hopeless I am on a ballroom floor.* Especially considering his destination for the evening was the godforsaken Grovington's ball.

With a practiced, graceful glide and head held high, Scarlett entered Grovington House unaccompanied and handed the butler her pelisse. At the beginning of her second season, her mother had stopped linking arms with her when they entered events. She'd crafted some excuse about Scarlett being too much taller, making it uncomfortable to match paces. The yip of disappointment her mother released every time Scarlett declined a gentleman's offer to escort her into the ballroom said otherwise.

The Grovington's ballroom was perfect for the first ball of the season. Large, sunken, rectangular, and well-lit by thousands of candles, a person could spot a friend all of the way across the room. And Scarlett did. As she stood by the entrance, she identified Mrs. Bethanne Riverston, daughter of Lord and Lady Wilkins, stepping away from her dance partner on the other side of the dance floor.

She strode towards her dear friend, skirting around the people along the edges of the dance floor. The massive room was somehow packed full to the brim, but this was not unexpected for the first event of the season. Everyone hadn't seen nor been seen since the end of the last season, and they were dressed in the finest, most colourful silks, cravats, baubles, and buttons they could afford. Scarlett avoided being stepped on by multiple sets of fashionably heeled shoes, which had the potential of doing some serious damage to toes.

A blonde man wearing obnoxiously bright tangerine silk obstructed her path. "Miss Halloway, lovely to see you."

"Lord Cullen." A curl fell into her eyes as she dipped her head. She blew it away.

Before she could continue on her way, he grabbed her forearm. "It feels as if it has been ages since we last met."

"Yes, last season. My drawing room. You almost upturned the entire tray of tea service in your rush to leave," Scarlett replied in a stuccoed beat.

Plucking Lord Cullen's grasping fingers from her arm one by one, she strained to free herself while surveying the crowd in search of Bethanne. Each finger she moved immediately snapped back into place against her skin.

"One could hardly blame me. You had refused my offer." He grasped harder. The tight grip of his fingers drained the color from her skin. His ice blue eyes glinted with anger, but his smile, which others deemed dazzling, hid his fury well from the crowd angling towards the pair.

"Rejection is merely an opportunity to *release one's grasp* on the false sense of control one has on life. Do you not agree?" Scarlett flicked her gaze from his face to her arm and back again.

He stared at her, blinking rapidly.

When he evidently did not understand her thickly-laid hint, she twisted her arm, releasing herself from his grip. He cried out as the movement splashed his drink onto the ruffles of his shirt. Scarlett could not help herself from releasing a miniscule giggle as she strode away.

"Bethanne, finally we are reunited." She sighed a breath of relief when she arrived at her friend's side.

"Finally? We saw each other in the country last week. What's happened?"

"Don't ask. It's a short but unimaginative story."

Bethanne quirked her brow, then turned to watch the bouncing dancers at the center of the room. "Did you hear more of the soldiers have just returned from the continent? " She paused to chew on her lip. "They're finally being sent home after cleaning up Napoleon's mess. Many are here tonight. It's good they're safely back, but I don't think I can even look at another red coat without tearing up." Her voice cracked in a graveled rasp.

A few years older than Scarlett, Bethanne had had a long engagement and short marriage to John Riverston, a soldier who met his end in Portugal shortly before victory was declared.

Scarlett nudged Bethanne in the ribs, pulling a smile to her face. "Don't fret. I shall do all the looking for you."

"I know I have officially packed away the lavender dresses, but I just don't think I'm ready for it all again." Bethanne plucked at the azure fabric of her ballgown.

"Even I'm not ready for the pressures of the marriage mart, and I've had two seasons of practice with no expectation of this season ending any differently, not unless the men here in London suddenly acquired more interests than drinks at the club and betting on horses. At least you have the experience of being married before."

"*Experience* is not how I would describe it," Bethanne mused. "I had barely been married before he left for the continent. And I doubt I ever will again."

"What do Lord and Lady Shackles think of this pronouncement?" Scarlett asked.

Those were the titles Bethanne lovingly used to describe her overprotective parents, the Wilkinses. Scarlett was comfortable referring to them as such given she and Bethanne were more like sisters whose natural ribbing jabbed at each other's nerves more than that of simply friends. As much as Scarlett would have known given she had no siblings. Her parents hadn't found it in them to do the necessary act twice apparently. Yet another example to not emulate in marriage.

Note to self, a marriage prospect must also be attractive. With that addition to Scarlett's requirements of a gentleman, all hope of ever leaving her parent's home was surely lost. All of the gentlemen her friends had fainted for over the years had never made her feel anything other than the muted thrum of boredom.

Bethanne's response steered Scarlett from her mental list making. "Her Highness Shackleton dotes upon me every minute of the day as any mama ought." Bethanne winced, but Scarlett shooed her on.

She was too excessively used to her own mother to care about whatever she might have been missing. At least her mother allowed her enough daily autonomy in the form of neglect to not earn the name *Shackle*. It was only the spare moments spent with her that would more likely earn the woman the name *Gallows* or *Guillotine*.

Bethanne continued, "His Most Dutiful Shackletry will not leave me alone either. He has tried setting me up with not three but four of his friends from Eton."

"How old are they? Fifty?"

Bethanne's nose crinkled. "Quite."

Pushing past Bethanne, Scarlett's mother joined their conversation and leaned in close to Scarlett's ear. "You might just be the most impetuous girl to ever exist."

"What, pray tell, has earned me this honor?" With a hand to her chest, Scarlett batted her eyelashes. Beside her, Bethanne sniggered.

Her mother ignored them both. "I hear you have made a mess of Lord Cullen. That is no way for you to encourage him to continue courting you."

"Good. I don't wish for him to court me any longer."

Her mother harrumphed, crossing and immediately uncrossing her arms when, steps away, Lady Irving grimaced at their tableau and leaned towards Lord Irving's ear. Lady Halloway recomposed herself and looped her arm with her daughter's, appearing as ever the dedicated mother she was not.

The act seemed to have worked. A man wearing a fine silk brocade waistcoat sauntered towards them with two glasses of lemonade in hand. "Lady Halloway, Miss Halloway, Mrs. Riverston. How are we tonight? To be back in the refined air of Mayfair is always a treat and in such rarefied company no less."

"Such a charmer as always, Lord Langley." Nearly swooning, her mother gripped onto Scarlett's arm, biting her nails into flesh.

There was little chance of escape this time, possibly when Scarlett needed it most.

Lord Langley, a marquess from Northamptonshire, had been her most persistent suitor both years prior. He'd attempted to call on her in the country a few times, and each time Scarlett had been conveniently sick with the ague or visiting distant relatives in Bath. What was actually convenient was how easy it was for Scarlett to bribe her lady's maid to shoo away the suitor by giving her a simple sweet bought from the village bakery.

Lord Langley seemed a perfectly nice man. Too loud and spirited, but many declared he was perhaps the politest available gentleman of the last few seasons, and, as a marquess, eligible to boot.

But Scarlett remembered differently. As children, he had not been so kind. He'd taunted her and deemed her incapable. However, now he was supposedly polite, and whatever errors he did make others easily overlooked for his height, trim figure, thick hair, dark blue eyes, and pretty much all attributes that most women, including her mother apparently, swooned over.

"Scarlett—I mean Miss Halloway." Lord Langley choked on his likely calculated misstep and thrust a glass towards her. "Would you like a lemonade?"

Jerking her head in Scarlett's direction, Bethanne's piercingly grey eyes searched Scarlett's face for answers. Her mother nearly broke her neck in her snap to catch Scarlett's gaze. She panted in her obvious wait to ask Scarlett if Lord Langley had any reason to use given names, any reasons involving life-long commitment.

Great… Now I shall have to deal with the whole Ton believing I'm nearly betrothed. A supposedly well-meaning man gets too familiar against my will, and I'm the one who must deal with the consequences.

"No, thank you." Scarlett's gaze pretended to search for

something across the room. "I'm due over that way for a dance with another gentleman." The hem of her gown swept the floor as she dipped an inch into a rushed curtsy.

Now she needed to make her excuse a reality, otherwise, during their ride home, she'd never hear the end of how the Marquess Langley was a bird in the hand she'd squandered. From her view, all the gentlemen not dancing were either married, and therefore were awkwardly yet understandably unavailable for a dance with an unmarried woman, or had visited her London drawing room last season, and she was not prepared to give any one of them false hope yet.

Then there were the soldiers, a fresh set of young and willing dance partners, who were gathered around the refreshment table housing the wine.

Too short, too drunk, too . . . hairy. She scanned the fringes of the group.

There was a trio of soldiers who, by the way they waved their drinks around, looked to be in a lively debate about something involving the ceiling. One in particular stood out to her, literally, as he was a whole head taller than the rest of the men and was as wide as two typical men standing side by side.

He was unconventionally, jaw-droppingly handsome with his brunette hair shorter than was fashionable and whiskers longer than acceptable, but what could a man do if a shave in the morning did not last all day? Perhaps ask his valet to shave him again. But this man was a soldier and likely did not have a valet. All the better as Scarlett found the short shimmering hairs along his cheeks and jaw to be uniquely, unrefinedly beautiful.

The glass he held was miniature in his massive hands, seemingly as easy to crush as a rose petal in hers. Yet he carried it around between the tips of his fingers with the greatest delicacy as if he was entirely aware everything around him could effortlessly break at his touch.

With every muscle in his thick neck flexing against his shirt collar as he laughed, he seemed too rugged to be wearing a starchly pressed red coat in a London ballroom. The knees of his trousers were smudged with black. Wherever this man belonged, it certainly was not this ballroom. By the way he shuffled his unbelievably large, polished shoes against the floor and tugged at the tight buttons of his waistcoat, it was clear he would be comfortable in less layers.

And Scarlett would have to agree. She, too, would be more comfortable if he were in less clothing.

That one. He's the one. He's perfect.

Chapter Three

S hall we dance?" A woman held out her slender, gloved hand to Tate.

His jaw hung, too stunned to speak for several seconds. He'd never been asked to dance by a woman before. Quite likely, it was the first time a woman had ever asked a man to whom she hadn't previously been introduced to dance in a crowded ballroom. Especially a woman as stunning as this one.

There was nothing about her physicality that particularly declared difference. She was beautiful. That much was sure. With her silky hair the color of milky tea, green eyes as sharp and piercing as mint, and enticing cupid's bow lips, she was one of the most handsome women he'd ever seen. But she carried her beauty as if it were the least interesting thing about her.

There was, however, a call to him in her demeanor. Something that spoke to the parts of him which were buried deep within the recesses of his soul. The self-assuredness of her posture. A hint of well-informedness in the slant of her brow. A spark of larger purpose in her black pupils which left him breathless. She knew something he did not, and he'd relish the opportunity to hear it.

He straightened his lapels. This was a lady, and, if she was asking him, it was because she must need his assistance. Nothing more—certainly nothing that involved her bowed upper lip. To aid was his duty. He was a soldier and a gentleman after all.

"Why, yes. I do believe we are long overdue." He handed his glass off to his friend Roberts, abandoning their conversation about the cornices in the ballroom, and nestled her hand into the crook of his arm.

The woman visibly squared her shoulders and offered him a sly smile. They walked arm in arm onto the dance floor as the musicians played the next piece, a waltz. Sweat beaded on his temples as he stumbled to take position on the floor.

The woman must have seen the flash of panic that crossed his face because she squeezed his shoulders and whispered, "Don't worry. I will lead." She winked one of her green eyes, sparkling like a dewy meadow in the morning.

Tate's eyes were light brown. His older brother, Richard, had always mocked him for it, calling him unrefined and muddy. Women seemed to always prefer his brother, so who was he to argue?

While it would appear to anyone in the crowd as though he was leading, the slight extra pressure of her hand on his shoulder directing his movements said otherwise. Using her face as a marker, he steadied himself as they whirled around in the puzzle of waltzing couples. She was so graceful. She made him, as bumbling as he was, feel graceful too. This woman had obviously trained extensively in movement to be able to lead a dance like this.

She held his eye contact and nodded to reassure him. With a hiccup, his nerves escaped as a chuckle. He wasn't used to women looking at him so levelly. Most women he encountered were much shorter than this one and acted coy and demure by looking up at men from under their eyelashes. Not him, of course. He'd observed women do so to his brother and friends.

"You are not so bad at this." The corners of her lips twisted, holding back laughter.

"Well, of course not. You obviously picked me out of any other soldier for my superior dancing skills." He raised a brow to mock his haughty tone.

She erupted into a fit of giggles, and, oh, there was never a less magical sound. For such a naturally beautiful woman, her laughter left her body in strangled gasps and spurts.

He couldn't help but chuckle at her laughter. For a brief moment, it was good to be home again, back in familiar ballrooms spending time with friends, which was most frequently how he spent his time at balls. In the past, before his army career, he would dance with the occasional woman, but only when his brother was too preoccupied dancing with her more attractive friends to find time to dance with the young lady. He always stepped in to remove her embarrassment, and, in turn, embarrassed himself on the dance floor.

This dance was different, however. This time, he'd been asked. Not his brother, who was somewhere else in the room likely surrounded by women fanning themselves. Him.

"I'm sorry I can't dance. I'm a man of science, not the arts."

"Ah, too busy in your study to practice the waltz, I presume?"

Tate sighed. "Sadly, no. I have been too busy on the continent lately to study my true passion."

"Which is?" She expertly guided their dancing around another couple.

Back on rhythm, Tate loosened his grip on her waist, noticing he was holding her tighter than was typically acceptable during a waltz. Close enough to capture her aroma. Paper and sun and baked spices. Homey yet entirely new. Novel. Thrilling.

He gulped down the flutters in his throat. "I'm fascinated by architecture."

"A soldier and an architect, what an accomplishment! This explains the charcoal on your trousers?"

Tate glanced down at his knees and laughed nervously. "I'm not an architect yet. My aspirations were delayed by my service. I'm hoping to study more now my commission is complete. Although, I suppose I should have changed my trousers before coming here tonight."

"I don't judge. I, too, wish I had more time for my true passions, but time is finite while the hungers of the mind are infinite."

The way her lips curved into an oddly contorted, sad sort of smile as she spoke was awfully distracting. Tate blinked rapidly to focus on listening.

She continued, "I would study all day if I were allowed. My lady's maid had to dress my hair in the library." The slope of her nose crinkled in a snorting giggle.

If Tate were a smoother man, he would have complimented her on how, with hair as lovely as hers, no one would have been the wiser. But he was not smooth, so instead he blurted, "Hair matters not."

The woman wordlessly questioned him with a slant of a brow.

He cleared his throat. "So what is your subject of study?"

"I consider myself a student of philosophy. At least, that is the only interest which I'm allowed to study. Although, most people seem to believe philosophy is also not appropriate for women." Her green eyes lit like the flash of lightning in a thundercloud.

Underneath Tate's palms, the woman's ribcage went rigid, no longer flexing with inhalation. She was holding her breath, awaiting his reply.

She's scared. This woman who showed no fear in approaching me, a burly soldier she does not know, who asked me to dance is scared. What have other men said to her to make her believe she must defend herself for having interests?

Tate lightly squeezed her willowy waist in one hand. "Perhaps that is because they have not stopped enough to listen to the wise things women, including yourself, say. So what is your latest philosophy?"

Too surprised to remember the next steps in the waltz, Scarlett slipped in the man's hold. She stumbled towards his broad chest. Wrapping his arms around her, he caught her and set her upright. The warmth of his body so near to hers radiated into her skin.

Had he just asked her to share her thoughts? He hadn't even done so under the veil of sarcasm. His dazzling golden-brown eyes had remained unrolled, and his pillowy lips had not smirked. And now, he was softly smiling at her, patiently waiting for her response. Not only had he asked, but he seemed as if he genuinely wanted to know her answer. He was not inquiring as an opportunity to brag or to flagellate her as other men she spoke with at balls would.

Recalling the beat of the dance, she redirected their movements to match the other dancers around them. It took her several moments longer than she was willing to admit to regain her ability to produce a coherent answer to his question.

"Earlier today, I argued that women ought not feign humility in a society which affords them so little freedom of choice. They should at minimum feel free to publicly pride themselves on their strengths." Her assertive tone hid the knot of nerves clustering in her throat. As this was the first time a handsome gentleman had ever truly listened to her speak on her ideas, she prepared to be lectured, scoffed at, or left alone on the dance floor.

Instead, he pursed his lips and nodded slowly. "A fine assertion, but you are assuming most women are feigning humility. Could not their meekness be genuine as they were not provided the opportunity to build strength in their areas of interest?"

Now, this man was not only listening, he was engaging in a bout of repartee. The nervous knot inside her unraveled and knitted into a giddy swath of exhilaration in her chest.

"And that is a fine counter, but I'm not assuming. I know they are because I've witnessed their skills, and I'm not holding up the charade anymore. Women know we have as many talents as men, beyond embroidery and the piano forte of course, and we should stop disguising them." The volume of her voice grew louder in her excitement.

Onlookers from the sides of the ballroom pointed at her, but she ignored their stares.

He shuffled their steps to the other side of the dance floor. "With how you portray yourself, I should think you have more talents than many men I know."

The air around Scarlett was suddenly scorching hot, and it was not due to the exercise of dancing. Her lips, in particular, burned. Did she want to kiss this man? She had only known him for mere minutes. She did not even know his name.

It was not as if this was the first time she had wished to take an attractive man by the face and plant a peck straight on his lips, propriety be damned. There was the sun-tanned groom at her parent's country estate to name one. But as this man had just given her the kindest compliment of her life, this was the only time she had to stop herself from doing so. She kept her mouth to herself even though his plump lower lip was terribly tempting.

Typically a woman of many words, she could only decide on two. "Thank you."

As the violinists' chords swelled with the final notes of the piece, his hands dropped from her waist. In the absence of his touch, her skin beneath all her layers of clothing chilled.

"Well now, I believe our dance has come to an end. What's your next move? Can I be of any more assistance?" He guided her off the dance floor.

Scarlett blinked in confusion for several seconds. "I did not ask you to dance for your assistance. I simply wanted to dance with you. You are the most eye-catching man in the room."

Despite being back on two steady legs, Tate tripped over his feet. *Is she flirting with me?* His cheeks burned.

"What is your name?" he blurted.

"Scarlett." She straightened her posture, squaring her shoulders to his.

She was indeed tall, still shorter than him, but she stood unashamedly high next to his height. Unlike his which made him appear like a giant beast, her height only enhanced her beauty like the sturdiest-stemmed flower in the bunch.

"Scarlett." The name rolled in his mouth like a smoky whisky. "And what shall I call you in polite society?"

"I asked you to dance. I believe we have skipped the need for introductions and can use given names freely." She snorted while laughing.

There was something endearing about the way this woman, Scarlett, could snort so loudly with such elegant features. One would think a face so delicate would be incapable of such sounds. As Tate had discovered, one would be severely wrong.

"Besides, I have had enough drama surrounding names tonight. I give you permission to just call me Scarlett."

"And if I were to call on you?" Hooking a finger into his collar, he tugged the choking fabric to clear his throat before making his best attempt at flirtation. "You know, to discuss how our studies are progressing."

"Then you may know me as Scarlett Halloway. And should I wish to call upon you?" She winked. "Where may you be staying?"

Perhaps Tate should have expected the woman who asked him to dance to also request to call on him, but he didn't.

Honestly, no one in his position would have expected so. He was convinced there was no precedence or experience on earth which could have prepared him for Scarlett.

"You? Call on me? Why yes." He cleared his throat. "I mean, I'm Tate. Tate L—"

Interrupting their delayed introductions, a man wedged himself between them and rested his arms around their shoulders. "I see two of my favorite people are meeting."

Scarlett shimmied out from under the man's arm. "Lord Langley, if you wouldn't mind, I'm busy having a conversation with—"

"My brother." Richard hollered.

Tate tried shrugging Richard off, but Richard's fingers clamped into his shoulder muscles.

Scarlett's complexion drained before his eyes. In a split second, the confident, forceful, wildly-intoxicating woman standing in front of him became a withered, shrunken shell.

"I must be going."

"Scarlett, please wait." Tate stepped towards her.

Her fiercely green gaze locked with his as she weaved into the crowd before disappearing entirely.

"You called her Scarlett?" Richard scoffed. "Has all your time on the continent left you without a sense of propriety? As a reminder, brother, we don't use given names here in England unless we are *quite* familiar with the person."

Tate's hands scrubbed down his face. His words mumbled into his palms. "I have not lost my manners. She gave me explicit permission."

"I see. Your huge size intimidated her so much during the waltz that she believed she must share her given name in case you crushed her and needed to explain who exactly it was you maimed." Richard snickered.

"She did not seem to mind my size." Tate turned his hands over, recalling the memory of her thin fingers in his meaty palms.

"I don't see how she could not."

Perhaps Richard was right. She had run away rather quickly. Was it because someone, someone being his brother, saw her with him? Did she not want others remembering she had danced with him?

As Tate trudged to rejoin his friends, Richard trailed closely behind him, speaking in his ear, "It's not as if there's much else you two could have discussed. Despite her oddities, which can be easily ignored by plugging one's ears with cotton, she's a coveted pick of the unmarried females here in Mayfair. Her dowry is rumored to be significant, and her appearance is certainly more than acceptable. And, you ... " Richard smacked Tate's back and chuckled. "Well, you are a behemoth, a second son, and a lowly soldier. Certainly nothing a London lady is setting her sights on."

"She hasn't set her sights on me, if that's what you're worried about. She asked me to dance, and we discussed our studies." Tate bit his tongue to keep her request to call on him to himself. He could no longer guarantee she'd made it in earnest. He continued, "That was all. Now would you leave me alone and go about your rakish pastimes already?"

"Of course I wasn't worried. I'm more afraid for you, brother." Richard pulled Tate in for a sideways embrace. "I don't wish for your feelings to be hurt while she uses you as a pawn to get my attention."

A pawn? Was Scarlett using Tate as a pawn? While she was obviously a very intelligent woman, she didn't seem the kind to play such games. She had been very direct. Straight-forward. Honest when other women would have been coy.

What was Tate thinking? He didn't know this woman. Perhaps Richard knew best. Richard had indeed spent considerably more time in London's social set than himself.

Or, for the first time in their relationship, did Richard see Tate as a threat? Richard obviously took an interest in this woman, but she hadn't danced with him. She'd danced with Tate.

It didn't matter. Unlike his brother and all the other men of the peerage, he was not here to find a wife. He was here to focus on his career. But first, he must get it off the ground floor. A long road of work was ahead for him to make a name for himself. It'd be worth the effort if he ever wanted to relinquish his reliance on Richard's support.

"How sweet of you," Tate mumbled to his brother. "I promise I won't be hurt. As I'll be focused on my next profession, I don't intend to spend much time at these types of events this season, so you needn't worry about me."

"Good. Promise me you'll still enjoy yourself at this one before you dive back into your studies?" Richard requested while walking backwards away from the clump of soldiers.

Tate nodded and retrieved his drink from his friend Roberts.

"What was that about?" Roberts asked.

"For the first time ever, it's possible a woman might prefer me, and, I'm not quite sure of this, but I think my brother might be jealous."

"The woman you danced with? What was she like?"

What was Scarlett like? Were there words eloquent enough to describe a woman so brave, so sharp, so striking?

"She's a force."

Chapter Four

That Scarlett Halloway was a deceitful, conniving rogue of a woman.

Richard stomped away from his brother's group of uncivilized, tavern-frequenting military friends.

A pickpocket would have had more morals than that woman, stealing away from his attentions with such an evident lie. Her empty dance card had hung plainly from her wrist. And to have the audacity to so flagrantly disregard propriety when making her lie a reality. Asking a man to dance? What delusion made her believe she was exempt from following the normal social conventions? She was still as absolutely ridiculous as she was when she was a sword-wielding laughing stock of a girl.

Disappointingly, it was this exact independence and unconventionality that Richard needed in a wife. Which meant he must tolerate it until he could get her to an altar. Then he could leave her to her fantastical whims while he enjoyed the private wonders of his life without the scrutiny of hopeful mamas and their marriage-minded daughters.

But he would never get that far if she insisted on flitting away from him at every encounter. The only sensible way to determine how to garner Scarlett's attention was to speak to her mother, for the woman had to bear Scarlett's eccentricities on a daily basis.

After his frequent visits to the Halloway's drawing room during calling hours, Richard had become acquainted with the woman well enough to know it wouldn't be difficult to locate her in the ballroom. Find any reflective surface, and she'd be there, preening herself like a parrot. As he expected, she was by a refreshments table, hovering over the punch bowl and pinching her cheeks.

"Lady Halloway, I don't know how your husband is comfortable allowing you to attend these events without a chaperone. You're so easily mistaken for one of the debutantes."

"Oh, my lord, you're too kind." Either from the pinching or his compliment, her cheeks were redder than strawberries.

Leaning against the table, Richard placed one hand to his brow and shook his head melodramatically. "It's my kindness which keeps me diligent in my quest for your daughter's hand. Without it, I would have lost faith long ago." He peered between his fingers to catch Lady Halloway's reaction.

She rested a heavily bejeweled hand on his arm. "While she may not, her father and I appreciate your patience. You see, my daughter is . . . independent to say the least. Her father has always expected me to control her, but I've never known how."

Richard set his hand on hers. "Might you have any useful insight to encourage her interest?"

"Honestly, I don't know my daughter well enough to say. She spends all her time with her head stuck in books in the library or walking that beast of hers in the park. I'm surprised you don't know her more than I do after these years of courting her. If you don't know her well enough to secure her attention, then why do you wish to marry *her*?"

Richard squinted at the peacock of a woman. That was the exact question he did not wish for people to ask. Did she know more than her bird brain let on? He must steer her away from scrutinizing his intentions. Flattery would do the trick. Every mother appreciated hearing how beautiful their daughter was.

He leaned in close. His breath fluttered the feathery hairs around the woman's face. "Her loveliness will make her the perfect marchioness. She must have inherited this from you. I cannot risk losing the chance to marry her simply because she has not allowed me to know her. As any man would, I will learn more about her in marriage."

"If you get that far." Lady Halloway whispered from the corner of her mouth as she waved her fingers at Lord and Lady Wordsworth. "My husband is a difficult man to get in front of. He's been holed up in his study consistently as of late. You won't be able to secure a meeting unless he's sure you're not wasting his time on a passing fancy."

"And should I happen to send over a few of my mother's vintage jewels to Halloway House? What assistance could you provide me then?"

The jewels had been gathering dust since his parents' deaths over a decade and a half ago anyways. Better to give them away than to leave them available for his servants to pilfer.

The woman's overly-manicured brows rose. "In that case, I believe I could speak with her father and figure out something for you."

Richard poured a glass of punch and took a quenching sip. "Oh, Lady Halloway, now it is you who is too kind."

Chapter Five

My brother. The words rang as Richard's irritatingly loud voice in Scarlett's head as she made her way to the terrace.

Tate, for that was now the name she could put to the attractive, whiskered face, was Lord Richard Langley's brother.

The gentle, curious soul with which she desired to become more acquainted was the brother of the most vexing man in all of London. Perhaps all of England. She could not say for the whole country, but Richard was definitely a contender.

She couldn't breathe. Her hands flew to her throat. Her lungs expanded tautly between the constricting laces of her corset.

The air stagnantly floating around her was as hot and thick as steam above a tub. It was impossible to tell whether this heat wave was caused by the large multitude of sweating people she weaved between in the ballroom, the captivating man she had just met, or his misfortunate relation to an utter lobcock.

Either way, she'd needed fresh air minutes ago, but the crowd blocking the way to the terrace doors was incredibly difficult to navigate.

Another sabre to make a way for me would very much come in handy right now. Scarlett hopped to see over the heads of the people around her, searching for a path. *Albeit it would have also been useful around Lord Cullen and Richard and any other unwanted suitor who dares interrupt my night. But no, women are not meant to wield weapons. We have only our wits which are easily ignored.*

Except Tate. Tate was the only man who hadn't ignored her. He'd listened and asked questions. He'd watched her intently as she spoke. And when he'd looked at her with those soft, welcoming, earthy brown eyes, her face had melted and gone numb. It was ironic, truly, that when a man finally wanted to know her thoughts, her mind nearly wiped clear.

Unable to shake Tate's warming gaze from her mind, Scarlett distractedly mazed through the crowd and accidentally trampled on Lord Neels's foot before whirling onto the terrace which overlooked the Grovington's garden. She promised herself she would make it up to him later. It was not her fault the man had unusually large feet.

Under the soft moonlight, she nearly collapsed onto the stone banister. Her lungs flooded with the crisp breeze which shook the leaves on the topiaried trees.

"Miss Halloway! Come here and meet our new friend," a gaggle of women on the other end of the terrace called to her.

The women skittered over to Scarlett before she had a chance to ask for a moment of relative peace. The quiet of the outdoors would have been the perfect place to contemplate the ramifications of Tate's unfortunate choice of family. And the way his muscular hands had felt as they glided along her waist. And the exact thickness of his neck with its veins which had bulged under his skin. Or how from the very first moment she had laid eyes on him, she felt an overwhelming, confounding sense of rightness. This deep thinking was meant to be accomplished in solitude. Preferably in her bedchamber, but out here would have done for now had she not been absorbed by the female flock.

Lady Grovington, the night's hostess, pulled forward a woman about Scarlett's age by her elbow to the front of the group. "Miss Halloway, meet Miss Camilla Bertram. She's in London for the season visiting her aunt, Lady Bertram, here." Lady Grovington gestured to an elderly lady seemingly half Scarlett's height who was blankly staring at the hostess's face.

"It's nice to meet you, Miss Bertram."

Miss Bertram dipped her blonde head. "And you, Miss Halloway. How was your time on the dance floor?"

"Lovely, as usual."

How did this woman know she had been dancing? Scarlett dabbed her brow with the back of her wrist. Her glove came up dry. It was not sweat which clued her.

"Usual is not how I would describe what I saw," another woman Scarlett recognized as the Duchess of Halfust chimed.

"I have heard you asked a man to dance."

The Duchess was the type of woman Scarlett had always dreaded becoming. Intelligent, artful, and cutting, but all these things only for the sake of gossip. As the Ton's most notorious rumormonger, the woman dealt in the currency of secrets. At her level of wealth, they were worth more than money itself.

"Your Grace, you jest. Scarlett knows better than to be so bold." Lady Lucy Bell, another unmarried miss, giggled and flipped a curl of her auburn hair off her shoulder. She nudged Miss Bertram's side. "We unmarried ladies are well aware of our fragile reputations. One small slip, and everyone thinks we are having an affair with a baron, or a duke, or a marquess. Or all three!"

With a panicked wheeze, Miss Bertram succumbed to a fit of coughing. Her blue eyes bulged from their sockets. Hiding her mouth behind her gloved wrist, she hiccuped as she composed herself.

Scarlett took a step back from her, allowing the woman more space to breathe around all these perfumed peeresses. "I don't see why asking a man to dance makes me bold. I wanted to dance. He would dance with me. I don't see the issue."

"I didn't say there was an issue, Miss Halloway. I only said it was an unusual choice," the Duchess corrected. "Though if you ask me, London has been a little too usual the last few years. The seasons have lost their entertainment."

Lucy bounced on her heels. "I'm hosting my annual musicale again this season. That is sure to be entertaining! Of course you are all invited, including you, Miss Bertram."

Seemingly absorbed by observing the party inside, Miss Bertram whipped her attention from the window to Lucy at the sound of her name and offered her a small, distracted smile.

"It will be lovely, dear, but not as diverting as scandal. Would you not agree, Miss Halloway?" The Duchess tilted her head, regarding Scarlett at an angle.

From this woman's unreadable expression, it was impossible for Scarlett to tell whether she was implying Scarlett had already been involved in a scandal or that she believed Scarlett would actually agree with her. Either way, Scarlett was too emotionally winded for this conversation.

"It's my understanding that scandal does not occur for the purpose of entertainment, Your Grace, but instead for a woman's decision to act freely or a man's decision to disregard a woman's wishes."

The Duchess picked at the fingers of her maroon silk gloves. "Then I wish to see many free women this season."

Scarlett squinted at the woman and sarcastically announced, "I shall do my best to oblige."

Lady Grovington shook her head. Her grey curls boinged. "Let us not give Miss Bertram here the wrong impression of London society. Our girl Scarlett is all talk. She has never been the object of any scandal, not unless wearing the wrong footwear for a promenade is a scandal now. She's just a sharp wit and an even sharper tongue. That is all."

"While I might not have caused any serious scandal, I'm

certainly not eligible for sainthood. Only you are, Lady Grovington."

Her mother might torture her if she learned Scarlett was not on board with her campaign to make her appear perfect. As if taking pins to the scalp wasn't already punishment enough. However, she couldn't stand the idea of being pedestaled as perfect. Perfection, or at least what Mayfair deemed perfect, was not perfect to her.

Perfection wasn't charm and manners and beauty. Perfection was honesty. It was the continuous quest for knowledge. It was a sun-soaked promenade in the park. It was her dog curled on her feet in the library. True perfection was the pursuit of one's deepest truths and the embodiment of self, as tarnished as one came.

"See there's that sharp wit of hers." Lady Grovington's wrinkles crinkled as she laughed. "Scarlett, you are an odd sort. Most young ladies would want to be complimented as such while you're trying to convince us you are not deserving of being one of Mayfair's coveted picks."

"It's because I never asked to be. I never wanted to be." Scarlett stared at the cracks in the stones of the terrace floor, avoiding eye contact with Lucy.

Lucy was also on her third season out. However, unlike Scarlett, her unsuccessful seasons were occupied by fruitless courtships which never led to the altar. It was a pity. The woman, again unlike Scarlett, so clearly wanted to be married. The desire to embrace the poor girl nearly overtook Scarlett.

That was until Lucy whispered to Miss Bertram, "Don't be fooled. Scarlett is no innocent prize. She once stole from a boys' fencing class and caused quite a fright."

Scarlett's fingernails dug into the flesh of her palms. Evidently, her mother was wrong; some people did still remember her theft. Was that truly the most impressive, and perhaps infamous, act she would be known for for the rest of her life? Not any of the countless, well-crafted, clever remarks she had made?

As Scarlett was silently seething, Miss Bertram shuffled to her side and murmured, "Frankly, I find you the least troubling one here. Innocence is overrated anyhow."

While leaning back to access the woman, Scarlett bumped into someone standing behind her. A deep "*ahem*" came from the figure. Scarlett turned around to see Lord Neels rocking on one steady foot.

"Miss Halloway, may I have the pleasure of your hand for this next dance?"

She could not injure this man twice in one night, even if one injury was physical while the other would be to his pride. "I would be happy to. Have a lovely evening, ladies. Lady Grovington, Your Grace, Lady Lucy . . . Miss Bertram." Scarlett bid her farewells, taking a second look at Camilla Bertram whose gaze was already locked on something or someone inside the ballroom.

Chapter Six

Reynolds, do you know anything about a Scarlett Halloway of Mayfair?" Tate asked the Langley House valet the next morning.

"No, sir. His lordship does not discuss such things with me." He shoved Tate's arm into his riding coat. With shoulders broad enough to give tailors nightmares, the assistance was very much a necessity and not simply a formality. "However, I can ask Callows if he has. He's much too knowledgeable on those such things for a butler. One would think he's one of the maids."

"The state of being well-informed on social matters needn't be exclusive to women." Tate patted him on the back. "But thank you, Reynolds. That will be all."

Creeping downstairs in his most comfortable boots, and most scuffed for he refused to allow Reynolds to touch them should he accidentally ruin the cozy indents around the ankles, Tate shuffled through the front hall and reached for the front door handle. He almost made it outdoors unnoticed until his brother marched out of the drawing room. Curse those squeaky polished marble floors. They were a fine choice architecturally, but damn were they loud. He had grown unaccustomed to the reverberating tendencies of cleanliness while in the mess and murk of war and forgot to adjust his movements accordingly to be more covert.

There was much more than tattle-taling floors that he had grown unaccustomed to in his family's London property while away. Had the gilt-framed mirrors always been so blinding? Or the ceilings so needlessly high? So much so his brother's voice could find a new purpose as a horn on a sea vessel.

"Tate!"

"Yes, Richard?"

"I wanted to ask you if you'll be in need of the family betrothal ring any time soon." Richard crossed his arms and leaned against the door frame. "See, it would break my heart if I thought I'd taken it before you had a chance to say to whom it should go. Mother and you were so close, and she was the last to wear it."

"I don't believe I will. Besides, I hardly remember mother."

And I know damn well, as the second son, I don't have rights to it. You want to rub yet another thing in my face.

Richard inspected his tailcoat sleeve and picked lint off the cuff. "Good because I believe, this year, I will."

Tate rolled his eyes, but Richard was too busy brushing the wrinkles from his breeches to notice. "Which of the lucky ladies are you finally choosing?"

"Miss Halloway." Richard smirked.

"Miss Halloway? The same Miss Halloway I danced with last night?"

Tate's ears began to ring. It was just the after effects of battle. He had learned from the other soldiers this could happen. Or was it caused by the thump of his heartbeat which had begun drumming in his head the second Richard had mentioned Scarlett.

Why should he care if Richard intended to marry the woman? It wasn't as if he'd formed some kind of attachment to her after one dance. Not unless thinking about someone every waking and dreaming hour since meeting was an attachment. No, that could not be considered one. Not yet at least. One needed to make evident gestures for it to become an attachment, and he would not, could not, do so. His career wouldn't suffer the distraction. He couldn't lose himself to the unpredictable waves of courtship else he would become sick.

"The very same!"

Richard's clap returned Tate's attention to the moment at hand before it could drift too far into a reverie. Tate had begun to imagine what such distractions would entail, like pulling a certain spirited whirlwind of a woman into his arms and sucking on that bowed upper lip of hers.

"So you intend to marry *the* Miss Halloway who quite literally ran away from you when you joined our conversation?" he asked.

Richard pointed a bony finger at him. "Who is to say she didn't run to get away from *you* because one dance with you was enough?"

Tate squared off to Richard and jutted his chin in the air. "I am. She asked to call on me just before you arrived."

A sputtering guffaw exploded from Richard's lips. "She? Asked to call? On you?"

"Yes, she did. And she gave me permission to call on her," Tate mumbled, not quite as confident as he had been seconds ago. His shoulders fell forwards, slumping his spine.

"She asked to call on you." Richard's shouting between bouts of laughter drowned Tate's words.

"If you have nothing else to say, I will be leaving for my ride."

Richard bent double, his face turning purple. "She. Asked. To call. On you."

The thud of the front door smothered the noise of his brother's laughter.

Rubbing his dark under eyes and yawning, he trudged to the stables to collect his horse.

"A ride in the park is what I need. The fresh morning air will give me clarity. And space from Richard," he mumbled to no one but himself. He had slept poorly with dreams fraught by a striking set of green eyes which haunted the back of his eyelids every time he blinked.

The park was nearly empty that morning. Mist hovered as high as his horse's knees. The trees were covered in a light layer of dew, giving the illusion of frost without the biting wind.

It'd been unseasonably cold that year, but that day felt like the exception.

He lost himself in the ride and his attempt to justify to himself why it'd be prudent for him to visit Scarlett that afternoon instead of working on his designs. It wouldn't be considered a gesture of affection, merely a polite formality to thank a new acquaintance for the lovely evening prior. Right? Or was he lying to himself?

If he was not to call on her, he wouldn't be able to focus on putting pencil to paper, distracted by thoughts of the way the cupid's bow of her upper lip stretched as she spoke. If he did call, he would be wasting precious time he should spend on strengthening his skills for his new career. But if he called, he might hear another one of her fascinating philosophies and feel inspired by her deep thinking, helping him to create something unique.

That was the hope at least. There was always the possibility he would instead be inspired to kiss her.

This was why being in the military had its benefits. One, there were no eloquent, soft-skinned, distracting women around. Two, one's responsibilities were clear and concise every moment of the day, every day of the week.

Without that structure, the freedom from responsibility was daunting. Tate could do anything with his days. And with the modest funds from his commission, he need not find a new profession, at least not while he was still a single man accepting his brother's generosity.

However, his mind and his hands hadn't received the message. They twitched with the desire to think, to create, to work. And maybe caress a sweet face framed by fawn-colored curls and set with a pair of sharply assessing green eyes. Green eyes which he would love to be scrutinized by if it meant one more moment with her.

However, if Richard did earn her hand, he might not have the opportunity for that one more moment.

This back and forth was maddening. It was decided.

He would call on her.

"Good morning, Tate!" An unexpected voice startled him from his musings.

Those were not the eyes of which he dreamed. A familiar wheat blonde with blue eyes stood before him. They belonged to his childhood best friend and neighbor from the country.

"Camilla, what are you doing in London?" His grin warmed his cheeks.

"What everyone else does. Trying to find a husband." She gestured to the area around them with a reticule in her hand.

Tate instantly paled. Cold beads of sweat dripped down the back of his neck. He had always loved Camilla's straight to the point manner of speaking, but this time it was a great deal less entertaining than when she had bluntly called his family's gardener a ragamuffin straight to the man's face for planting carrot seeds too deep.

His terror must have registered to Camilla because she quickly followed with, "Not you, Tate. How about we discuss this over tea? It's been a long while since we last saw each other."

"Yes, this Tuesday perhaps?" Tate's mouth twitched in a nervous smile.

"It's a date." She clapped resolutely, then resumed her stroll.

Tate's encounter running into Camilla in London was a surprise, but what wasn't a revelation was the news she wasn't interested in marrying him. Even though she was merely the daughter of a country gentryman, she was likely hoping to find someone who wasn't just a second son with a courtesy title, a soldier, and, as his brother so lovingly put it, a *behemoth*. Since she cared enough to journey this far to find a husband, she was liable to set her sights on a baron of minor, guaranteed wealth at the very least. Someone like Lord Neels perhaps. Not Lord Neels exactly because she could catch his notorious bad luck like a fever.

While it was a relief she didn't hold Tate to the expectation he would marry her, which had been set forth by their fathers, did she have to be so quick to reassure him he wasn't the match she hoped to make? He may not be as lithesome or cleanly shaven as other men in England. However, at the very least, he had his height, his intelligence, his newly acquired muscles from his military service to his credit. Although, the muscles had opted to grow beneath his layer of softness instead of fully replacing it.

Tate observed his trunk-like legs flex against the tight fabric of his breeches while he balanced himself on his trotting horse. Maybe his brother was right. No normal woman would want a man as large as him. Which would explain why no woman had ever favored him over his brother, or his friend Roberts, or any of his other male acquaintances for that matter.

Except there had been one. One woman who chose him around a mass of other possible options.

Scarlett.

And if he was not mistaken, he heard her distinctive laugh coming from somewhere in the park. Unless that was in his mind.

Lord, please do not add going mad to the list of reasons a woman would avoid me.

Thankfully, a person up ahead came into view. She was waving her arms around in the direction of her dog who was hopping through the clover. The dog threw himself down onto the ground and rolled in the grass. His tongue flopped out of his mouth. As he wiggled around on his back with four paws to the sky, the woman doubled over in laughter.

Yes, that was most definitely Scarlett. No other woman would so unashamedly snort like that.

Tate cracked his horse's reins to get a closer look. She wore a light blue dress which rippled around her body in the breeze, revealing the luscious curve of her hips underneath. The curves up top, however, weren't as well hidden. Unlike most young ladies in public, she didn't wear a spencer, only a shawl which slipped over her shoulders. In the fog, her lively countenance shone like a single lit taper in the dark.

As he rode closer, he attempted to craft something clever or witty to say to her. He came up short. Words had never been his strong suit. He was much more comfortable with numbers and working with his hands.

"I hope for the sake of the horse, you ride better than you dance." She was speaking to him first. Again.

He choked on his tongue. Why did this woman make him feel the need to pause every time she spoke? She had a knack for catching him off guard. There was something about her manners that gave off an air of impertinence. She always began speaking to one as if already in the middle of a conversation.

"Tate?" She lifted a brow.

The brow led him to gaze at those eyes. Those eyes. His gaze dropped yet again, this time to her mouth, a perfect rose-colored curve which twisted up at the ends as if in on a jest only she knew.

He quaked at the use of his given name coming from those lips. So intimate. Why had he allowed her to call him as such? He should have known hearing his name from her mouth would have been better suited for a bedchamber.

"Why did you ask me to dance yesterday?" He blurted while stepping down from his horse to walk alongside her.

What in his right mind was that? Any air of refined civility was entirely blown away by his runaway mouth. Oh, well. It was too late now to fix. The stone was set.

"I already told you. Because I wanted to."

"Yes, but why me? I was amongst a bevy of suitable young dance partners."

After whistling for her dog to keep up with their walking pace, Scarlett stated frankly, "Because you caught my eye."

Tate dragged his boots in the gravel, kicking up dust. "Ah, I see. Then it's because I was the largest in the room."

"No. I first noticed you because of your size, but I chose you because of the gentle way you carried yourself. You struck me as conscientious. Your handsomeness was an added benefit. I do, however, prefer your face at night when it's not so freshly shaven." Eyes widening and a crimson blush striking her cheeks, she whipped her gaze towards her dog who was pouncing after butterflies.

With her level of self-possession, he had not expected her to be capable of a blush. He had an obvious effect on her. A swell of something rocked through him. Something which struck right to his core. And, if he was being honest, his trousers.

"Noted." He stroked his smooth jawline with his free hand.

Reynolds would now have one less task to accomplish in the mornings.

He changed the subject to something she would be more comfortable discussing. "Who is your friend here?"

"This," she gestured to the red, fuzzy creature chasing in circles to catch his own tail, "is my boy Brissot. He was supposed to be my father's hunting dog, but I acquired him."

"Acquired him?"

Everything about this woman, down to the origins of her dog, was a mystery he wished to unfurl against his better judgment. Richard had announced this morning he would propose to her, had he not? Around her, he was no longer sure that had happened. Indeed, he was not sure any moment not with her had ever occurred.

"More like rescued him." She sighed breathily.

He was, at the very least, sure he wanted that breath on his skin.

She continued, "You see, he was not quite smart enough for the birding fields, so my father wanted to be rid of him. I believed it unfair he should ever be made to work without the ability to decide in the first place, so I scooped him up. He's been mine ever since."

"He is . . . unconventional." Tate found himself smiling at the dog who was bouncing up and down in an effort to catch the birds flying overhead.

"You can speak the truth. He is a nincompoop. Not to be confused with his namesake."

"Who?"

"Brissot. Jacques-Pierre Brissot." Scarlett stared at Tate incredulously.

"Ah, yes, the French philosopher." Tate stroked his chin. "I believe I read a work of his condemning the death penalty. I hear he had some unpopular opinions on the labour of the trade in the Caribbean as well, ones which I quite agree with."

Tate sensed Scarlett relax with relief, and he could not blame her. He had experienced enough hard days of labor in the service to know no one should ever be made to work without compensation.

"My Brissot does not have quite so thorough an understanding of liberty, nor such a righteous cause. But I love him in spite of his . . . peculiarities. By calling out his name whenever he trails off, I can only hope I am reminding those within earshot about the importance of freedom." Her hand reached out, her fingers brushing Tate's bicep. "Now is my turn to ask a question. Why do you have to be the Marquess's brother?"

Tate took her hand and tucked it into the crook of his elbow as they walked. "If it would help you to know, I, too, wish we were unrelated. He's a right and utter arse."

"He *is* an arse," she emphasized.

A dumbstruck chuckle rumbled from Tate's throat. Not only had this woman clearly stated her preference for himself, but now she was actually disparaging his brother. That was a first.

"What?" Her voice squeaked. "You said it before I did. Until now, I had only ever thought it. Everyone says he's such a gentleman, but I see through his act." Her eyes squinted in suspicion. "How he treated me when we were children doesn't help his case. I'm sure you can recall the particular incident. You must have been there."

"What incident?"

And there it was. Scarlett had asked to determine if he already knew her greatest embarrassment, hoping he did and that she would not need to dredge it up. It'd be convenient if he already knew she was considered wild and willful and had been involved in a scandal. She wouldn't need to tell him she was flawed.

But he had asked. Now she must relive it, if only to give him an honest picture of the woman standing before him. And if he decided she was too much? If he never spoke to her again? Well, her life would look no different than it currently did.

Only, it would then be somehow lonelier.

If anyone would understand her actions, it'd be the man who happily accepted her invitation to dance. Any other man would worry about his pride or reputation. Tate seemed to be a kindred spirit of unconventionality.

She shut her eyes for a moment, taking in the reinforcing warmth of his arm under her touch before he had the chance to remove it.

A resolute sigh blew from her lips. "You know the incident involving the sabre. It happened not far from here. You must have been one of the fencing students."

"I have no idea what you're referring to." His eyebrows furrowed in confusion.

"Come now! You seriously don't remember when I stole the sabre from the fencing class? When I ran around and challenged anyone who approached me to duel me for it? When I tore a hole in the instructor's jacket and slashed a few ladies' skirts?"

Tate shook his head.

"Actually, it happened over here." She unweaved her arm from his and skipped up the path and down into the flat, open portion of lawn.

Tate followed closely behind. Brissot sprinted towards them, jumping for attention until a bug hopped in the grass. He chased after it.

"It went like this. I nabbed the sabre from behind Fitzhenry Neels back—you know Lord Neels?" After Tate nodded, she continued, "Then I ran. Everyone was chasing me. I was surrounded here and took position to fight."

Sliding into a lunge, she pointed an imaginary sabre at Tate. He held up his hands in surrender. Her nose scrunched in a snorting giggle.

"Then everybody began yelling at me, including your brother. After I got a few goods strikes in, I was made to surrender." She mimicked swiping the sabre, then returned to Tate's side.

"I believe I would have remembered that." A swirl of Tate's rich brown hair fell onto his forehead as he chuckled heartily.

Scarlett's hands twitched with the desire to brush the hair back. Could she truly be lucky enough to have found the only man in the peerage who'd never heard of the terror she'd caused? And now she was relaying it to him as if it was something for which she prided herself. Stupid girl.

"I must not have been there. Richard and I were placed in different fencing levels because of our age gap." Collecting himself, Tate swiped the heel of his palm over his forehead, pushing his hair back. "So you enjoy fencing?"

"I used to. Until I was told I could not." She shrugged, keeping her secret butter-knife fencing she still practiced in her bedchamber to herself. This impressive man whom she'd only just met didn't need to know about her pathetic hobby. It might turn him off from her. "I took up philosophy in its place and vowed to wield a sharp wit instead. Although, I still can't help the occasional need for physical defense."

"Against who?" Tate's hands balled into fists at his sides. "If I learn my brother's been—"

"Not your brother. Others. But I can defend myself." Scarlett reached out and smoothed open his palms, then tucked her hand back into the crook of his arm to keep herself from sliding her touch further to the forearm muscles which roped under his jacket sleeve.

"From the sound of it, you truly can. I know I would never wish to be at the end of a blade in your hands." His steadying gaze quickened her breath. His eyes were the color of her favorite delicacy, chocolate.

She was at a loss for words. This man didn't judge her for her mistakes. Instead, he took her seriously for her interests and even jumped to her defence, but didn't force his assistance, believing her capable on her own. And he looked damningly alluring while doing so. He was far superior to the knights in her maid's romance novels.

Could he be the match she'd been waiting so long to make?

A marriage to him would be a union of equals, to be sure. And to have found him at a glance? What were the odds?

Her mouth opened, but nothing came out except a puff of air. Her brain, too, was breezing past full sentences. The only fully-realized thoughts that surfaced were imaginings of him touching her. Perhaps he could hook his thick fingers into her dress, pull her in close, and lock her between the swells of his biceps. Or he could brush her cheekbone with his thumb before bringing his face so close to hers she could truly examine the flecks of copper in his irises. All she had was the certainty that if he made a move for her, she would definitely not defend herself. Even, and perhaps especially, if that move was eventually a proposal of marriage.

T ate had to shift the conversation. Quick. If he didn't, he'd end up kissing Scarlett's delicately parted lips.

He cleared his throat in the hopes the act would also clear his mind. What topic was so upsetting it would force his attention from the lickable curve of her clavicle? Architecture? No, cupolas looked too much like . . . Well, too much like the rounded structures beneath her bodice. Philosophy? No, eros was also too distracting of a subject. Family? Yes, family was beyond irritating enough to distract him.

"Well, it seems you and I are the only ones to know just how much of a prig Richard is. I have to face his true personality all the time now that I've returned. Which is why I plan to stay far away from any event he attends and instead focus on my work."

"That's too bad." Her gaze lingered on him, then traveled to her dog where he was intensely sniffing the gravel in the center of the path.

The huffs of air flowing through Brissot's nostrils could be heard yards away. After breathing in too much dust, he shuddered in a sneeze, his red fur standing on end.

Tate leaned forward, hoping to recapture her gaze. "Why?"

"Because I was looking forward to seeing you at such events. My parents are forcing me to attend nearly all this season, and I could use someone there with whom I may *discuss my studies.*" Her tongue darted out to wet her lips before her mouth curved into a sly smile.

Scarlett was using his line on him to flirt. Despite all odds, she was keen on him. On Tate Langley. Not Richard Langley, the *Marquess*. Tate Langley, soldier and aspiring architect. And behemoth. At least according to her, he was a *handsome* behemoth.

He wrung the back of his neck. "Well, I could . . . " His words trailed off.

Apparently, he was the kind of man who considered rerouting all of his priorities for a woman who called him handsome. And, with that convincing smile of hers, he couldn't even be upset about it!

He must keep his head on straight and think. Given her forwardness, perhaps there was a way he could focus both on developing his new career and courting her. Both would require time and dedication, but she seemed persistent enough to make it clear for him. The question then remained if he was successful, could he support a wife on the funds left from his commission before he achieved income from his designs?

He squeezed his eyes shut, blocking Scarlett from his vision. Did he just think of her as his future wife when she'd only suggested they attend a few fêtes together?

Now he was actually going mad. He should be spending his time entirely focused on his work, but instead he was promenading with a beautiful woman on his arm and dreaming about her becoming his wife, imagining what it would be like to listen to her inspirational pronouncements all day. If not mad, he was most certainly delusional if he thought he could have both things, his career aspirations and a woman more intoxicating than he could have ever dreamed.

Besides, there was always the fact that Richard had announced his intention to marry Scarlett that morning. He seemed to keep forgetting that bit.

"Perhaps you could tell me which events you are to attend?" The words tumbled off his tongue before the logical portion of his mind could restrain them.

Scarlett ceased walking, pulled her hand from his arm, and leaned in close. Despite the privacy of this sparsely populated swath of the park, her voice whispered in a hushed, sultry tone,

"I've avoided all other gentlemen's suits up until now, so I may be mistaken, but is courting not supposed to be like a dance? Where is the sport in it if I tell you what step to take next?"

He gulped. She could not keep talking that way. It was the slipperiness of her consonants. It was the wetness of her vowels. Her mouth. It was all too goddamn maddening.

"With me, there's none. No sport, no ambiguous repartee, no guessing, no waiting games. No bouts." He tossed her a knowing, slanted smile. "There's only honesty. You seem like the type of woman who respects straightforwardness."

Stepping close enough to her the breeze ceased its flow between their bodies, Tate planted his hands on her shoulders. The soft tip of a curl caught under his fingertips. He rubbed the pad of his thumb over it, feeling the heat of her skin underneath the strands.

He took a deep breath. "I honestly wish to see you again, Scarlett. I did not return to London to join the marriage mart. I'm here to find work, but now I've also found you—Actually, you found me."

They chuckled together, hers ending in a hiccup of a snort.

He continued, "And the only dancing I aim to do is another waltz with you. Hopefully next time I can ask you to dance and lead without hurting your toes."

He braced in expectation. She would run. Flee from his forwardness. Escape from him and the park and eventually be betrothed to his brother, leaving him with his charcoal and drafting paper.

But she didn't run nor flee. She didn't even flinch.

The sunshine broke through the fog, reflecting within the verdure of her eyes as she beamed up at him. "Next time, I will let you lead. I know you'd never hurt me, even by accident."

Tate stopped breathing. He had to physically force his lungs to expand again.

What miracle or head injury had caused this woman to see him as no one had before? Not a single person in his entire life had ever said such kind things to him. Actually, they'd said the exact opposite. His father had regularly warned him to take care in shutting doors because he would snap off the knobs or to take a seat slowly otherwise he may shear the legs off a chair. The typical warnings from a parent to their son. If their son was a behemoth.

Overcome by his emotions, he gripped Scarlett by her slight frame and enveloped her in an embrace. A stitch in his waistcoat popped as he wrapped his arms around her.

Where he feared she would feel frail under the control of his muscles, she was in fact warmly firm but soft where it mattered. The plushness of her rapidly palpitating breasts pressed against his chest. The velvet skin of her bare arms. The hushed humming coming from the back of her throat.

Now he was hard where it mattered. He shifted his hips sideways to avoid prodding her.

Her hands slid up the girth of his middle and onto his chest. Between them, she laid her cheek. He rested his chin on her head. Her coiffure tickled his shaven cheeks.

"I will be attending the Duchess of Halfurst's stargazing event." Her voice was muffled by the linen of his shirt.

Against the desire, the need, to keep his hands on her, Tate released her from his embrace. "I will be there."

Chapter Seven

B rissot nudged Scarlett's elbow with his frigid nose, leaving behind a moist impression.

She tousled the tuft of fur at the crown of his head. "Well, Brissot, it appears for once I have news which will make mother rejoice. He may not be titled, but at least I have a marriage prospect. One I believe I could actually *enjoy* a lifetime with."

To her delight, Tate had offered to escort her home, but she had declined, saving him from a possible encounter with her parents. Their attachment was too new to expect him to endure such torture. If she'd let him, her mother would have scolded her for promenading with her suitor unaccompanied without the watchful eye of a chaperone. It was enough she was allowed to walk Brissot in the park without their lady's maid following her every move, which was more for her mother's benefit than her own. Lady Halloway had quite the penchant for trips to Mr. Monahugh's Millinery. As she had exclaimed, she could not very well be expected to carry around all her hat boxes by herself.

Upon return to Halloway House, Scarlett tracked down her mother who was frantically pacing in the hall outside her father's study. The woman's gnawing teeth tore at her fingernails.

"Mother, you will never believe this—"

"Shhh, Scarlett. I'm trying to hear what is happening inside."

Scarlett knotted her jittering hands behind her back and continued, unperturbed by her mother's all too common dismissal, "You will be happy to know I have finally found someone who I may be interested in marrying. Lord Langley truly deserves the title of gentleman."

"You are forgetting your manners dear. It's best you call his lordship the Marquess Langley, not Lord Langley. And I'm pleased to hear you wish to marry him because he's in there," she pointed a chewed nail at the door, "as we speak asking your father for his blessing."

"No, I'm speaking of the Marquess's brother, Lord Tate Langley. He is—Wait. Did you just say Lord Richard Langley is in there asking father for my hand?"

"Yes, girl. Now be quiet," her mother hissed.

She need not have asked. She knew by the haunting laugh carrying through the cracks around the door Richard was in there, adulating her father who already did not need any more reason to push Scarlett out of the home than the fact she was one-and-twenty and a female.

Not that she didn't wish to leave. She did, beyond anything

else she could want in life. But to leave for the hands of Richard would be like never leaving at all. Her cage would only be slightly shinier.

Her stomach lurched. Her insides twisted, suffocating her lungs and stopping her heart. Internally, everything was a breathless, blue shade of nausea, like the stench of the waves over a fishing net. A sickness only she could cure. No one else around knew nor cared who Richard truly was.

Twisting the tarnished knob in a rusty snap, she flung the door open and stomped into her father's study without so much as a knock.

"Rose, did I not instruct you to control the girl?" Lord Halloway, for that was what Scarlett was instructed to call her father, shook a fist at her mother and slammed his drink onto his desk. Brandy sloshed onto the wood.

Her mother cowered. "I'm sorry, Hubert. She slipped right past me."

Richard adjusted his waistcoat as he rose from a tattered suede armchair. His tooth-filled smile flashed at her. "Scarlett, dearest, it's lovely to see you this fine afternoon. I hear you've been walking in the park. I'm glad to know my intended cares to invigorate her constitution by manner of long promenades."

Her mother's cheeks stretched in a strained, placid expression. "We ensure Scarlett regularly exercises her body and mind to maintain her health."

That much was true. Scarlett's mind was indeed sharpened enough to pluck two distinct words from Richard's address.

"Your intended? I am not your intended." She slowly shook her head, which suddenly weighed two stone more than it had in the park. When she stopped moving, the room continued to spin around her in a blur.

Richard approached her, taking her hands in his. In her vertigoed vision, his nose was by his ear, his eyes were touching, and his mouth was upside down. A menacing sight.

"As of last night, you were right. We hadn't yet sought your father's blessing, but he has given it now," he said.

With a shudder rolling over her skin, she took her hands back and slipped them into the folds of her skirts, wiping her palms on the muslin. "But I never gave my acceptance. I was never asked."

"A man of the Marquess's stature need not ask and wait for your acceptance. Of course you would say yes." Lady Halloway's squawking whisper drove like a stake through Scarlett's ears and into her brain.

Of course you would say yes. Of course nothing. There was absolutely nothing about her interactions with Richard—which could be described as anything but cordial—that implied and warranted such confidence.

Scarlett shook her mother away and yelled to everyone present in the room, "Well, I wouldn't have said yes even if his lordship *had* cared to ask me. Now when his brother asks in due time, that will likely be a different story." She ended her statement with a definitive plant of her hands on her hips.

In a splintering crash, her father's desk chair tumbled to

the ground. He stood, looming over the room like a wall of incoming thunderclouds above a field. "The deal has been struck, girl. You will marry by month's end."

"Scarlett, I suggest you retire to your room. If you keep talking, you will only make things worse." Her mother fiddled with the gold and ruby necklace dangling above her sternum.

Was that jewel new? Scarlett was familiar with her mother's many gems and trinkets. This one wasn't one which had before hung above the woman's vanity mirror. With its bevel and inlay, it appeared to be an antique. But it was most definitely new to her mother.

She pinched the gem off her mother's dress and held it on its chain before the woman's eyes. "Where did you get this necklace?"

Richard spoke over Scarlett, "Miss Halloway, I understand your trepidation. Any young lady is bound to feel nervous about the prospect of marriage. However, I promise you, you will have a happy life enjoying the off season at my country home, Walden Manor, and every season around your family and friends here in Mayfair."

"A lady need not ask for more," her father's gruff voice rumbled. He gulped down the remainder of the brandy in his glass.

Scarlett's vision glazed with the film of tears. She dared not blink, forcing the draft of the room to dry them.

It was all outside her control. The still dizzying atmosphere of the room, her betrothal, her life, whom she was told she must marry. All of it. Entirely decided for her. Leaving her behind, feeling battered. Completely without defense.

Maybe with the exception of her words. Perhaps she could talk herself out of this. Her parents ought to be reasonable. There were no actual papers on her father's desk Richard could have signed for her hand, and her parents had allowed her to wait this long. Why not a little longer? Just until her courtship with Tate naturally reached marriage. That couldn't be longer than by the end of the season, which didn't seem a ridiculous wait.

She finally allowed herself to blink. Her cheeks remained unstained.

She soundlessly glided closer to her father's desk, wringing her hands behind her back. "A lady can indeed ask for much more. She can ask for friendship, for understanding, for passion. She can ask for a husband who fosters her interests rather than mocking them. None of which I receive from his lordship."

The floorboard beneath her father's feet creaked as he trembled with rage. The grinding of his clenched teeth echoed off the walnut-paneled walls.

So, that was clearly not the solution. Scarlett backed away.

Tugging Scarlett by the wrist, her mother hurried them both from the room and dragged her upstairs. "Stay in your bedchamber until your father cools."

Scarlett's wrist cramped from her mother's vised fingers. Once free, she rubbed the sore joint. "And then may we again discuss the falsity of this betrothal?"

"No, you heard your father correctly. The deal has been struck," her mother whispered.

She shut Scarlett inside the darkening room. The sun was setting, and no staff had stopped by to light the candles.

Scarlett paced a rut into the threadbare rug of her bedchamber. *How could my parents so easily sign me away to a man they should know I hate?*

The deal has been struck. The deal.

They wanted me to find a match this season because my seasons have been costly, but they didn't specify I must do so right away.

Her mother's jewelry was new. The deal.

They were bribed.

They sold me.

Chapter Eight

As it turned out, the only person more conniving than Scarlett Halloway was Richard's brother, Tate Langley. Richard never would have suspected it from that oaf.

Scarlett and Tate had only danced together once, and yet she was declaring she would marry him. After one measly moment at a ball, the girl was convinced his brother made a better match than him.

Ridiculous girl.

What had Tate said or done to her to persuade her of this? Whatever it was, the man was smarter than Richard had previously given him credit. However, thanks to his own genius, Richard held the secret to handling a conniving person.

Be conniving right back.

He'd given Scarlett's mother jewels. He'd settled on a rather financially beneficial deal—for her father—after discovering her dowry was nowhere near what it'd been rumored. He should have guessed by the disrepaired state of their home. He'd originally chalked it up to their eccentric personalities.

Neither of his actions would apparently be enough to get her to the altar without a fight.

Perhaps instead of giving, he should take.

Take his beast of a brother who'd somehow bouldered his way into Scarlett's heart away from her. Then, with no other prospects, she would go willingly to the chapel, and this whole mess would be behind him. He would be free to enjoy more pleasurable company.

His new approach led him to a soot-covered building, the offices of Bosworth, Cragett, & Stubs, Regimental Agency, located outside of Mayfair on grimy Clipton Street.

Stephen Bosworth was not expecting him, but he'd be welcome as a former client. His unscheduled visit did, however, mean he was forced to wait alone in the man's office for longer than he appreciated.

Luckily, the space was comfortably tidy. With the occasional visitor from Mayfair, Mr. Bosworth couldn't afford to lose business over an unkempt workspace. The ledge of the one window overlooking the bustling street was dustless. The leather chairs were soft and freshly buffed. The man's desk was set in an orderly fashion with a neat stack of papers and arranged nicknacks.

The housekeeper and Callows should take notes. As if Richard's butler Callows would take the time out of his day's worth of gossiping to actually perform his duties. That man would have a heyday with the current dramatics of Richard's love life, and he would probably root for Tate as their parents always had. Their father had had an odd way of showing it, but Tate at least caught his attention. It was more than Richard could say for himself.

Not in Mayfair, though. No, this was his realm, where he shined.

"Marquess Langley, let me guess, it's been almost four years exactly since we last did business?" Mr. Bosworth shook Richard's hand as he entered the room and gestured for Richard to take a seat.

"Yes, my brother has completed his commission–" Richard began.

"And you are here to find him another. How thoughtful of you."

The man had the manners to keep a clean office, but not to interrupt? It was no wonder he worked with soldiers.

Richard inspected and straightened his cuffs. "He's considering finishing his army career, but I want to find him a new commission, one which is difficult to refuse."

"Then India is the right choice." Mr. Bosworth leaned back in his seat and rested on hand atop his large belly.

"India?"

Mr. Bosworth opened his desk drawer and produced a snuff box. "British India. A treaty was recently signed. The Treaty of Sugauli or some such. They are looking for officers to build up their presence in the area. It's an exciting opportunity I doubt he could deny."

"How much?" Richard rubbed his palms together.

Sending his brother away had been the hope. He never would have dreamed he'd be lucky enough to find a way to send him clear across the world. With Tate on the other hemisphere, he would not interrupt Richard's plans to marry Scarlett and would never have the chance to discover why Richard needed her in particular.

Deep-set wrinkles carved into Mr. Bosworth's face as he inhaled a pinch of snuff. "As you know, my fee is twenty percent. Got to pay for relocation to a better part of town somehow, right?"

He held out the snuff to Richard who pushed it back into the man's hand.

"How much is the commission, Mr. Bosworth?"

Mr. Bosworth shrugged and took another pinch. "Two thousand pounds."

Considering the Langley wealth, two thousand pounds was a very small price to pay to remove any competition in Richard's mission to obtain a distractible, loathsome wife who would leave him to his own devices.

More like vices. Richard hardened from the mere thought of—no, he couldn't allow himself to be distracted until the matters were settled.

He slapped the man's desk. "He'll take it."

Mr. Bosworth wiped his nostrils with a handkerchief. "You don't wish to consult him first? It's he who will have to sail to the other side of the world."

Richard drummed his fingers on his chair's armrests and shook his head. "No. I know my brother. He will be delighted."

"As with last time, he must be present to sign the final paperwork," Mr. Bosworth warned. "Preferably well before the regiment leaves on the thirty-first of the month."

"He will be. I will make sure of it." Richard's chair scraped the wood floor as he stood. "T'was a pleasure doing business with you, Mr. Bosworth!"

Chapter Nine

"S ir, Reynolds informed me you wished to know more about a young lady. Miss Halloway. Is now a good time?" Callows, the Langley House butler, poked his grey-haired head into Tate's bedchamber.

Tate dropped his pencil and wiped his charcoal smudged fingers on his trousers. "As good a time as any I suppose."

He'd worked tirelessly on designing a concept for a building, but the style of the cupola was alluding him. If anyone were to take his designs seriously enough to hire him, he must have an extensive portfolio to demonstrate his range. And to do so, he'd need to focus enough on drawing without Scarlett floating into his thoughts. Or the way her hair had spilled out of her coiffure and over her decolletage when she'd demonstrated a skilled flèche with her invisible sword in the park. Or how much he couldn't wait to see her next.

Tate had never imagined himself to be the type of man who

was so easily distracted by a woman. He'd always been focused, dedicated to his service and his craft. He'd certainly not expected to be distracted by such a unique woman either. But if any woman was worth the time he should be spending on building a solid foundation for his occupation, it was Scarlett, a woman as challenging and inspiring as any craft or science worth the study.

Callows set down a tray of hot chocolate and biscuits on Tate's desk, then wrung his hands. "Well, I'm sure you know about the . . . *event* in the park many years ago."

After over a day of concentrated efforts, Tate's stomach rumbled for sustenance. Thankful Callows had remembered he preferred chocolate to tea—despite the ingrained memory of his father's insistence upon it being fattening—he sipped the scalding liquid, burning himself from impatience. He scarfed down a biscuit to sooth his tongue and choked on a crumby chuckle. "Yes. I am aware."

"The maids have also told me she has turned down a number of offers the last few years. Many say she's an eccentric with no interest in marriage." Callows dropped his voice to a dusting of a whisper and leaned in. "And, at her age, nearing the status of an old maid."

This man was well-informed indeed. Not to mention a touch over-dramatic.

While Scarlett was no doubt unique, she had seemed to be interested in a serious courtship, which typically preceded marriage. Maybe she simply wasn't interested in marriage to any of the men who had asked so far. He didn't see how this made her *eccentric*. If her previous suitors were anything like Richard, he could understand why she remained unmarried.

But old maid? *Blegh*. What a disgusting concept. She was no more than a couple of years younger than Tate himself. What did that make him given he, too, had never neared marriage? An old stable boy? A decrepit footman? An ancient valet?

He laughed to himself. When Callows quirked a brow, he coughed into his fist. "The crumbs. They tickled. Do go on." He took a sip of his chocolate.

Callows stared at him dubiously, then continued, "This year, I have noticed his lordship is particularly motivated to secure her hand. In fact, I hear he has found success."

Tate's hand accidentally tipped too far, spilling a scalding amount of chocolate into his mouth. He spat and sputtered until he could cry out, "Found success? How?"

Callows handed Tate a serviette from the tray. "Her father has given his blessing. Supposedly, he's quite the reclusive hothead. However, his lordship somehow secured a meeting with him."

Did this mean Richard had succeeded in his proclamation, no, his threat? Was Scarlett engaged?

A pain akin to a splitting punch hit Tate square in the chest. Had he just been shot? He'd witnessed it enough times on the continent to know the recoiling force the action took to a man's body.

He stood abruptly and tossed his cup onto the saucer. It rolled along the porcelain edge before settling into place.

Bolting from the room, he didn't stay to make sure it landed.

"Sir? Have I overstepped?" Callows yelled after him.

"Thank you for the help, Callows. I must offer my brother my *congratulations*," Tate's voice bellowed in the hall.

He stomped through the house, shoving open door after door until he found Richard eating alone in the dining room.

"Richard, tell me how it is you have convinced the father of a woman who has no desire to marry you to give you his blessing."

Setting down his fork, Richard gestured to a seat across the table. "Tate, welcome. Would you like to join me for a midday repast?"

"No." Tate struggled to cross his arms in the confines of his tailcoat.

More often than not, he found himself missing the moveable attire of his military days, preferring them to the stiff, pressed styles of London. More movement meant more range. More range meant a better chance he could pummel Richard should their disagreement come to fists as they often had when they were children. However, this time Tate might be able to get in a few punches. Perhaps even win. He was undoubtedly bigger than Richard now.

"Fine choice." Richard untucked his serviette from his shirt collar. "You are large enough as is. More food will not help your situation. Honestly, I don't know how the army used you given how much of a target you are."

Tate's fingernails bit into the wooden frame of a dining chair. "Answer my question. How have you obtained Lord Halloway's blessing?"

"Money." A grin stretched across Richard's face. "And it's not just his blessing. I have an agreement. A verbal one, but an agreement nonetheless." His eyelids narrowed to slits. "Now how do you already know this? It only happened yesterday. Did Callows tell you?"

"Yes, of course Callows told me." Tate slammed an impatient palm onto the chairback. The wood creaked under the force. "So, you are telling me you bribed him for her hand?"

Richard rolled his eyes. "I need quieter servants." He stood, throwing his serviette onto his plate and crossed the room towards Tate. "Yes. I bribed him. And, while I have you here, I would also like you to know you have a new commission. You are headed to India. Allow me to help you pack." He slapped Tate's back and ushered him into the hall.

India? Why India? It wasn't the first time Richard had tried to get rid of him, but India? If his brother had paid for another commission so far away, it meant he was indeed threatened by Tate's presence. He'd had his suspicion, but boy was it more delicious than he'd imagined. To be the object of Richard's, the beloved charmer of all, jealousy was the last thing he'd thought would happen with his life.

What it also meant? He was a serious contender for Scarlett's heart. Whatever he'd done, consciously or not, intended flirtation or misunderstood nervous ramblings, had worked. She'd formed an attachment to him as well. She may even have been in the early stages of love as he suspected of himself.

Tate's chest puffed. A flood of confidence coated his tongue as he yelled, "I sure as hell am not," and sprinted to the front door.

"Where are you going?"

Throwing the door open, Tate tossed back, "To tell Scarlett she and I must elope. They can't ask a married man to travel across the world if war is not in question, and you can't marry an already married woman."

He flew down the carved stone front steps and bolted towards the stables. Behind him, the second slam of the door told him Richard was fast on his heels.

"You can't be serious. You've just met her!"

"More serious than you who knows nothing about her!" Tate slid on the straw of the stable floor, shut the door behind him, and dropped the lock into place. He pressed his back against it to keep Richard's ramming shoulders from busting through.

He must get to Scarlett first. It wasn't the slow, sustained courtship he'd planned, but it'd have to do under the circumstances. He couldn't allow his brother to squelch the spirit of such a marvelous woman.

She couldn't marry a man that would treat her like a trophy and douse her fire. She needed—no, not needed for it was evident she didn't need a husband—she wanted someone to fuel her flame. To stand behind her as she released herself into the world and discovered who she could make of herself. And, employed or professionless, architect or no, Tate was certain he was that man.

Chapter Ten

I f the Lord and Lady Halloway, for that was how Scarlett mentally referred to her parents since the *betrothal*, believed they could get away with accepting a bribe for her hand, they were as misinformed as someone who believed Confucius created Confucianism by himself, as if Mencius did not exist.

Her parents may as well have struck a deal for Richard to marry an armchair because she certainly would not be standing before a vicar with him. The only way they could force her to that altar would be strapped to that chair. Which would never happen.

She need only find a way to remove herself from the legally binding contract which she hadn't signed. It was verbal, so she couldn't have anyways even if they had asked her. Oh, the joys of being a young, unmarried woman at the will of the King's laws, or lack thereof. Because, really, it should be illegal for her father to make such an important decision for her.

But, as she had learned from Voltaire, no issue goes unresolved when faced with persistent thought.

Although, her sustained thinking had formed a headache at the base of her skull. It was spreading.

She needed a distraction from her troubles, and Bethanne happily accepted her invitation to escape with a little shopping as she, too, was now fielding the woes of an unwanted courtship. Much to her annoyance, Lord and Lady Shackles-Wilkins had minorly succeeded in their quest to wrangle their daughter's errant love life.

Scarlett and Bethanne perused a rack of new ribbons, bonnets, and reticules at Mr. Monahugh's Millinery where Scarlett bought nothing. Better not add a log to the fire of the financial woes fueling her unwanted engagement. Although, she was tempted by a first-edition of Sir Francis Bacon's essays at the bookstore.

She did, however, ask Bethanne if they could make a stop at the cobbler for repairs to a few of her ripped slippers. Those occasional butter knife fencing sessions she conducted in the privacy and secrecy of her own bedchamber weren't so occasional and wreaked havoc on her shoes.

By the end of their three-hour-long spree, her hands were emptier than when it began. But the true success of their trip was entirely due to the lack of mentions of redcoats, men, marquesses, or their ungodly handsome brothers.

To quench the thirst brought on by holding their tongues, they stopped for tea at Gunter's Tea Shop. The tinkle of the ringing doorbell caught Scarlett's attention as she bit into her scone.

Camilla Bertram, the woman she had met out on the Grovington's terrace, entered the shop. She glanced at Scarlett. "Goodday."

"Goodday." Crumbs fell from Scarlett's lips. She dabbed her mouth with a serviette. "Would you like to join us?"

Bethanne tilted her head in Scarlett's direction and pursed her lips.

"My mother was right. My curious nature has finally had the better of me," Scarlett whispered behind her serviette.

Camilla scanned the other tables occupied by older ladies, courting couples, and two women who were both with child, then turned a scowl back to Scarlett. "Yes, I would love to."

The tea shop attendant brought Camilla a cup and poured her a portion of steaming cinnamon tea, Scarlett's favorite, from their pot while Scarlett introduced her to Bethanne.

"Are you new to town?" Bethanne asked.

Camilla nodded. Her cheeks plumped into a smile. They were freckleless and nearly flawless, irritatingly so. "I'm visiting for the season. My parents sent me here to live with my aunt. She has offered to sponsor me to help me find a husband because there are apparently no suitable ones in the country anymore." At her final few words, there was an almost imperceptible roll to Camilla's eyes.

"Where in the country?" Bethanne spread a tab of butter onto her scone.

"Northamptonshire," Camilla answered.

"So you must know the Marquess Langley and his brother!" Bethanne's elbow jabbed Scarlett in the ribs.

"Yes, I know them very well. Lord Tate Langley and I were close in our childhood. In fact, my parents were more than hoping I would run into him here."

Scarlett blanched. Was it suddenly too hot in here? It must be the tea. It could also be the fact that she was sweating from the idea this woman could hold hopes to marry Tate. Was that how she'd known Scarlett had been dancing at the Grovington's Ball when they met? Had she been watching Scarlett dance with her love?

The clouds outside broke, sending a ray of sunshine through the window which reflected upon Camilla's blonde hair and beaming face. Why did her romantic rival have to have the aura equivalent to a warm summer's day when Scarlett's was more of an oncoming raincloud? Captivating from afar. Irritating to most when set upon them. Life dealt with an unfair hand.

But she couldn't blame Camilla. One need only glance at the way the man's stubble shimmered on his devastatingly distracting jawline or how his shoulders strained tightly against his clothing to understand why a woman would come so far to track him down.

Scarlett wiggled in her seat, the cushion of the chair suddenly feeling incredibly hot against her buttocks. "Did Lord Tate ever—"

Bethanne jumped in to speak before Scarlett. "We have put a

moratorium on speaking about men today, so let us instead hear what your life is like in the country."

The women enjoyed their tea while having a rousing conversation about the books they'd read in the off-season. For Scarlett, that was the hard-to-find copy of Confucius. For Bethanne, a fashion magazine. And for Camilla, a volume on botany. The topic somehow developed into a mutual wish for the freedoms of the country to be brought to London. Bethanne suggested a picnic sometime soon to mimic country living. All three agreed the idea sounded divine, especially Scarlett who'd had to stay in London this last off-season for some reason her father had refused to explain.

Despite being Scarlett's competition for Tate, Camilla made for frustratingly good company. By the time the pot was empty, Scarlett and Bethanne offered to escort Camilla home through the park. Being without a lady's maid, she happily accepted.

As they strolled along the cobbled path, Lord Neels tried waving them down. When he dismounted his horse, he accidentally stepped in what Scarlett hoped was a mud puddle. The man looked like a territorial cock in a hen yard by the way he scraped his shoes in the grass.

"I swear, that man has the worst luck," Bethanne giggled.

The three ladies were too busy quietly—or, in Scarlett's case, not so quietly—laughing behind their hands to notice another man coming their way.

"Ah, Miss Halloway." Lord Cullen approached them from behind and whirled Scarlett around by the shoulder. "I see you weren't too busy to take a stroll in the park today despite how it appeared, considering you could not take the time to reply to my calling card."

She shoved his hand off her. It left behind a clammy, cold phantom on her skin through the fabric of her sleeve. "Lord Cullen, I've tried being polite. I've tried being witty. Now I don't know how much clearer I can be. I am nothing to you. You are nothing to me."

"You jest. You're being a typical woman, acting disinterested around me, the Earl of Cullen, to attract my attention. You play the coy coquette well, miss. Your humble sensibilities keep you from admitting freely there's something between us." His lip curled in a snarling smirk.

"Ha!" Scarlett genuinely guffawed. "Be not mistaken, *my lord*. This is not false humility. This is pride. It's my pride which keeps me from stooping to your level, so much so I can't consider you a gentleman, let alone a suitable one." She planted her feet to the ground, ready for the parry.

Lord Cullen's precisely manicured blonde hair fell over his sweaty forehead as he shook with anger. "Did you not hear me? I'm an earl! You could not do better than me."

"Lord Langley is after her, and he is a marquess, so she can, in fact, do better than you," Bethanne interrupted, returning a wink and a grin to Scarlett's shaky grimace.

At least Camilla was on Scarlett's side. She scowled deeply at Bethanne's quip.

Lord Cullen sputtered, then continued, "It's my right to

possess a woman of your beauty, and I'm sure I could convince you of this if you would stop being so . . . so . . . " His words trailed off.

"Impertinent? Wild? Willful?" Bethanne suggested.

Scarlett glared at her. "You are not helping."

"Ugh!" Lord Cullen growled. "It's no matter. I shall make you see reason!"

Gripping Scarlett's forearms, Lord Cullen pulled her against his chest. It was sunken, scrawny with rib bones jabbing her breasts. Revulsion spit bile into the back of her throat.

A soft hush came over the few people in the park around them. Even the wind stopped whistling through the trees, and the birds ceased their melodies. No one came to her aid, all likely too afraid of what a man of Lord Cullen's stature could do to them should they oppose his wishes.

He even attempted to appease the onlookers by yelling out, "There's nothing to see here. The lady is feeling faint, and a fit has come upon her."

As uncomfortably close as she was to his mouth, the stench of alcohol on his breath nearly intoxicated her second hand. She tugged her arms, but his grasp remained firm, so she did the first thing which came to her mind. She kneed him between his legs.

Straight in the bollocks.

Chapter Eleven

Cracking the reins, Tate rushed his horse through the park towards Halloway House. The pounding clops of Richard's horse, a golden perlino Arabian, followed closely after him.

Wind whipped Tate's cheeks. He leaned forward closer to his horse's mane, hoping to increase his speed and reach Scarlett enough seconds before Richard did. He estimated it would only take him five to haul her onto his horse and off to Scotland. Eloping wouldn't be exactly that easy, but he'd work out the logistics later.

He rounded the bend around oak trees at a speed shy of throwing him from his saddle. When they reached the clearing around the corner, his horse whinnied and rose on its hind legs. Tate's leg muscles screamed as they latched onto the horse's sides, keeping him seated. In a reflexive flash, he pulled back on the reins. His horse skirted to a halt. Dust billowed in a cloud around them. As it cleared with the breeze, a grouping of people mere yards away came into view.

Richard's horse dodged around his and halted. "Woah! What the devil are you doing, Tate? You could have caused us to wreck."

Tate's mouth opened to retort, but a voice from somewhere in the crowd interrupted, yelling, "I shall make you see reason!"

From his height advantage atop his horse, Tate had a clear view of what the crowd was gathering around. A man was clutching a woman's arms, pulling her this way and that. Dirt kicked up around their feet in their struggle.

Tate and Richard maneuvered their horses around the other onlookers. As they drew closer, the woman's identity became clear. Light brunette hair. Spark green eyes. Tall frame with generously supple curves wrapped in a periwinkle morning dress like a bow on a present just for him.

Tate's stomach wretched. It was Scarlett who writhed in the brute's clasp.

He leapt from his horse. Richard was quick to copy. They darted through the front rows of the crowd, only to skid to a stop at the front when Scarlett's leg swung upwards in a gloriously swift kick to Lord Cullen's bollocks.

Howling, the man dropped to his knees. His face purpled with veins throbbing at the surface of his forehead. His eyes bulged from their sockets. He slithered onto his stomach and squirmed in the dirt, collecting mud on his finery.

Richard left the crowd in a rush to Lord Cullen's side. Lord

Cullen swatted at him, preferring to roll as a ball on the ground. Richard dragged the man up by the armpits.

Tate was frozen. His jaw hung open as an involuntary chuckle rumbled from his mouth. He couldn't wait for the day when he'd get to retell this story as Scarlett had told her account about stealing the sword.

Who was the woman who had kicked an earl in the balls in front of a mass of people in broad daylight? That was Scarlett. His Scarlett. Not Richard's. His. What a force of a woman.

The crowd in front of Scarlett was a blur of richly dyed gowns and top hats. A roar of blood rushed in her ears, muffling Lord Cullen's cries. Her breath tore through her throat like sand against bare skin. Her legs twitched, and her arms dangled numbly against her sides. She blinked repeatedly, refocusing her vision.

Just as they had once before in her life, members of the Ton stood around her, whispering behind lace fans and shaking their heads. However, this time she wouldn't be forced to apologize. This time, no one was at her side, gripping her arm and pulling her away from the scene she'd caused. She'd never before been allowed to actualize the full extent of her bouting skills. She was entirely at a loss for what this moment precedented.

If this had been a fencing match, she would have been declared the victor, and what did the victor do upon triumph? A traditional salute.

But this was not a fencing match. No, by the enthralled expressions of the crowd, it felt more like a show, and Scarlett was the performer. It was a consolation to the onlookers' purses that they hadn't paid for this production because she wasn't trained in acting.

The only acting she knew was pretending as if this veneer of Mayfair did not bother her. And she was horrible at it.

Impulsively and with one grand sweep of an arm through the air, she bowed.

Her bonnet flopped over her eyes. As she straightened, she replaced it over her pinned curls. She was met with the sound of silence.

She spun on her heel and sprinted through the trees, yelling over her shoulder for no one to follow. Not even her friends could console her in a moment such as this, neither lady being equipped with the experience of severe social embarrassment to be of any assistance. Luckily, this time, she didn't have any stolen items for which anyone need chase her or any sabre weighing down her strides.

Her fast footfalls crunched on pine needles and undergrowth. As she reached a quiet, wooded portion of the park, she slowed and stopped to catch her breath against a tree trunk. With her eyes closed and her focus on the gentle rustle of the wind through the leaves, she could almost forget she'd made a scene by injuring an influential nobleman in front of tens of people who were bound to share the experience with hundreds more.

A horse's clop drew near and halted in front of her. She squeezed eyelids tighter. Goodness, let it not be her governess, who'd been dismissed ages ago, here by some slippage of time to verbally lash her. Or, heaven forbid, a constable.

The rider's soothing, familiar voice reverberated with laughter, "You weren't jesting when you said you could defend yourself."

"Tate." Her face dropped into her hands. Salty rivulets of tears drained through the gaps between her fingers.

If anyone was to witness her reckless behavior, why did it have to be the one man with whom she could picture a future? He likely wouldn't want a wife who resolved her disputes by damaging a man's most sensitive body part. No man would. He'd be worried she'd be waiting to strike with a raised boot any time he made a mistake.

"I'm fine. You can leave me here. You shouldn't be seen with me after what I've done," she muttered into her palms.

There was no response. She waited to hear the diminishing clop of horse hooves. Instead, there was only the swish of fabric. Then a set of warm, thick arms wrapped around her slumped figure.

After sloughing off his coat to free his arms from the restrictive sleeves, Tate pulled Scarlett close against his chest. Thankfully, she'd picked a rarely frequented copse to take her shelter, and he could console her without fear of prying eyes.

Her tears soaked through his shirt. As her shaking frame calmed in his embrace, she nuzzled her cheek against the bare triangle of skin peeking between his open collar. With the chaotic morning he'd had, there had been no time to don a cravat. He couldn't be more grateful for that fact now. When next would he have the opportunity for her to touch a sliver of his naked skin? *Possibly never if Richard has his way.*

Tate dared not break the embrace first. It'd take the strength of ten men to separate him from this woman in this moment. This brave, strong, powerful woman. She deserved every moment of comfort he could provide after her courageous effort to protect herself.

"Please, don't let go." Her whispering breath tickled the hair on his chest.

"I'm here. You have me."

He slid his back along the tree trunk and sat, leaning against its base with Scarlett pressed to him seated in his lap. They sat this way for minutes until Scarlett's sniffling ceased and she glanced up at him. Her tearful green eyes danced like emeralds with the most intricate *jardins*.

"You must find my behaviour dishonorable." Her hand swiped at the few remaining droplets hanging from her jaw.

He shook his head.

She blinked. "If not dishonorable, then wild at the very least."

He flicked his thumb across her cheek, catching the last droplet. "No, I don't believe you to be wild."

"But he's a nobleman, and I damaged his . . . his . . . " she stuttered.

In her discomfort, she shifted in her seat on his thighs, unconsciously rubbing her buttocks against the front of his trousers. He scooted down, leaning further from the tree trunk to hide his growing cock from her with some much needed space from her generously cushioned backside. Now was no time to be aroused, but, no matter how much he told himself that, his member had other opinions.

He filled in her silence with a smirk. "His bollocks."

"His manhood." She playfully rolled her eyes. "A man of his rank doesn't have such things happen to him. Imagine it was your brother I hurt."

Listening to Scarlett speak of manhood while sitting in his lap was tantalizingly uncomfortable. But, the mention of his brother was like being shoved into an ice cold lake. And he would know. Richard had done so to him before at their family's country home, Walden Manor.

Tate cleared his throat. "All the better."

She lightly slapped his chest. "I'm being serious."

"As am I. You were in danger, and you did what was best for yourself. I'm not ashamed of your behaviour. I'm proud of it. And so should you be."

Even though Scarlett's radiance was beginning to shine anew, his words felt inadequate. He yearned to give her the reassurance she so evidently needed. Reassurance that what she did was right. That who she was was right.

With a sweep of his fingers against her silk skin, he brushed a strand of hair from her face. His hand did not part from her. Instead it cupped her neck and pulled her closer to him. He used his gaze, flicking to and from her lips, to ask if this was what she wanted.

A soft inhalation coursed through her parted mouth. She nodded and hesitantly closed the space between them, lightly grazing her lips on his. Parting from him for the briefest of moments, she glanced at him and sighed through a soft smile, then quickly returned her mouth to his with enough ferocity to meld their lips together.

Tate's tongue darted out and swiped her bottom lip. To his unexpected delight, her mouth opened at his touch. There it was, her aroma of baked spices. Her mouth was spiced. Her lips tasted of something fresh from the oven. Still steaming. It was cinnamon.

All his senses were lost to her. The softness of her mewing, whispers of moans tickling his lips. The searing heat of her essence. The outlines of her soft curves fitting into him like a key in a lock. She was *so right.*

He groaned deep within his chest, shaking himself to his core. He traced his fingers up the nape of her neck and through her hair, pulling her in tighter to his search. It was not until her tongue explored his, dancing like a slow waltz, that he could experience the full flavor of her. She was sweet and spicy, like an overripe apple tartlet served on a porcelain platter in the heat of summer.

Hungry for more of her taste, Tate's mouth left hers. She released a breathy murmur of disappointment followed by an intoxicating moan when his lips brushed down the sensitive skin of her neck. His mouth dragged along the long curve as her head lulled, opening herself to him. Her pulse throbbed against his tongue as he licked beneath her ear. Her hands fluttered against his chest, and he hoped she was reaching to undo his buttons.

A chirp from a bird on a branch overhead lifted him from his daze. Damn him and his lustful stupor. He must remember they were in public. She'd worried enough over her reputation for the day. Hell, for the year. He'd be devastated if he added to her lament.

For that very same reason, eloping to evade their troubles was exactly the wrong decision. What had he been thinking? She was a brilliant young lady. A daughter of a viscount. He couldn't be the reason she would be shunned.

As much as he desired to trail further down, all the way to the pillowy mounds straining to keep rhythm with her pant against the hem of her bodice, he stopped himself.

To Scarlett's utter dismay, Tate's mouth left her neck. He pulled away from her and leaned back against the tree. "I can't let myself be carried away. You deserve more than this."

"*We* got carried away," she corrected. "And I *do* deserve more than this. How about we get started on the more now?"

She swirled a fingertip on the pulsing skin of his neck where the whiskers under his jawline shimmered with the light of the sun. It was obvious he continued not to shave for her. Her mind hazed with the unfamiliar pulsating sensation in her base clouding all sense of rationality.

His hand engulfed hers, pulling her wandering fingers from his chest to a chaste kiss at his mouth. "But this was never my intention. I rushed here to speak to you about pressing matters and was distracted by your marvelously swift kick of justice."

Scarlett's cheeks heated in a blush. Was he truly impressed by her actions? A wave of pride and satisfaction washed through her, followed by a tidal current of despair when she remembered the news he wouldn't be so impressed to hear; she was betrothed. To his brother. The Most Dishonorable Marquess of Langley.

She found her hands at his chest again, latching onto his shirt collar. "Tate, you must know I want *you*."

"I know—"

She cut him short, hoping to hurry past this ugliness to the part where he pledged his undying devotion to her and helped her escape her arranged engagement somehow. "But my father has promised me to Richard."

"I know," he said through a low growl undulating from his throat.

He ran his touch along her waist and squeezed. The sensation left her hot and ridden with a tingle which danced over her skin.

"You know?"

"Richard told me." He took a deep breath. "That is not all."

"Oh?"

What could be worse than the possible end of their burgeoning courtship? Had he given her the plague? It wouldn't be the worst way out of marrying Richard.

After another squeeze to her waist, Tate set her on the grass next to him, gathered his coat, and stood. With his back to Scarlett, he spoke while adjusting his horse's saddle, "Richard is trying to force me back into the military."

His stiff shoulders slumped. The muscles of his back flexed underneath his shirt. They were rigid and taut all the way down his spine.

"Oh." Scarlett's mouth froze open, allowing for her involuntary sounds of disappointment to escape. "Oh."

For being a woman who prided herself on her wit and well-crafted words, she lost them all when in Tate's presence. However, the idea of him leaving London, being away from her for who knew how long, was a prospect worthy of silence.

Not quite the plague. She wasn't that dramatic. It was, however, certainly worse than the influenza. And like Hippocrates, she, too, believed this disease afflicting their courtship wasn't caused by a god. It was caused by the devil named Richard.

She rose and approached him, gliding her touch along his arm to turn him back towards her. Tears pooled in the corners of his eyes.

Intellectually, she'd understood men to be capable of crying. They were, in fact, anatomically as capable as women. But she'd never before witnessed a man express his emotions so freely.

It was a blessing she hadn't, for his tears struck her as the shock one feels as one falls asleep. One minute still. The next lurching inside and feeling as though she was tumbling. She wished to hold him close in her arms as he had her, but her arm span would likely not reach past his sides.

Instead, her hands clasped his and shook. "He can't make you go if you don't wish."

Tate swatted his wet cheeks with his sleeves. "Of course I don't wish to leave. I'm finally free to pursue my passion. And, for the first time, a woman finds me, a colossus behemoth, attractive enough to court. At this moment, I have everything. I have the chance for both a fulfilling career and marriage for love. And he will take it all from me."

Did he just say love? Now she was no longer wild for kicking a gentleman's manhood. She was wild for the steaming fervor rising within her after he basically admitted to loving her. Was it thrill or trepidation? No, it must simply be shock for love was a charade, and she was surprised an intelligent man such as Tate would believe in it.

What they had was not the blossoming of love. It was a friendship based on intellectual understanding and a heavy dose of lust. The perfect combination for a contented marriage. How to make that wedding happen, however, was a puzzle she'd yet to solve. And she'd need to sooner than she would have liked.

They'd just met earlier this week. Luckily, however, so much had happened so early into the season that she'd seen enough from him to already know he would make a wonderful husband. His qualities—his conscientiousness, his gentleness, his understanding—were what every suitor before him had been missing. Love was the one quality she didn't require, yet he seemed keen to give it regardless.

As it was obvious he'd accidentally admitted his love in his frustration, this was gratefully not the time to discuss the momentum of their courtship, or her unpopular opinions on the unreality of the emotion. This was, however, the perfect time to nip his confounding self-doubt in the bud.

"You are no behemoth." She leaned into him and reached up to place a kiss on the dip of his clavicle where his heartbeat leapt under his skin, where a cravat should have been.

Knowing him, he had likely forgotten it when dressing this morning, too distracted by his busy, ambitious brain. What adorable dishevelment. With this man, forgetting clothes was certainly the more satisfying option than expensive finery. The less he wore, the better.

And the more she thought about how he might look naked—like whether or not his chest had the same soft hair as his face—the less space her brain had to ponder on the concept of love.

She snaked her hands up his torso, feeling every rise and fall of muscle and flesh under her palms. Under her touch, he was substantial. Substantially large. Substantially powerful. So much man and all for her to explore. Someday. Hopefully. At least not here while they were in the park and could be easily discovered.

"You are mighty. No one, not even your brother, can make you do anything."

Tate looped Scarlett's arm in his and guided them towards the path which led in the direction of her home, towing his horse behind him. "He made me sign a commission once before. He could again. I currently rely on his generosity for support. I cannot go against his wishes. If I do, he will revoke his assistance, and I will be without housing."

Using the end of her fingertips, she brushed the light hairs of his forearm which escaped from his shirt cuff. Underneath her touch, his muscles flexed, sending ripples up to his elbow. How could this man not see how strong he was? How capable he was of standing on his own two feet? How could he believe anyone could control him?

Family was an understandable force upon any person, no matter how many muscles one had or how much one guarded oneself. Her parents were a testament to that fact. However, they could sometimes be swayed, could they not?

"Richard must occasionally be a reasonable person, especially for his brother. Perhaps if you told him about your aspirations, he would relent."

"He's always known and never cared." Tate grimaced. "When I'd first expressed to him my desire to become an architect after years of reading and studying the craft, he announced I would be joining the army the very next day, stating it was a better use of a frame my size. He told me I'd never be worthy of the Langley name unless I returned from service looking more presentable, less 'bear-like.' He personally escorted me to sign the commission papers."

"Why did you let him force you?"

"For the same reason you allowed people to tell you you could not fence." He glanced at her. Pain deepened the color of his chocolate eyes. "The pressure. The ridicule. I listened to all of it. He raised me, Scarlett. Our parents died nearly two decades ago. His opinion was the only one I had."

His words slapped Scarlett like a bitter gust of wind. It was possible he was right, but why did he have to express it in such frustratingly clear language?

She scuffed her heels on the ground in a trudge as they strolled. He hadn't said such things to hurt her, but they had.

Was it possible she would have been allowed to continue fencing if she had been more persistent? If she had disregarded all of the naysayers?

It wasn't worth wondering now. Either way, she was still a

scandalous woman who resulted to physical defense in the most unladylike forms. She was also a woman courting a man who would soon be gone, leaving her stuck in her parents home, holed up in the library amongst her dead philosophers and their pretty words. Or worse, stuck in a hateful marriage to Richard.

Unless . . .

Unless she fought again. She would have to do so in front of all of the ton's judgmental gazes without kicks to bollocks or swords this time.

If she showed everyone the purpose of her desperate acts, perhaps they would sympathize and help her. Some would still disapprove, but, with the good opinion of enough of the right people, she might just be able to win.

She stopped in her tracks, tugging Tate to a halt. She brushed her palm over his scruffy cheek, pinched his chin, and pulled his face in an inch from hers.

"You now have one other opinion. Mine. And I need you to stay."

Her lips planted a soft, lingering kiss on his. He tasted sweet and stuck to her like honey. The warmth from his mouth left her as snug as when she wrapped herself in a blanket on the chaise in the library. It felt comfortable. Right.

Like something she'd never felt before.

When she came up for air, her whisper brushed his lips. "We will fight this." She refused to define what *this* was. "We will fight Richard. He can't force you to sign the commission, and he won't become my husband."

Her legs marching with newfound determination, she led them again in their journey.

Chapter Twelve

Richard's shoulder ached from holding Lord Cullen's entire body weight against his side. They stumbled towards the two women Scarlett had left behind, exactly in line with her typical style of thoughtless, reckless behavior.

What if Mrs. Riverston and Miss Bertram had been accosted as well? She'd left them to fend for themselves.

"Miss Bertram, I hadn't known you were in London," Richard grunted, schluffing Lord Cullen up to keep the man from sliding back onto the ground.

"My lord, I hadn't known I needed to inform you of my whereabouts." Camilla's tone frosted the air around her words. It'd been an unusually cold year thus far, but she was far colder.

Lord Cullen mumbled something about pain and damned women.

Richard ignored him. "I suppose you do not. You're a free woman."

"Am I? Thank you for informing me that I, an unmarried woman, am free enough to not share her traveling plans with her neighbor." Camilla clipped her speech in short syllables. "Wait, no. Not just a neighbor. The lord over *all* of Northamptonshire. He's certainly not interested in where I go to visit family and find a husband." She glared at him, the delicate slopes of her eyelashes scrunching together.

Before a response could form on Richard's tongue, Camilla weaved her arm with Scarlett's friend's, and they stomped away.

Why was she so upset? He was the one who deserved to be frustrated. She really ought to have told him sooner she would be coming for the season. She couldn't have expected him to be thrilled about her surprise visit. He'd spoken with her before leaving the country, so what more did she expect from him?

Distracted, he dumped Lord Cullen against a tree. "Do you need my assistance to take you home or can you go from here? I take it you are in no condition to ride."

"I Im, um, harrumph" Julian Cullen groaned.

Richard nodded as if he understood any of the blabber. "I have matters to attend to, so I shall leave you to your . . . recovery."

Crinkling his nose in disdain, he circled his hands in Julian's direction, then mounted his horse and rode out of the park, away from wherever Scarlett and Tate had run off to. Hopefully separately. Whatever damage they could do in one afternoon would not be enough to combat the plans he'd been about to set in motion before Tate so rudely interrupted his morning.

He'd only chased the man on horseback with the hope to scare Tate out of all of it before he'd have to resort to more serious measures. As with anything involving Scarlett, that hadn't worked, and his plans were still a necessity.

Tate's threat to elope with Scarlett had to have been a bluff. If he ever had a hope of achieving his ill-conceived dream of designing structures for London's elite, he would know he could not make such an idiotic decision. The Ton does not mix with ilk who so brazenly disregard propriety. For that much, Richard was certain. However, if Tate was here, constantly flitting around Richard's bride, he ran the risk of ruining the contract for Scarlett's hand. Or worse. The lubber could somehow manage to muck it all up.

Richard brushed the dust off his sleeve that Julian had smeared on him. Despite the fact Julian was horrendous, he was a necessary evil. Amongst all of Scarlett's suitors, Richard had the advantage, but it didn't hurt to have Lord Cullen around to lower Scarlett's expectations of what made a man a true gentleman. If not for that, Richard wouldn't have befriended the vulgar man in the Halloway drawing room seasons ago.

His friendship with Julian also provided him with another unexpected benefit, the knowledge of where to procure the services of men willing to work around the fringes of the law to—accomplish tasks. One could call them thugs as Julian did. But Richard preferred the term *hireable men*. These hireable men were exactly what Richard needed to ensure Tate's absence. He'd planned to head to the meeting with these men earlier in the morning before all the inconvenient disruptions.

On matters of inconvenience, it was incredibly difficult to plan all of this while his mind was preoccupied with the dissection of his interaction with Camilla.

"What does she think she's doing here in Mayfair? Does she really think she can upset me with her presence?" Richard muttered to himself as he rode down back alleys to his destination. "Well, I will not be shaken."

It had only left him mildly annoyed, but not upset. Maybe a little exasperated. Definitely a touch frustrated, but not upset. But her mere existence frustrated him. She need not be in London to accomplish that.

He couldn't allow her visit to disrupt him from his ultimate goal. Was this her intention in coming to London?

No. He wouldn't allow himself to be distracted again. There would be plenty of time for distractions of all kinds once he was a married man out of the Ton's watchful gaze.

For the briefest moment, he would be far away from their gaze currently at his destination. He'd received directions from Julian to an address on a street he didn't recognize in a neighborhood he never frequented and, upon arrival, was guided through the front of the butcher's shop, past the bloody cutting block, and into a back room where five men were playing cards in dim lighting.

"How did you hear about us?" A burly man wearing a patched jacket drummed his hands on a card table. A thick scar ran along the back of his left hand.

"You came highly recommended by Julian Cullen."

"We 'aven't heard of 'im." A lanky fellow crossed his arms as he leaned against a stack of boxes along the wall. "Maybe you should go back 'ome to your butler and ask 'im to take care of your little troubles."

Richard's skin jolted in fright as he hadn't noticed the man's presence before he'd spoken. "Why does it matter how I came to know of your services? Are you up to the task or not?"

"Post here likes to scare off our customers. Not sure if he's trying to make sure you have the stomach or he just hates the money." The man with the scar shuffled a deck of cards.

"Post?" Richard asked.

"Yeah. Name's Post. Like Lamp Post. On account of my 'eight, you see." Post kicked a leg out and gestured with bony, twig-like fingers to the length of the appendage.

"Well, Post," Richard eyed the scarred man incredulously before continuing, "I have the stomach and the purse. Just don't hurt him. He's my brother, after all."

While Tate's removal from his entanglement with Scarlett was imperative, she would never forgive Richard if Tate was hurt. She had kicked Julian in the bollocks for merely touching her. Imagine what she would do to him if Tate came out of all this injured. She might just rip Richard's bollocks off completely. He shuddered at the thought.

"Dependin' on 'ow difficult this gets, I might need back-up. Can you pay for my friend 'ere too?" Post pointed at the rotund man who had been leaning with his elbows on the card table and silently glaring at Richard since he entered the room.

"What is your friend's name? Boulder?" Richard sniggered.

The big man growled, and Post answered, "Yeah. 'Ow'd you know? That Lord Cullen told you too much of our operations 'ere."

"Quiet, Post. The gentleman is jesting." The scarred man threw a nearly empty water glass at the lad.

Post caught it in time, but liquid sloshed down his trouser legs. The man looked like he'd pissed himself.

Richard sighed and checked his silver pocket watch. "Whatever it takes to get those papers signed before the regiment leaves." He dropped a small bag of coins on the card table, shook the men's hands, and sneered at the smudge one of them left on his palm. His shoes left streaks on the floor in his hurry out the door.

If those dirty men are half capable of their jobs, his brother would soon be on a boat to India and out of his hair.

Chapter Thirteen

After the incident in the park, Tate had escorted Scarlett home, during which they'd shared a lengthy discussion about his opinions of columns and her assertion that the support they provided was merely superficial given the existence of walls. To which, he had explained the importance of the structure that not only served a vital purpose, but was also a point of beauty.

In the moment, their conversation hadn't felt real. Scarlett had asked him questions about the art and science of architecture. How a woman as lovely as her could care about such things was mind-boggling. It was the most delightful time he had ever had in his life.

When they'd arrived at her family's townhouse, she'd introduced him to her butler as her suitor. The man was the first person to be officially informed of their defiant courtship.

Tate had rocked on heels, full of exhilaration, while listening to Scarlett call him her beau. Although, he was unsure how much of the conversation Forbush had actually heard. He'd nodded his head the entire time and called Tate "Mr. Radley" repeatedly, even after Scarlett had corrected him. The man's lack of hearing could have easily been caused by Brissot's ear-splitting whine which had traveled through the crack in the front door and stopped when Tate had scratched the pup under his furry chin.

Tate tapped one of his pencils on his desk with a rapid ticking beat. Today wouldn't be filled with nearly as much excitement.

If only there'd be a repeat of yesterday's spicy, warming kisses with Scarlett. He'd seat her here on his lap and press his lips to hers until they swelled. He'd throw his papers from his desk, including the nearly perfected archway he should be focusing on redrafting, then prop her up on the tabletop. She might beg him to press himself so close to her in an embrace her legs would part for him. She'd be radiant sprawled open against the coolness of the wood. The sun would cast light from the window shining across the room onto her breasts like mountains in front of the sunrise. Her eyes the hint of green which hued the early morning sky around them.

Phew. Remember to think with the proper head. Musings of Scarlett were flitting through his tired mind with abandon. Which was perhaps the reason why his designs were suddenly taking on a much more luscious, daring shape.

But no, he wouldn't see—or touch or feel or taste—Scarlett that day. Nor would he have any chance of squandering his brother's determination to ruin their lives because he was scheduled to visit Camilla for tea.

A yawn stretched his cheeks painfully wide. He'd hardly slept for worry of Camilla's purpose for this visit. When she'd unexpectedly encountered him in the park, she'd claimed she didn't intend to make him her husband. What if she'd said so simply because she was instructed to by her father with the hopes reverse logic would pique his interest? It had not.

Just as Richard had always been, Camilla was dutifully concerned with her father's wishes. The man had always made it quite clear he hoped Tate would someday marry Camilla. It wouldn't be surprising if Camilla held those same hopes as well.

Who had he become, suddenly concerned by the attentions of two women? The attention of one alone was an entirely new experience, and that was the one he wished to keep for the rest of his life if he could. Rejecting Camilla would be a first for him, and it'd be more tortuous than the process of measuring rafter spacing. How did his brother reject ladies so often without remorse?

Please, let me be wrong. It would be so much easier if Camilla was interested in a baron with the guaranteed wealth of a firstborn, a Lord Neels sort, and not him.

There was nothing wrong with her per se. Growing up, they'd enjoyed many a day together exploring their families' adjoining properties. She was humorous and adventurous, but she was never anything more than a friend. It hadn't been clear to him why their friendship had never blossomed into more until he'd met Scarlett; unbeknownst to him, he'd been waiting for the woman who sparked inspiration.

"Knock, knock." Richard opened his bedchamber door without permission, beaming from cheek to cheek. "I hear you are to meet with Camilla today. It would have been nice if you'd told me she was in town." His smile was so tight his lips turned parchment white.

"Why should you care? Are you not betrothed to Miss Halloway? Because if not, it'd make my life a whole lot easier." Tate raked his hand through his hair and trailed it down his smooth, shaven face.

Reynolds had shaved him clean this morning. If Scarlett was correct his appearance was more attractive with a little stubble, then Camilla would not see him unshaven.

A pencil he'd forgotten behind his ear fell onto the desk. *So that's where I put that.* This wider gauge pencil had disappeared hours ago.

Richard raised his brows and fiddled with his waistcoat buttons. "No, I am. I just find it fascinating you claim such an interest in *my* intended, but you're calling on your old flame instead."

"Camilla and I are friends. Scarlett is rational. She will understand." Tate finished sorting his drafting supplies and crossed the room, pushing past Richard.

At least, he hoped she would. How would he explain to her that, despite the beliefs of others, Camilla was never his intended?

"So you mean to say Scarlett does not yet know you're visiting Camilla? She's a hot-head. She will dislike it as much as Camilla's father will be upset to hear you have no intention of marrying his daughter."

Tate bounded down the hall, out of the house, and away from Richard's goading.

Lady Bertram's home was barely outside of Mayfair on Parks Lane. With grime-covered rendered stone and crumbling bricks, it was shabbier than all of the London houses with which he was acquainted.

Granted, he was no stranger to humble lodgings. The housing in the military had been short of nonexistent by intention. Which was why it came as no surprise to him that the scribbled designs he'd created during his service were nowhere near passable.

Mrs. Bertram's housekeeper opened the door a crack. Her nose and mouth squeezed through the opening. "Who is it?"

"Lord Tate Langley here to see Ms. Bertram."

"You are expected in the drawing room, sir." She swung the door open and scurried off.

Thanks to an open door on his left, Tate found the drawing room himself. An unpolished silver tray lined with sweets and a chipped china teapot were staged on a table in front of the settee.

Camilla was seated in a chair across the tableau, teacup in hand. "I have asked my aunt to give us privacy."

Privacy? Why did they need privacy? Tate held his breath and perched on the settee. His wide frame posed difficulties when attempting to sit completely on such delicate furniture.

A long silence ensued. The shuffle of the housekeeper's steps carried in from the hall.

Camilla cleared her throat and tilted her head in the direction of the service, waiting for him to grab a cup of tea or plate of food. Their entire friendship, she'd refused to play the hostess role expected of her, and it only endeared him more to her as it was the most familiarity he'd had in his young life. Why should propriety force her to serve him? It should not. As she would say, she was a country miss, not a maid.

Instead of serving himself, he sat on his hands as his nerves had kept him from eating or drinking anything yet that day. They shared an awkward glance and set of forced smiles before breaking the silence simultaneously.

"I don't wish to marry you–"

"I am in love with someone else."

"You're in love?" Tate blurted. A rush of relief relaxed his tense muscles.

Camilla unsuccessfully hid a sheepish smile behind her teacup. "Yes. Although, I don't know if it will come to anything."

With his stomach free from its knot of nerves, it grumbled loud enough to widen Camilla's eyes.

He grabbed a biscuit from the tray. "Does he love you back? The person is a 'he,' I assume? Please correct me if I'm wrong."

If she loved a woman, there'd be no better person for her to confide in than himself as her oldest friend. Unlike the House of Lords, he was certainly not one to judge. He'd witnessed and heard of many new things while on the continent, including two ladies who had exited a room together at a brothel whose pub had the best ale in France. As long as she was in love and didn't wish to marry him, he'd be seated at the front aisle of the chapel, ready to wish her many happy returns with her bride.

"Yes, I believe *he* may love me." Camilla blushed. "What have you learned in your years on the continent, Tate Langley?"

"I have learned from others to be courageous. To finally become a man who is brave enough to tell you, as lovely of a person as you are, I have never held the feelings for you that you deserve." He took another bite of the biscuit and twitched his lips into a smile. The baked good crumbled in his mouth, all buttery, sugary goodness.

"A weaker woman wouldn't have taken that comment so well," she laughed dryly, "but I've never felt anything for you either. Our future together was only ever an idea in our fathers' minds. Luckily for you, you don't have to face your father to tell him so as I do."

"My father is dead."

"Precisely." She swirled her teacup as she gazed out the window.

She then caught him up on life in Northamptonshire, including how much her younger sister, Lilith, had become quite the prattler after her debut, for a half hour until Tate's rumbling stomach signaled it was soon time to leave. Otherwise, he'd eat through their pantry. He'd not had a full meal in over a day.

From their discussion, he discovered Camilla was right; her relationship was most likely doomed from the start as she was in love with a Mr. Watters, her father's solicitor. With tight lips and shifty eyes, she'd been rather quick to finish speaking of her secret courtship, so Tate had dropped the matter.

"Before I go . . . " He toyed with the fringe of the pillow next to him, rolling the strings between his fingertips. "How do you know Miss Scarlett Halloway? I saw you with her in the park yesterday."

"We've recently become acquainted. We ran into one another at Gunter's. She's a real crush, you know."

"I know. I know." He sighed. "Camilla, I believe I love her."

Camilla gasped. "Tate Langley! Why didn't you say so sooner?"

He shrugged and stared at his distorted reflection in the silver tea tray. His nose appeared wider than his eyes and his cheeks fatter than apples.

The truth deep within his heart said he loved her long before this realization. Honestly, from the moment she held out her hand and asked him to dance, and he would go through trials and torture to be with her if he had to. Even if one of those trials was believing Scarlett would truly wish to be with a man like him.

His eyelids squeezed shut as he mumbled, "I think I want to marry her, but there's a ratbag of an obstacle in my way."

Her smile vanished. "Is it Richard?" She didn't wait for Tate's response to continue while throwing her hands up in the air, "I don't know why that man insists on convincing everyone he doesn't have a heart."

"Because he doesn't. A second cock is where his heart should be," Tate grumbled.

Camilla stuttered. "Well, that is just not true. He's quite—Nevermind. It's no matter. I'll see if I can talk him out of torturing you."

What could Camilla do to get his brother to stop being such an entitled prig? Wait. Why was he questioning whatever method she planned to employ? Any help to save the dream life at the tips of his fingers before it was ripped from him would be much appreciated.

As he bounded down Bertram House's mossy stone steps, he chuckled to himself. He'd been so unnecessarily nervous. Of course Camilla did not want to marry him. She'd only ever known him as the man he was before. Quiet, reserved, introspective, dutiful.

Recently, the other sides of himself—his drive, his artistry, his confidence—had flourished because they found inspiration. Scarlett.

Before, he accepted his brother's insults as truth. Now he would leave the room before the desire to punch Richard took control of his fists.

Before, he took his brother's advice on everything, including what to do with his life. Now he would stand up for himself and become the architect he'd always dreamed of becoming.

Before, he would have let his brother have the woman who interested him. Now he would fight for her until he could no longer, until she was standing at an altar. Or maybe he wouldn't give up even then.

Chapter Fourteen

Scarlett had promised Tate they would fight. Together, they'd take down Richard's plan to control their lives. And the fight would begin at the Duchess of Halfurst's stargazing soiree.

She planned to target a blow to Richard's ego with a proper demonstration to the Ton who her real suitor was. This would likely include some heavy flirtation with Tate, which didn't require any convincing on her own part. Perhaps she'd even secure a clandestine kiss. It'd be easy enough considering it was all she'd been dreaming of doing for the days since their encounter in the park. The feel of his mouth on her neck haunted her very spirit with shiverings and gooseflesh.

If only she could spot him through the dark covering of night amongst the multitude of other young people in attendance. Starlight wasn't sufficient to determine who was who in the guests milling about the lawn, and voices were indistinguishable in the din of clinking champagne glasses and coos directed at the constellations above.

It'd been quite surprising her mother had approved of her attendance at the event considering the Duchess's reputation. Besides being a notorious gossip, she was known for playing matchmaker to the unmarried members of the Ton. As a rich widow of a duke privy to the Ton's innermost secrets, what more was she expected to do with her time?

To the Duchess's credit, her events usually were an acclaimed crush not to be missed. Last year, she hosted a tasting of vintage wines her late husband had collected from his many travels on the continent. This year, her focus was astronomy with the acquisition of her new, positionable telescope.

Because the Duchess's invitation had claimed there would be plenty of chaperones in attendance, Scarlett's mother had even suggested she attend unaccompanied. She would have regretted her choice if she knew the chaperones were merely the oldest married couples of the Ton, so old they struggled to stay awake for this necessarily late event. Their heads bobbed as they dozed in the chairs set up on the veranda.

But it played perfectly into Scarlett's plan. Without the guiding hand of a chaperone, she could spend the entire night pasted to Tate's side. Once everyone witnessed to whom she'd actually set her cap, or feathered headpiece, her parents couldn't force her down the aisle to partake in a sham.

After waiting in a candlelit queue for far too long and listening to everyone else gush about the amazing view of

Orion's belt, she took her turn gazing through the telescope.

"Beautiful," a whisper beside her blew through the curls around her neck.

She squinted harder against the eyepiece. "Are they? It's difficult for me to see."

Stepping away, she rubbed her irritated eyes and pivoted to view the speaker.

"No, I meant you." Richard's waved hair was set faultlessly unmoveable above his plastered smirk.

"My lord, how nice to see you." Sarcasm weighed down her monotone voice.

He stepped closer to her, dipping his head down in line with hers. "You are more lovely than the stars."

She backed away from him, bumping into Lord Neels in the queue behind her. "I would never compare myself to a heavenly body."

"I don't know what you mean. I see a heavenly body before me." Richard's gaze raked over her form.

Her arms crossed over her chest in an attempt to hide her ample cleavage. "I need some air."

"But we are outdoors."

"I know." She stomped away further into the garden.

Perhaps she could catch sight of Tate from a better vantage point. She wouldn't see him back there near Richard where disgust clouded her vision.

"It's dark. I should accompany you. " He called after her. "Someone may be lurking in the hedges."

"I assume you know full well I can protect myself." She tossed over her shoulder.

Was Richard's attendance at this event why her mother allowed her to go unaccompanied? Had she hoped he would be able to solidify his engagement to Scarlett with a tried and true compromising? The thought made Scarlett shudder.

She thanked the stars Lord Cullen was not, to her knowledge, in attendance. He was likely still nursing his wounds. Giggling to herself, she distractedly plucked leaves from the nearby bushes and tore them to little pieces.

Her footsteps ambled along the darkening path. The Duchess had evidently ordered the candles to be spaced further apart this far out in the garden. She craned her neck and rose to her toes to survey the crowd from afar. Tate's large form was nowhere to be found.

"Pst," someone hissed from down an unlit path through a line of tall laurel bushes.

Clutching her chest, Scarlett gasped. Her heart thumped arrhythmically against her palm. "Who the devil is there?"

"Tate. I'm surprised it's possible to catch you off guard." His rich, calming voice carried from a few paces away. "Why were you laughing?"

"The better question is why are you hiding in the bushes?" She stepped into the shrubbery.

The rapidity of her heart's thumping didn't slow at the sight of him. At night, the shadows defining the lines of his neck and jaw were sharper, carving unimaginable beauty into his form. The darkness of his eyes reflected the stars, a miniature recreation of nature's greatest enigma. His warmth radiated from him, drawing her in closer and away from the coolness of dusk.

"As it turns out, I did not receive an invitation," he rasped, "but I still came because I knew you wanted me here."

"How could Richard be invited and not you?"

Tate sighed. A soft smile curved his lips. "Scarlett, my brother is much more eligible than I am. No one cares about the second son if the firstborn is still unwed."

Her fists planted on her hips. "I beg to differ."

"You're the only one." Gazing down at her, his earthy eyes glistened like amber in the starlight. "If everyone declared me eligible, including your parents, I don't believe we'd be in this mess."

"Well, this puts a damper on our plan." She gritted her teeth.

If no one could see him as an interloper, then how were they to show everyone they were courting? How were they to convince everyone he was a much better match for her than Richard so that eventually, maybe, Richard would change his mind? How else would Tate learn he could stand up to his brother and discover he need not relent to Richard's whims?

Frustration balled her hands into knuckled fists at her sides. Her face grew hot despite the chilled gusts of the night.

This was all a great deal more difficult than she'd imagined. The true aspects which make someone worthy of respect, of reverence—of what others might call love and she called mutual respect—were entirely lost upon these people. Tate's conscientiousness was worth more than a hundred Richards, men who charmed themselves into seeming kind and good when they were really unscrupulous deceivers.

Tate grabbed her by the arms and knelt slightly, bringing his face down to hers. "We will return to the battle strategy after tonight. There's no need to fight every moment for what you want. I know neither of us have much experience with serious courtship, but I also know, sometimes, it's about enjoyment. Let us not forget moments like this are just about you and me." He leaned into her, mere inches away. "And should someone happen upon us here in the laurels, well then I'll make sure they know you shouldn't marry Richard. Reputations be damned. But for now, let us watch the stars. That is the point of tonight, is it not?"

Scarlett inhaled sharply, this time not with fear. Her lungs took in the deepest breaths her bodice would allow. "But you are not watching the stars right now."

"Am I not?" His lips stretched into a crooked smile.

"No, you are looking at me." She twisted her hands in her skirts to keep them from grabbing his arm, his hands, his face, his anything.

"Fine." He twisted away from her and tilted his head up to the sky. "I'm glad I can't view them through the telescope. I prefer to see them naked."

"As do I. They're more honest that way." She bit her lip to keep from giggling at his horrid attempt to change the subject from less tense, tightly-wound topics.

T ate shoved his thumbs into the waistband of his trousers. If he didn't occupy his hands, he'd dig his fingers into her hair and crush his mouth to hers. And, despite what he'd said, their reputations were not so unimportant for their futures that he could damn them so thoughtlessly. If he were to kiss her here in the minimal privacy of the Duchess's gardens, he'd need to exercise restraint. This was no place for the throws of passion from his daydreams.

Scarlett swayed closer to him. The fabric of her dress swished against his leg. "It's almost as if the stars are begging you to step forward to know them better until you look back and find you are on uncharted grounds."

"Exactly. As if you have come this far, why not continue? Why not see the journey through until you can hold one?" He licked his lips, enjoying the way hers shined from the distant candlelight as she spoke.

Scarlett's bosom rose and fell with short, rapid breaths threatening to spill over the low-cut neckline of her midnight blue gown. Tate's pulse quickened.

"I thought you were a man of science. I'm surprised you wouldn't enjoy the technological advancement of the telescope." Her airy voice weaved into the breeze blowing through the laurel leaves.

"I am a man of science, only practical science. Things I can see with my own two eyes. Things I can touch with my own two hands." He lifted them to demonstrate.

Scarlett appeared to be mesmerized by his palms until she shook her head and snapped her gaze up to his. Their breathing seemed the sole noise cutting through the palpable silence.

Beyond the thick shrubbery, the rest of the party grew louder as they chattered and complimented each other on their astronomically-themed outfits of blue and black silks and shiny precious stones. All nonsense in comparison to the construction of the heavens before them.

Tate wiped his moist palms on his waistcoat. Now was the time. They were alone in relative peacefulness under the majesty of a celestial sky. He had Scarlett's full attention as she wasn't preoccupied with worries about Richard or her parents. She was here, savoring a moment alone with him just as they had when they first danced. There would be no better moment to express himself.

"Scarlett . . . "

"Yes?" Her jade eyes brightened with a knee-buckling smile swung his way.

His fingers twitched to graze the bare skin of her cheek, but he halted.

"I could have given up when Richard claimed you, or when he threatened my career . . . " He cleared his throat. "Or when

I didn't receive an invitation to the sphere in which you're a welcome member, but I didn't. I'm here because I've realized something," his voice split with the hope swelling in his chest. "I lo—"

Tate's words were abruptly mumbled against Scarlett's lips as she crashed into him. She threw her arms over his neck, pressing the whole length of her body against his. His wind blew from his lungs at the force of her embrace.

Her lips lapped over his. Top. Then bottom. Then top again. As ocean waves on a shore, sucking him into her current.

A moan rolled from the depths of him. He wrapped his arms around her, hands timidly grazing the upper curve of her buttocks through her gown. It was pert and firm at first touch, but it molded to his palm as she relaxed in his grasp.

He should let go, step away. He shouldn't allow this to go on further. They were hardly hidden in the gardens of England's most tongue-wagging woman for god's sakes. If they were successful in their plan, they'd have plenty of moments like this—minutes of her softly moaning into him, hours with her molding herself to his length—in the future once they were married.

But what if they weren't successful? What if he would be cast away to India without the memory of feeling her in whole, in truth, bare before him? There was no greater way to fall ill to love than to let it go unlived.

He held tighter to her, gripping her with a force likely too strong for her sensibilities. But he wouldn't release her. Not yet.

Instead of pulling away from his tight grasp, she whimpered. Oh, if it wasn't the most intoxicating noise which had ever reached his ears. His heart leapt as she trailed her touch down from the back of his neck to his shoulders and down his biceps. Her fingers squeezed into his arms.

Her tongue swiped across his lower lip. He opened for her. Astonished as he was by her boldness, he must remember this was Scarlett. His Scarlett. And for some reason he dared not question, she'd been clear she found him attractive despite what others had said before about his ungentlemanly appearance and oversized frame.

Perhaps she even returned his feelings of devotion. Of love.

S carlett couldn't help herself.

It was in the way Tate's mouth drew her closer when he began speaking the words she'd never thought could affect her so. Perhaps due to the improbability she would ever find a person who in turn inspired similarly strong feelings within herself.

Not love, of course. Enduring affection, to be sure, was the more logical name for this—this warmth she felt whenever he was near.

And, oh, is he so delectably close now. According to the

thrumming in her core, so was she. Close to an unknown, heightened euphoria with which she had never before been acquainted.

Her fingernails dug into his arm muscles. They flexed under her touch. A wave of tingling heat washed from her head to her base. His muscles were as hard to the touch as they appeared.

Her hands trailed further, over to his chest and down his front, discovering him. His heat. Where he was soft and comforting. And where he was *unbelievably* hard.

His mouth dotted kisses across her cheek, stopping to nibble on her earlobe. A shock coursed through her at the decadent touch where she'd never before believed to have feeling. He left a fiery trail down her neck, but didn't stop there. His lips brushed lower at the crest of her bosom as his fingers reached for the neckline of her bodice.

He gazed up at her, his mouth still working between the tops of her bosoms to send reminders to her pulsating core. She pushed closer to his touch. Her head fell back, leaving her to stare at the stars above. His hands tugged the lace-edged front of her gown down over her bosom.

The night breeze blew over her bare breasts, bringing her nipples to hard points. If the air was not enough to send shivers from the crown of her head to her toes, his wet mouth surely was. It pulled one nipple into its warmth. His hand kneaded the other breast, thumb stroking the nipple.

She was stricken. A burst of melting, dousing fire. Everything in her was hot, sweltering in swirling dizziness. She was liquid beginning to drip.

Her knees gave way to her pleasure. One of his arms looped behind her, holding her steadfastly to him.

Pressed to his length, a rigid column poked at her hip through the fabric of her skirts. One need only visit a museum to know what it was. It was hunger. It was need.

Her eyelids closed over her blurred vision.

"I want you. I need you." The words escaped her, a dare to be as wild in passion as she was in war.

His moan shook her breast. He deepened his kiss, flicking his tongue over her nipple. Then his hands slid to cup her bottom, gripping so roughly he elevated her off the ground. As a reflex, she gasped at the touch. Her gasp set him off. He released a low growl of passion and lifted her into the air, sliding his hands down her thighs to guide her legs around his waist.

Scarlett's skirts rose, bunching around her stomach. His hands rocked her hips up and down, rubbing her core against the hard front of his trousers.

A sun began to rise within her. She was on uncharted ground, approaching her star, and was so close to catching it in her grasp.

Until oncoming voices broke through their symphony of panting.

"The moon can be better observed from this angle," cried the Duchess's shattering voice.

"Is the moon a star?" Lady Lucy Bell's recognizable lilt inquired.

In the dark protection of the laurels, Scarlett slid down Tate's front. He bit his lower lip and groaned. His hands balled into tight fists, presumably to distract himself from another tightly wound body part which he'd pressed to her core, nearly sending her over the edge of her unknown precipice.

The cool air scratched Scarlett's throat as she struggled to catch her breath. Hollow and unclaimed, she rushed to adjust her rumpled clothing.

From the rustle of skirt hems on grass, footfalls drew nearer.

Her mouth hung agape. She stood, frozen, unsure of her next move. There was no sword, or butter knife, in her hands. This was no time for a flèche or a riposte. Nor were there any words she could say which would explain their flushed cheeks and Tate's wrinkled trousers.

Tate straightened her dress sleeves and whispered, "Run. They can't see you here like this with me."

"But—" She began to protest.

"It will not help. Go!" His bronzed eyes pleaded to her.

Scarlett sprinted down the path, careful not to land her steps on the slick, dewy patches of lawn. Her strides muffled into landscaped undergrowth of ferns and vining ivy. Sneaking around the shadowed edges of the garden, she believed she remained unseen by the other guests.

She tiptoed behind the seated, napping chaperones. Once safely past the open French doors and inside the Duchess's empty drawing room, she finally exhaled the breath she'd held since leaving the laurels. She leaned against a wall and pressed a hand to her chest to calm her racing heart.

If I was seen, I am caught. I will bravely face the societal consequences of my actions alone. Tate will not be implicated. Her mind ran as fast as her pulse. *His career would be ruined before it even began.*

"My dear, are you unwell?"

Scarlett twitched and yelped in surprise.

It was the Duchess. How was this woman everywhere at all times? It was no wonder she was a magnificent gossip.

"I believe I'm just chilled," Scarlett stuttered. Her palms rubbed her arms.

The Duchess led Scarlett by the elbow to a settee. "Yes. You do appear rather flushed. Let us say it's from the cold."

Scarlett stalled. With an indignantly raised chin, she gazed at the woman through slitted eyes.

The Duchess held her stare with a blank, unreadable expression.

This was the first time Scarlett really examined the woman. The Duchess couldn't have been more than six years her senior. Her hair, brilliantly sleek and darker than dried tea leaves, allowed the diamonds hanging from her ears to sparkle. Her eyes were shockingly black, so dark one couldn't distinguish the pupil from the iris. Her skin was tanned, like burnished copper. She wore a dress that was spun of threads of silver with a scandalously low neckline and a fashionably high waistline.

"Your Grace—"

"Please, call me Ava." She peered pointedly under her lashes.

"Scarlett, my gardens are just that, mine. What happens in them is my information to share . . . Or not share."

Her butler brought over a tray holding two glasses of brandy. Ava motioned for Scarlett to take one.

"Have you noticed that Lord Cullen is not in attendance tonight?"

"Yes." Scarlett choked out the word through a cough. Her throat burned from the drink.

"That is because I wanted to thank you." Ava paused to sip, emptying her snifter. "I heard what happened in the park."

What a surprise, Scarlett thought, straining to keep from rolling her eyes. She was likely the first to hear of it. And after she did, hundreds more followed. Best to go straight to the source of gossip with Scarlett's own explanation of the event in question.

"I was merely defending myself."

Ava waved her hand in dismissal. "Dear, no one understands you more than I do. I always respect an unusual solution to a usual issue." She handed her empty glass off to her butler, then ordered him, "Leave us."

After the butler shut the door behind him, she leaned in close to Scarlett. "I don't see why anyone should care to know that you were stargazing *alone* in my laurels." She gave Scarlett a knowing look. "However, I will keep this knowledge to myself as I don't wish to send my friend into any scandal. And, as my friend, I want you to teach me how to defend myself as you did."

Scarlett's eyes blinked, slowly reopening to ensure the scene playing out before her was indeed happening. Yes, there the woman was, tapping her fingers on her knee expectantly.

She was waiting for what? For Scarlett to jump with joy over the prospect of being coerced into teaching other women how to behave as ridiculously as herself?

"Your Grace."

"Ava."

"Duchess—"

"*Ava*," she corrected again.

Scarlett sighed. "Ava, what I did was wrong. It's best to protect oneself with knowledge and well-timed words, not violence."

"And when words and knowledge are not sufficient?"

Scarlett held her tongue.

"I see nothing wrong with your methods. And neither did many of the women with whom I have spoken. We all understand why you did what you did, and we want to know how to employ your methods when we are faced with similar . . . situations. So you will teach me and a few other friends." Ava's tone did not question. It ordered. "Now, I have already told the staff to bring your carriage around." Ava stood. Her dress elegantly swooshed around her form as if it was fashioned from rays of moonlight.

Scarlett followed suit. "I don't know how I can show my gratitude."

"Nonsense, it's you who will be owed the gratitude. After your lessons, of course." She grinned at Scarlett. Her mouth curved into what seemed a genuine gesture of glee.

With the end punctuation of Lady Ava Halfurt's front door shutting behind her, Scarlett had effectually made an ally of the Ton's most notorious gossip. And unwillingly became a tutor. Perhaps the most unconventional tutor to ever exist.

Chapter Fifteen

All these days later, Scarlett swore her skin still tingled from Tate's gliding touch when she allowed herself the diversion of remembering their starlit tryst. Which she did. Frequently.

At breakfast, her mother had asked her if she was ill, and she hadn't realized why until she lowered her gaze to find her fork hovering inches from her open mouth. It was a blessing drool hadn't run down her chin because her mother wouldn't have believed it came from the kippers on the utensil.

While she should have been pestering her parents about revoking Richard's contract, all she could do was sit in her library everyday with the illusion of reading a book written by Descartes.

Her father stopped by to lecture her about being unpatriotic and how women were filling their heads with too much nonsensical information. Then he asked her what her thoughts were. As she'd been stuck on page twenty for the last day and a half, her answer was exactly what he likely expected, a series of mumbles and a shrug.

I've read Descartes before. If only I said without the mind, the body is nothing, and without the body, the mind is everything. Scarlett thumped her forehead with the book.

Both Tate's mind and body were everything to her . . . As was his bravery for sneaking into the Duchess's property just to see her. She'd always remember the kind, caressing words he'd spoken to calm her down and the way his calloused palms had dragged up her thighs and grasped the sensitive roundness of her buttocks. The slight pain of the sheer strength in his grip—sparklingly pleasant—was unforgettable. Even more haunting was the pressure which had risen between her legs while she'd rocked against him. What would have happened with that pressure had they not been interrupted? Would she have boiled over like a teapot or crumbled like rubble from a wall of fallen bricks? She couldn't wait to find out.

But, she must. When would be the next time she could have a moment alone with him? Too long from now. Even if it was at the Wilkins' picnic in a few days, that would also be too long from now.

She groaned, startling Brissot where he lay in a sun spot on the floor. His head snapped up so fast his ears flipped inside out, revealing the cavernous openings one could assume went straight through without a brain blocking the path. Scarlett threaded her fingers into the warmth of his red blaze of fur to soothe him.

Of course now she wasn't distracted, she formed a quality retort to her father's insult. *If nonsense is in the books I read, then I hope many people's heads are filled with nonsense indeed for it's better than having an empty head as you do, father.* That would show him about women's education. If only she'd been reading Wollstonecraft, then perhaps she would have quoted a line or two as well. Although, he doubtfully would have listened to her entire diatribe. She really needed to learn how to shorten her ideas. No one, besides Tate, ever listened to the whole thing.

At least the library was comfortable with its overly-stuffed, sundrenched chaise in front of large, paneled windows. The air wafted with the toasty scent of old books, ones she always knew where to find in their shelves because only she ever touched them.

She could stay here everyday until her mind rotted from reliving the memory of Tate's body entwining with hers and his lips exploring her bare skin too many times. She didn't trust herself to leave the house in this state. She'd probably get herself run over by a carriage.

Because her parents believed her to be ill, she'd sent away every caller, including Richard and Lord Cullen, with a smile before curling back over her book. As such, when someone entered the library, she assumed it was Forbush with another calling card.

"I'm still not taking callers, Forbush. I'm unwell," she yelled while shaking her head. With his hearing abilities, he understood motions better than speech, so she always employed body language when speaking with him.

"You don't appear ill to me." Her mother's shrill voice carried across the room. "Your complexion is actually very bright considering you haven't left the house in days."

"Mother!" Scarlett's hand fluttered to her brow. "My complexion is bright because I'm feverish. It's from the sweat."

Lady Halloway sauntered towards the chaise. Her glower scanned Scarlett from head to toe. "Then I take it you can't join me to pick out your wedding china?"

Scarlett faked a cough into her fist. "Certainly not. I'm much too sick."

The back of her mother's hand tested her forehead. "You are not sick."

"Fine. I am not. But I have an appointment with Bethanne today I must keep."

This was a lie, one Scarlett must now hold herself to. Running the risk of being trampled by a carriage was worth it to avoid shopping with her mother, especially for a wedding she was certain she would keep from happening somehow. If only she could get her mind to function properly again.

"Very well. But you won't be getting out of the visit to the dressmaker's for your wedding gown and trousseau." Her mother wagged a finger.

"Or what? You will bribe me? It won't work. We don't have the same taste in jewelry." Lifting her book in front of her face, Scarlett peered over the edge of the gilded spine, glaring pointedly at her mother's newly acquired pendant.

Lady Halloway huffed, the breath fogging the gems of her gaudy necklace.

Scarlett did have one thing she could do while she was out, and it wasn't a visit with Bethanne. A recent missive from her friend had informed her that Bethanne was quite busy fending off a persistent suitor of the unwanted soldier variety. Scarlett had offered to help, but Bethanne had said she would handle it on her own, which, after the lifetime of friendship, revealed that Bethanne was secretly happy to be dancing the dance of courtship again. "Unwanted" to Bethanne simply meant unexpected.

No, it was Tate she wanted to see. She couldn't wait here, mind-numb and drenching her skirts, until the next time she could have a chance encounter alone with him. But she could not very well tell her mother she was planning to call on a man. Let alone a man who wasn't her supposed intended.

Tate was sure to be working on his sketches, but he would make time for her. And perhaps they could disregard the usual, polite pastimes of calling hours to immediately pick up where they'd left off in the garden. She fanned herself with her book at the thought.

Scarlett gathered a number of stares while briskly walking Brissot unaccompanied down the streets of Mayfair to Langley House. With a slight twist of her lip, she looked back at each and every person who passed her by as if they were the ones who were unusual.

Lord Drafton and Lord Neels gave her a wide berth, walking with their hands in front of their trousers. While distracted by Scarlett, Lord Neels accidentally tripped over a carriage wheel rut in the lane. The motion sent his cupped hands jerking into the front of his buckskins. He yelped in pain.

The expression the Langley House butler gave her was the worst of them all. His dumbstruck mouth hung open from the moment she knocked on the door to when she asked to call on Lord Tate Langley. No one could call the man unprofessional because he regained enough composure to wordlessly show her and Brissot into the drawing room.

They waited for a quarter of an hour, pacing back and forth in front of the marble fireplace mantel. Brissot inspected the ash residue inside the hearth, sneezing repeatedly when he stuck his nose a little too close. Grey snot flew from his nostrils, sticking onto the canary-yellow, floral-papered walls.

"I told you to keep your distance, but you never listen," Scarlett scolded her pet. Then she wiped his face with the only cloth she could find, a crocheted doily. She hid the soiled cloth underneath a cushion.

It was nearly tea time, so there was no way Tate was still asleep. She hadn't seen him riding in the park. It was unlikely he was at the club this early. Chances were he was shut away in his room, slumped over his desk. So why was he taking so long?

"Scarlett, what a pleasure." Richard sauntered into the room.

Merde. After Descartes, French was on her mind. *Had I not been clear that I wish to speak with Lord Tate Langley, not this prig?*

R ichard couldn't have asked for a better way to get Scarlett alone to learn more about her odd attachment to his brother than for her to volunteer herself to him. Well, not to him, per se. She had told Callows she was here to see Tate, but Richard was the Lord of the house. He made the decisions, and he decided she was here to see him.

"Richard–"

"I'm so glad we are finally using familiar names now," he interrupted her.

Her brunette bun at the base of her neck nearly unraveled with the force of her eye roll. "*My lord,* I was hoping to speak with your brother."

"My brother? What brother?" He straightened his cravat, glancing at her with a smirk.

Her nostrils flared. "Tate."

"Ah. Yes. Tate. He's unavailable at the moment. Do sit." He gestured to the damask silk settee.

"I will, but only to wait for him." She fell onto the nearby seat. Her lilac skirts billowed in a cloud around her.

Her dog—what was his name? Biscuit?—curled at her feet.

Richard scooted in next to her on the settee. "What brings

you and Biscuit here this afternoon?"

He rested his hand on her thigh. She flicked him. Now his hand sported a bright, red splotch. The bitch.

"His name is Brissot. After the journalist philosopher. You should know this as you've been visiting my drawing room every week for the past three seasons." She paused. Her head swiveled around. "Speaking of which, ought we not be supervised by one of your staff right now as my lady's maid does? Where is your butler? Even a maid would do."

"Callows is busy collecting the tea service. Besides, there's not much precedence on the societal procedures for when a young, unmarried, unaccompanied woman calls on a man in his own home." The words rolled off his tongue like sherry in a glass. "Besides, we're betrothed now. We can spend some time alone together. That leads me to my next question. Scarlett—"

"Tea, my lord." Callows entered the room carrying a tray so polished it could function as a mirror, exactly to Richard's specifications.

Richard shot daggers at Callows. While his butler was his most competent manservant, the man's timing was suspicious. He always served Richard well, but could he favor Tate? He wouldn't be the first. Mother had always babied the boy, filling his head with absurd dreams.

"I can't stay for tea." She leaned forward to rise, tugging Brissot's lead for him to follow.

"You really must." Richard reached for her wrist to pull her back into her seat.

Apparently he was taking notes from Julian Cullen now, but how else was he supposed to hold this woman's attention? His morals forced his fingers to quickly release her, but her dog ensured he wouldn't come that close again.

Brissot jumped to her aid, literally. He leapt at Richard, snarling through his barred teeth. Once Richard shuffled away to the far end of the settee, Brissot laid back down at Scarlett's feet.

Richard's teeth chattered. "Watch that mutt of yours."

She patted her pup on his head and fed him a biscuit from the tray. "He knows it's better to defend the honor of the one he loves than to seek the approval of the one he does not."

"He'll know me soon enough once we are married."

Her unladylike laughter etched through the air in the room like a hungry pig in its pen. "There's no reason to trouble yourself. We won't be getting married. I think Brissot will make sure of that."

Richard's fingernails scratched at the mahogany wood arm of the furniture. The gall of this woman. Her parents had agreed she was his, yet he still had to work to ensure her irritating arse made it to the altar when he needed her there.

"How have you been occupying your afternoons lately? You haven't been available when I've called."

Scarlett was silent.

"Have you been enjoying the weather? It's been refreshingly cool."

She nodded while busying her mouth with a biscuit.

If he couldn't get her to talk through normal conversation, then it was time to capture her interest.

"Did you know my brother and Miss Bertram are close friends?"

Scarlett snapped her sickeningly green gaze up from her plate. "Yes, I did know they used to spend time together when they were young."

Richard chuckled from his chest. "Oh, not just then. Why, if I'm not mistaken, he called on her just the other day. He was there for quite some time in fact."

"I—I did not know that," she stuttered.

He dug in further, leaning closer to her side. "How could it be exactly that you formed an attachment to Tate if he's preoccupied with another woman?"

Tate was, in fact, not at all involved with Camilla. That much had always been obvious. For the longest time, Richard had guessed Tate might have even preferred men considering how little interest he showed in their busty blonde neighbor. He'd indeed hoped Tate did, for it would have meant Richard had less competition for the ladies.

Because Scarlett didn't know the full truth about his brother and neighbor's friendship, she just might be willing to share any pertinent information about her and Tate's faux courtship if she believed Tate to be disloyal. If Richard could retrieve the information from her to use as leverage, he'd be allowed to keep up with the *activities* he enjoyed once they were married. And with whom he enjoyed them.

"We danced at the Grovington's Ball."

A loose thread tickled the palm resting on his stomach. He ripped it from his waistcoat's hem, then scoffed, peering sideways at the woman. "Is that all? Why would you need to call on him after one meager ball that was two weeks ago?"

"We also met briefly in the park on one or more occasions." Scarlett's expression remained unchanged.

There was no way she was being entirely truthful. Not with the fervor of devotion she'd expressed for his oaf of a brother. Time to strike again.

"Ah. I hear he also met with Camilla in the park. It doesn't seem like you've had enough interaction with him to form as deep an attachment as you claim. Unless..." He paused to feign a gasp. "I'd hate to hear he's taken liberties with you you feel you must hold yourself to. At his size, he's a bear who believes he can force anyone to do what he wants out of fear."

"He's only ever been a gentleman with me." The tip of her nose pointed to the ceiling.

A break in the clouds outside beamed a ray of sunshine through the windows and onto her face. Under the light, not a bead of sweat nor twitch of the lip revealed whether or not she was lying.

There must be something she was hiding. She'd been missing for most of the Duchess's party, which happened to be the same night his brother had returned home with leaves stuck in his hair.

Scarlett held her inscrutable expression and sipped the cup of tea Callows had poured for her minutes ago. It was bound to be tepid by now, but she swallowed it with a smile as if it was soothingly warm.

If she was lying, she was a hell of a good liar. He'd have to keep that in mind for when they married soon.

He leaned back into a plush, velvet cushion and stretched his arms over the seatback. "Will you be attending the next ball? I will be there and hope to claim your first and last waltz of the night."

"I will. Even so, I make no promises for my dance card." Her attention swiveled to Callows who walked past the open doorway. "Will Tate be available soon?"

Richard tisked and inhaled through clenched teeth. "Did I forget to mention he isn't home? He went out on some errand for his little sketches. I don't know why he wastes his time. He'll be leaving with the regiment soon enough. Before the end of the month, I believe."

Scarlett and her dog stood simultaneously. "Well, I really must be going. My mother will be worried."

Another lie. Richard was familiar enough with Lady Halloway to know she would only be worried once she heard the rumors about Scarlett visiting Langley House unaccompanied. Rumors which would inevitably originate from the Langley House staff member who was lurking outside the doorway.

Before Scarlett left, Richard bowed and kissed her hand. She wiped it on her skirts and rushed herself and Brissot out of the drawing room.

Her voice carried in from the hall, "Oh, hello Camilla. I'm surprised to see you here."

Camilla was here? Perfect. Absolutely perfect. She couldn't have come at a better time. Just as he could use her for his needs. Just as the thrill of a win was pulsing through him.

He sprinted to the doorway and leaned into the hall against the doorframe. "Ms. Bertram, come to see Tate I assume?"

Camilla scowled at him. "Actually, Richard, I have come—"

With a hand to her lower back, Richard led Camilla into the room. His fingers splayed against the soft muslin covering the elegant curve of her spine. "Please, step inside. You may wait in the drawing room until he is available."

Scarlett opened her mouth, but Richard swung the door shut in her face before she could speak.

Chapter Sixteen

Practically the whole Ton was invited to the picnic Scarlett's friend Mrs. Bethanne Riverston and her parents, the Lord and Lady Wilkins, were hosting in the park, including Tate, to his surprise.

By the time he arrived, the lawns were already busy with crowds playing games and enjoying refreshments *en plein aire*. Because the event was outdoors, members of the Ton brought their well-mannered pups with them. Scarlett was sure to have Brissot, which would make spotting her in the crowd easy next to her flaming red dog.

At a full head, or in some cases two, taller than everyone, Tate need not crane his neck over the crowds to catch sight of his lady seated on a blanket in front of the river with her friend. Wrapped around her ankle peeking from out her skirts was a leather strap, Brissot's lead, likely to keep her pup from running after the others.

A leather strap did look fetching around her skin. That was something he'd surely keep in mind . . .

Assuming he'd need to weave through the crowd, his shoulders slumped forward and his chest curved into himself. Before he could prepare to make the dozens of apologies for stepping on toes, the other guests parted for him with a clear path. Their eyes followed his every step. He tossed a nervous grin at each of them, particularly the elderly ladies who clutched themselves as he passed, appearing bothered by his mountainous frame looming above them. He kept his distance, pasted his arms to his sides, and mumbled polite how-do-you-dos.

At his quiet, unrefined niceties, they gasped, fluttered themselves with their fans, and plastered scandalized expressions on their faces before cracking into shy smiles like little girls. One of them dropped her lace-edged fan, and Tate bent to retrieve it. As he straightened and held out the item, his gaze caught on an odd man who was leaning against a tree behind the lady.

The man was surrounded by picnic-goers who were using the tree's shade to protect themselves from the sun, but none talked with him. He was tall, thin, and wearing the ruffled shirt of outdated garb. He had a sneer for a face and stared directly at Tate.

While the man obviously had an issue with someone here, Tate didn't recognize him. He must have mistaken him for another soldier, albeit another of the sturdily-built soldiers who were not so uncommon considering the number of begrudging Scots who were forcefully shoved into their ranks by King George. Now many of his fellow army lads had returned from the continent, they were sure to be popular amongst the business they'd left behind for months or years. Perhaps this man was a creditor seeking payment. It would explain his knuckle cracking a bit more.

A small cough broke Tate's concentration on the man. The elderly lady in front of him with a swirling mass of white fluff curled around her face held out her hand expectantly, awaiting the return of her fan.

"My apologies, Lady Burton. It seems the sun must be getting to my head." Tate's cheeks burned with embarrassment.

He pivoted on his heel to escape the flock of fanning grandmamas before he committed yet another social faux pas. As if being a giant was not bad enough. Along the way to Scarlett, he stopped to fetch drinks.

"Afternoon, ladies. May I join you?" He held out two of the lemonades to the women.

Scarlett nodded. A lock of her hair had slipped from her up-do and fell across her face.

After he sat, he reached out to tuck the loose coil behind her ear. Her head swerved away from his hand as she leaned forward to reach Brissot. Her fingers nimbly untangled one of his legs from his lead.

Free from his self-inflicted entanglement, Brissot sprung up, leapt over Scarlett's outstretched legs, and curled up between them. His tongue flopped out of his mouth when Tate scratched behind his ear.

Mrs. Riverston directed a flash of a strained smile at Tate before turning back to Scarlett. "So, you were just about to tell me how the Duchess's event was?"

Tate greatly wanted to know the answer to this question. He had no clue what had happened to her after he'd taken liberties with her in the gardens. His gaze probed her expression.

Scarlett's cheeks streaked crimson. She stared unflinchingly at Mrs. Riverston, sending no flick of her lash-rimmed gaze in his direction. "It was fine. I spoke with the Duchess for some time at the end."

Mrs. Riverston's mouth twitched into a scowl. "Why? Since when do you consort with a gossip?"

"She wanted to know if I'd be willing to instruct her in self defense." Scarlett scrunched her nose at Mrs. Riverston's judgmental tone. "Besides, Ava is much more than a gossip."

"The Duchess wants you to tutor her? What an exciting opportunity." Tate slapped his knee.

At the loud noise, Brissot twitched, then he licked and gnawed on Tate's fingers, evidently upset his belly had gone without a rub for all of two seconds.

"Yes, it is," Scarlett clipped. Her demeanor was colder than the glass of lemonade propped between his thighs.

She glanced at him, and her eyes, those enchanting emeralds, glimmered between tense, angry corners of butter-soft skin. Was she upset with him?

What could he have done? Was she angry he hadn't called on her the last few days? He'd been too busy making exciting steps in his career that he couldn't wait to tell her about. If only she'd give him her attention long enough for him to share.

Or was she upset he hadn't allowed for them to be caught in the Duchess's hedges and revealed their relationship in some grand, impractical gesture? Or, worse, could it be she regretted their clandestine moment in the first place?

His forehead hurt from his inner line of questioning. Hadn't they been clear they wouldn't do this confusing dance in courtship? She knew how horrid he was at dancing. He massaged his throbbing temple and returned his focus to the conversation at hand.

"So you call her Ava now?" Mrs. Riverston questioned.

"Yes, she is my friend," Scarlett said.

"I am your friend." Mrs. Riverston furrowed her brow and smoothed her skirts. "I'm sorry that I'm not comfortable being as free and unobstructed as you or *Ava*."

Tate couldn't help but notice the two ladies' voices were growing louder by the word, drawing the attention of every person and animal in the vicinity. He hunkered down and focused on patting Brissot's upturned chest.

Scarlett's eyes rolled so slowly it appeared for a brief moment as if they shut. "Regardless, you're still my friend. One can have more than one friend. Especially if one needs their friend's help in learning how to protect oneself. You must admit, Bethanne, some of us women find we must be more 'unobstructed' if we are to remain 'free.'"

It could have been the wind, but the small, black hairs around Mrs. Riverston's forehead suddenly stood straight upright. "Are you implying I am not as desirable as you? Because I, too, have a man who won't leave me alone, and I haven't found the need to kick him in the crotch."

Oof. Who was kicking whom now? Scarlett had told him Bethanne was going through a difficult time in her grief over losing her husband, but Scarlett didn't deserve to bear the brunt of her lashes alone. As a reflex to the insult, Tate reached his hand out to graze Scarlett's. Her fingertips brushed his palm lightly before she pulled away and tucked her hands under crossed arms.

Finally, some sign of his normal, affectionate Scarlett. At least for a miniscule moment. He must get her alone to understand what he'd done wrong. Soon. If they were to have any semblance of a pleasant and effective afternoon of proving their courtship to anyone.

Scarlett wanted him to fight for their relationship. Today, he came prepared only to find she evidently was not. Had he, by some evil magic, swapped bodies with Richard in his sleep? No, the elderly ladies wouldn't have given him a five-foot clearance if that were the case.

Scarlett's sultry voice cut through his turmoil. "I did not say that. Bethanne, have I done something to offend you?"

"No. Nevermind."

In the silence between the ladies, Brissot barked at Lady

Irving's pair of primped poodles. Tate waved an apology at the lady as she passed.

"Who is this man who won't leave you alone? I'd be happy to speak with him. A friend of Scarlett is a friend of mine." He chuckled nervously. Anything he could do to improve Scarlett's mood.

She answered for Mrs. Riverston, "You probably don't know him. Her new beau is a Mr. Roberts."

"He is not my beau," Mrs. Riverston squealed. "How did you even know that?"

"Ava told me during our first lesson yesterday. She felt the need to talk the entire time I was teaching her about the body's weak points."

Mrs. Riverston picked at the grass and mumbled, "Your friendship with her has turned you into a gossip already."

"Mr. Roberts as in Calvin Roberts?" Tate's throat burned from swallowing his lemonade too quickly. "He's my greatest friend."

"Really?" Both ladies asked simultaneously.

"We attended Eton together and both served. So he's bothering you?"

"He is—" Mrs. Riverston started.

Scarlett interrupted, "Be honest. Lord Tate Langley here won't see through your coy behaviors of courtship."

Lord Tate Langley? Did she just call me Lord Tate Langley? Tate's chest hollowed out from the invisible blow of formality.

"He is not. We are courting in earnest," Mrs. Riverston's

whisper could hardly be heard over the cheering from a nearby game of battledore and shuttlecock.

Tate coughed to recover his cheery tone. "That's splendid. Intriguing, but splendid nonetheless."

"Why intriguing?" Scarlett inquired.

"Well, Roberts is . . . " He stroked his stubble in search of the correct description of his friend, then quickly removed his touch from his jawline when Scarlett's eyes widened.

She tore her gaze from his. It was all too painful, this courtship quadrille to which he had never learned the steps.

"Do you mean to say Calvin is more than a fair bit of a rake? A rogue? A flirt?" Mrs. Riverston sagely offered.

Tate stared at her quizzically. "All of those. Yes."

Mrs. Riverston swallowed a sip of lemonade. "I am aware of his reputation."

Tate glanced up at a murmuring commotion coming from the other guests and recognized the oncoming figure. "Speak of the devil."

Calvin Roberts, a lengthy, slender man with curly black hair, sauntered to their group.

Roberts had been Tate's friend for over a decade, since their time at Eton. In every class, they'd both been the odd ones out being gentle-bred orphans by such a young age. However, Roberts had had it better. His older brother was considerably older than him and was, therefore, better at raising his younger brother than Richard had been with Tate. Perhaps that was because Roberts had at least been easier to raise than his sister.

Miss Juliana Roberts was a handful.

Then, there was the irritating fact Roberts had always had more luck than himself in other more recreational matters. While Tate had always hunkered over his desk, Roberts had been shamelessly busy studying less bookish interests. Women.

Even now as he approached them, he winked at a few or more ladies who were gawking at his traditionally-attractive appearance. Tate had once heard Roberts liken himself to Adonis and had subsequently held back the desire to vomit.

"Tate, I wouldn't have known where to find you if it weren't for all of the loud discussions about a giant in attendance." Roberts ruffled Tate's hair. "Will you introduce me to this lovely miss beside you? I do not, of course, speak of Bethanne here as we are already *well* acquainted." He spoke with clear bravado and held a lingering smolder in Mrs. Riverston's direction.

Scarlett looked to her friend and raised her brows so high her forehead disappeared into her curls. Mrs. Riverston's cheeks flushed crimson.

Tate rose and offered his hand for Scarlett to join him. Mrs. Riverston followed suit.

He kept Scarlett's hand and placed it in the crook of his arm no matter how much she tugged, then jovially announced, "This is Miss Halloway. This is Mr. Calvin Roberts, brother of Viscount Dabbs."

"My friends just call me Roberts. So you are the infamous Miss Halloway Beth here has told me so much about. I believe we briefly met at the Grovington's Ball when you so wickedly stole my fine friend away for a dance."

"Beth?" Scarlett's head tilted as she glanced at Mrs. Riverston. "I'm sorry to say *Beth* has told me very little about you. It seems as if she has been too . . . *preoccupied* to tell me much these past few weeks. Come now, *Beth*, how have you depicted me to deserve the title of infamous?"

"Preoccupied, indeed." Roberts leaned towards Mrs. Riverston with a knowing grin carved into his face.

"I merely described you as willful. Forceful may have also been said," Mrs. Riverston admitted with a finger to her dimple.

"I prefer forceful." Tate smirked. His thumb stroked the backside of Scarlett's hand, but not for long as she slipped from his arm to adjust her bonnet when it flapped in the wind.

"Everyone is allowed a little obstinacy from time to time." Scarlett's lips slid into a sly smile directed at Roberts.

Scarlett's rosebud mouth opened its bloom to another man. Tate's lungs collapsed. The all-too-familiar feeling of being invisible despite his colossal height swept over him.

He shuffled his feet and swayed towards Scarlett's ear. "May we speak in private?"

"I don't know. Do you need to speak with Camilla privately as well?" Scarlett whispered back. Her consonants struck like hammer on stone.

Speak with Camilla? Why would he need to speak with Camilla? He wasn't even sure if she was here at the picnic, and it didn't matter if she was. All that mattered was he was here with Scarlett having the chance to court her publicly despite her betrothal to his brother like she wished, and she was acting as if he was as odious, as deserving of a proper bollock smashing, as Lord Cullen.

This was a waste of his time. He could be—should be—busy trying to save his future career from being confined to the notebooks he would scribble in during a boat ride across the world. As if he wouldn't be too seasick to sketch.

Roberts interrupted his reeling. "Well, that was awfully incriminating. Miss Halloway, what have you done?"

Scarlett took a deep breath exactly as she had before she'd told Tate her controversial history, then began, "When I was eleven, I may or may not have thought it was unfair for only the boys of the Ton to learn to fence, so I stole a sword from a lesson in the park."

"Ah, that's not so bad–" Roberts glanced away from her for a moment to pet Brissot who was digging at the checkered blanket on the ground. The fabric rumpled under his paws.

Mrs. Riverston jumped in, "And then she ran around, demanding anyone who approached her in order to retrieve said sword to fight her for it."

"Still–"

"I ended up slashing three ladies' skirts and cut a hole in the instructor's jacket."

At that, Roberts' attention snapped from Brissot to Scarlett, who had a sheepishly proud grin on her face. Roberts' expression was slack-jawed. Mrs. Riverston pushed his chin to shut his mouth.

Was it just Tate or did she actually sound more proud of herself with this retelling than she had when she'd first reenacted it for him? Was it that she was coming to accept what she'd done was rather valiant? Or had Roberts just given her the reaction she'd hoped to receive from himself? He prickled inside at the idea she could be finding more pleasure from another man's opinion of her than his own. What was the point of all this if she didn't respect the gravity of his adoration for her?

"Come now, you all cannot tell me you didn't get into similar antics as children." Scarlett playfully slapped Roberts on the shoulder.

Roberts shrugged. "Of course, some."

Mrs. Riverston's coiffure came undone from shaking her head too vigorously. Then, under Scarlett's glare, she admitted, "Well, I guess there was that one time you and I stole all of Cook's eggs and threw them out the third story window. We ended up hitting Fitzhenry directly on the head."

Everyone stifled laughter except Tate.

"Well, I didn't," he admitted. He dared not look at his friends' presumably pitying faces, instead watching Brissot who was growling at a nearby set of ducks. The fur along the dog's spine pointed to the clouds above. The striped birds waddled into the river.

"You mean to tell me you and Richard never got into any trouble? I find that difficult to believe." Scarlett's green eyes locked with his for the first time that afternoon.

"We certainly got in trouble, but not for any diverting

reasons." The corners of his lips twitched in a tiny half smile. "My father expected perfection out of Richard and myself. Our free time outside of lessons was spent studying. For Richard, that meant studying the estate's books and the ways of gentlemanly behavior. For me, that meant having my nose in a scientific journal or book of historical architecture at all times."

"Perhaps that would explain why you've never had a successful courtship," Roberts jabbed him in the ribs with his sharp elbow.

"No, that's because I am a giant. Remember?" Tate glimpsed Mrs. Riverston and Roberts exchange amorous glances, evidently too busy flirting to listen. "Speaking of successful courtships, I should leave you two to yours."

Mrs. Riverston raised one finger in the air as if she was about to protest, but Tate walked away when Roberts snaked an arm around her waist.

"Come now, you dolt. You know I didn't mean it," Roberts yelled after him.

Tate huffed as he kicked the ground. Of course Roberts didn't mean it, but the man never ceased being a shit-sack when women were around.

There was no point in staying if it meant he'd have to watch others fall in love while standing next to the woman who he longed to sweep into his arms and kiss until that attitude of hers melted away. But, it would not be. She'd made it evident he was unwanted.

Chapter Seventeen

"Where do you think you're going?" Scarlett's silk slippers soaked in grass stains as she stomped after Tate. Brissot ran alongside her, skidding to a stop every time he got ahead of his lead, which made pacing her steps incredibly awkward.

"Away, as you so obviously do not want me here," Tate tossed over his shoulder.

"Tate, slow down. Please. At least for Brissot's sake. He is going to choke himself."

Tate stopped. Scarlett and Brissot caught up to his side.

"So I am 'Tate' again, not *Lord* Tate Langley?" Tate took Brissot's lead and thrust his arm out for her to take.

Winded, as her preferred form of exercise involved a lot less running and a lot more weaponry, she gladly accepted the support. "You are technically not my intended, so it would be most improper to call you by your given name."

They continued walking around the other picnic-goers, this

time at a more leisurely pace.

"Since when do you follow the rules of proper comportment?"

"Since I last broke them to call on you only to learn from Richard that I am not the only woman you're courting."

A chill wind blew a cloud overhead, casting a shadow over the picnic. Scarlett's skin puckered with gooseflesh.

Tate shimmied out of his tailcoat and placed it over her shoulders. It enveloped her frame, leaving only a sliver of her chest visible between the lapels.

He stared at that sliver of chest, blinking repeatedly. "You called on me? When?"

Inside her grew a warming fizz of laughter at how obviously inept he was at hiding his lustful feelings, but she suppressed it. She wrapped herself tighter in his coat. "Perhaps when you were busy visiting another woman. Although, it would have to be a third because Camilla also stopped by with the intention of visiting you."

"What are you talking about?" His thick brows creased together in confusion.

Could he seriously not know or was this his way of avoiding the subject? With how pestering Richard was, there seemed very little chance he hadn't heard about the incident involving his other lover.

Her fingers dug into his thick forearm muscle. "I tried calling on you three days ago. You were not home, but Richard told me you'd met with Camilla and strongly implied whatever was between the two of you is not over."

"Is that why you've been so upset with me? You're jealous?" Tate's hand pressed to his stomach as it shook from laughter.

Was he seriously laughing? This was no laughing matter. She pulled away from him, but he pulled her right back against his side, so close her skirts flattened against his leg.

"There's never been anything between Camilla and I. Since she's been here, we've met for tea, once," he held up a single finger, "to catch up. She's actually in love with someone else. Why would you believe anything that comes from Richard's mouth?"

"What he said made sense. Camilla has known you for so long. I was afraid she came to London to find you."

"I cannot believe you were jealous. That you imagined me capable of handling more than one woman." Tate's palm brushed over his scruffy cheek as he scrubbed his exasperated expression. "Trust me, Scarlett, you are more than enough for me."

"I can't tell if that's a compliment."

"I didn't intend for it to be."

She slapped both her hands on his chest. Laughter bubbled from her throat and snorted out of her mouth. Relief came with it, enveloping her in pure giddiness.

Tate had never been involved with another woman. Why had she been so jealous? Because the thought of him holding another woman, kissing another woman, made her shake with rage. This whole forming-an-attachment-to-someone thing was a great deal more emotionally taxing than she'd expected. She had always been intentional in exercising her mind and body, but her heart? That had proven itself weak from disuse.

Loud murmurs around her yanked her from her reverie. The people around them snuck glances and whispered in each other's ears. One, Lord Burton, not so quietly whispered, "Is she not engaged to the Marquess Langley? Who's that man she's with?"

Another, Miss Mason, asked a second debutante beside her, "Is she the girl who injured Lord Cullen? How could Lady Wilkins invite such a person to her event?"

One gentleman, Lord Neels, was so flabbergasted to see Scarlett and Tate publicly courting that he didn't watch where he was walking and ended up absolutely coating his shoes in Lady Loewe's schnauzer's droppings. He cursed and trudged away with his head hung low.

Scarlett and Tate glanced at each other and strained themselves to keep from laughing. She bit her lip, and he pressed a fist to his mouth.

He sniggered as he spoke, "I don't think we can effectively convince everyone we make a better match than Richard and yourself if we're found laughing at their messes."

"Or perhaps we could if they believe us to have an equally improper sense of humor. They surely don't want the next Marchioness Langley to laugh at shit jokes. But where is the beauty of life if not seen in comparison to the ugly."

"I quite agree," he said while wiping tears from the corners of his eyes.

The pair straightened up as an elderly lady approached them.

Her outstretched hands clutched Scarlett's and Tate's arms. "I don't care what everyone else says. I think you two would make a charming couple. I know love when I see it."

"Thank you, Lady Callahan." Scarlett took the lady's gnarled knuckles in hers, quickly squeezing and releasing as the dampness of nerves began to drench her palms.

The woman had used The Word. *Love.* Scarlett hadn't even used that word with Tate yet. He had begun to say it, but she hadn't. She had kissed him instead, which she believed to be as clear of a reply for that moment as she could have given. Perhaps he wouldn't notice.

Tate tilted his head and gazed at Scarlett with raised brows.

He noticed.

Lady Callahan spoke to Tate this time, "This one was quite the wild child for so long. Be sure to not kill her spirit. It's what keeps us women alive longer than you men."

"I promise." Tate chuckled.

After Lady Callahan patted Brissot on his head and went on her way towards a tent set up to protect guests from the sun, Tate cleared his throat. "So . . . She was kinder than most."

Good. He didn't want to discuss The Word. She wasn't prepared to discuss The Word and might never be. The Word and all it entailed hadn't been a part of the pertinent life instruction her governess and tutors had provided her, and her parents certainly hadn't set a healthy example. The only time she saw *love* was in novels. They were intangible fantasies. Charades. They weren't truthful like her preferred reading of philosophy which discussed the reality of existence.

Maybe someday, once they were married, The Word would just slip out in conversation. It might become as innocuous as saying hello or goodday. By that point, she might not feel like The Word was some big, fantastical, frightening prospect with expectations she'd be held to. Expectations she couldn't fulfill because she was incapable of being the helpless damsel in a sweeping love story. Maybe then she would be ready.

But, for now, she excitedly grabbed his hands, entwining her fingers with his. "She was more than kind. She is Lady Grovington's aunt. My mother greatly respects—no—is quite honestly envious of Lady Grovington." Scarlett was practically bouncing with joy. "If she hears I'm publicly courting you and not Richard, she may recommend to my father they dissolve the contract for my hand and—*Ouch*!" She yelped. A pang shot through her calf.

"Are you alright? What happened?" Tate's face scrunched in concern. He handed her Brissot's lead and bent to inspect her leg which she hovered in the air. "Does this hurt?" He prodded her calf.

It smarted. She winced at his gentle touch. "Not too bad. I think I'm mostly unharmed. It was merely a shock."

On the ground behind her leg sat a pall-mall ball.

Tate picked it up. "I believe this is the offending object. You have been—*oof*!" Another ball rolled over his foot and onto the grass beneath him.

Scarlett searched the crowd for the culprits, her gaze landing on two men swinging around mallets. "We should have known."

A stone's throw away, Lord Cullen and Richard waved and walked up to them.

"Think we could have our balls back?" Lord Cullen asked, holding his hand out expectantly with beckoning fingers.

"That depends. How much did my kick damage them?" Scarlett quipped. She tossed them back at his chest.

Tate snorted and coughed to recover himself. Was that how she sounded when she snorted? Her mother was wrong; it wasn't so bad. It was perhaps even endearing, at least when it came from the softly pointed tip of Tate's nose. She wished to plant a light kiss there.

"Brother, you're quite the gentleman to accompany my intended to today's event." Sarcasm dripped from Richard's mouth. "You see, I scheduled plans with Lord Cullen, so I wasn't available. I'm happy to see she is not cooped up. She could use the fresh air to clear her head of all the philosophical jargon she loves so much. Granted, I'm surprised you didn't accompany Miss Bertram."

Scarlett's skin itched with the desire to curse, yell, punch, or run. She was unsure which. But she couldn't. Everyone was watching them, waiting for her to do something of that sort. Be typical, ridiculous Scarlett. Just waiting to have an excuse to call her a silly little girl again.

Her face masked to the most pious expression she could muster. Batting eyelashes, pouty lip, and all. "Trust me, *my lord*, my head has never been clearer."

"Richard, Lord Cullen, I believe you owe Scarlett an apology," Tate demanded.

"An apology?" Spittle flew from Lord Cullen's lips. "Given Scarlett is my friend's intended, he needn't apologize for anything when she should have already forgiven him. He will soon—In three weeks time, correct?"

"Yes, that is the date the vicar gave me," Richard murmured while scratching a mud scuff off his boot leg.

Lord Cullen hummed his agreement and continued, "In three weeks, he will legally have the right to do whatever he wants with her–*Ah*!" His speech transformed into a piercing scream as he fell to his knees.

Behind him, Ava stood with a pall-mall mallet slung over her shoulder. She flashed Scarlett a smile, before hovering over the fallen man. "My apologies, Lord Cullen. My ball was near your feet, and I thought I could maneuver it around you without you noticing."

"But you hit the back of my knee," he cried through gritted teeth.

"My aim is awful. Truly." Ava put on a real show of her regret. She dropped to her knees next to Lord Cullen and fluttered a hand to her forehead. Was there even a tear falling down her cheek?

"Was that hit learned after just one lesson?" Tate whispered in Scarlett's ear.

"Yes. She's a natural," she replied with a giggle. "Although, I didn't teach her the dramatics. I suppose I should review the differences between defensive and offensive maneuvers."

A crowd gathered around them, gasping and fanning themselves. The gathering was perfect for a little demonstration.

Scarlett snatched the opportunity Ava had inadvertently given her. She turned to Tate, rested a hand on his forearm, and loudly inquired, "Dear, do you think you could assist our friend here to a chair where he might recover? He will have no hope to attend *our wedding* if he can't walk."

Tate gave a brief quizzical stare, but understood the signal of her tight grip on his arm, and replied, "Of course, *my love*."

There was The Word again. Her throat tightened.

When Tate pulled Lord Cullen off the ground, the crowd applauded. Richard tried to assist with outstretched arms, but Tate shooed him away.

"Come now, brother. He is too much weight for you. We can't have you getting injured as well. You're to be my best man," Tate proclaimed.

In the excitement of the onlookers, someone's less-than-well-trained dog inched closer to Scarlett and Brissot. Scarlett glimpsed down just as the small, yippy thing snapped at Brissot.

He howled in fear and took off with his tail tucked, Scarlett in tow. They were headed straight for the river. She dug her heels into the grass as best she could, but she was no match for Brissot's speed. While running to keep up with her pup, Tate's coat flew off of her shoulders. In a wet flash, they plummeted straight into the waters with a resounding splash.

Tate was leading Lord Cullen towards a chair under the tent when a watery slap resonated from outside. His gaze whipped over to where Scarlett had been standing, only to find faces of the Ton he hardly recognized. After years away on the continent, the people he supposedly tacitly belonged to looked more foreign than familiar.

He dropped Lord Cullen into the nearest chair, unsure if the man's backside landed in the seat properly. Not as if he cared. The man sure deserved worse than bruised buttocks. Lord Cullen moaned in agony as Tate sprinted to the river.

Scarlett and Brissot both were sheep caught in a rainstorm where they stood in the shallows of the water. Brissot's red fur clung to his sides, making him appear one stone lighter. Scarlett's mint green gown was suctioned to her body, and her hair was matted to the back of her neck.

Tate jumped down the small drop from the riverside into the water. His arms wrapped around Scarlett's waist. He shivered at the feel of her curved figure under his touch, not only because the water soaking him though her clothing was frigid. He lifted her back onto the solid ground, then he picked Brissot up from his torso and set him next to her. Brissot's fur drenched his shirt.

Every little outline of his body beneath was on full display through the now see-through white linen. His fingers plucked at it, trying to pull it away from his form, but it merely stuck right back onto the stomach he considered not trim enough and the chest which had been described before as too wide.

There was nothing to be done. Everyone had seen him now, including Scarlett. Would she still find him as attractive as she had before now she knew he wasn't hiding a set of six cut abdominal muscles under his clothing?

When he jumped back up from the river, his boots sloshed with every movement. Brissot took his opportunity on dry land to shake all of the excess water off onto Scarlett and Tate. They shielded themselves with their arms to avoid the spray, but their clothing was splattered with muck.

They looked to the people who witnessed the blunder then back again to each other. Scarlett's dress was now speckled brown like a pheasant, and Tate's poor, favorite boots slipped down to his ankles and poured river water onto the grass. A fish may have even come out of one. It was hard to tell, but Brissot definitely pounced at something and swallowed before either one of them could pry his jaws open.

A clamour of laughter doubled them over. Scarlett clutched at her sides, guffawing in her classic style. Tate held himself up with his hands on his knees.

They were both dripping. Brissot and his red fur was a sodden pile of autumn leaves. Whatever parts of Tate's outfit which had been white were now tan. Scarlett's wet ensemble was nearly clear and hugged her curves in an unfashionable manner, yet pleasing to the eye nonetheless.

Tate refused to share this view of her with the rest of the people present. He should be the only one to see the way her swollen top led to a waist he could glide between his palms down to her perfectly rounded bottom. He *would* be the only one. He would make sure of it. Soon, if he had a say in the matter.

"I think we ought to get you out of those clothes."

"Is that a promise?" she whispered, raking her gaze over his drenched upper half.

Tate raised his eyebrows. *So she is not deterred by my level of exposure.* By the moistening of her lips, it appeared the exact opposite.

Again with her flirting. Such a temptress! He couldn't take it. At least not with how hard her nipples were poking through the lightweight fabric of her bodice. Nor with how tightly her skirt hugged her hips. The hips of a Grecian goddess which begged to be squeezed by his hands and his hands only.

He retrieved his jacket from the grass and returned it to her shoulders, buttoning it to cover her. "I would like to remain the only man who will see your form, and that won't happen if we stay here."

Scarlett's eyes widened.

He chuckled. When he'd first met Scarlett, he hadn't believed there was much he could say or do for which she would not have a witty remark or well-planned next move, but he gladly was mistaken. It let him know, at least when it came to him, Scarlett didn't feel the need to prepare. To guard or protect herself. She knew she was safe with him.

Scarlett called out to a woman in the front of the crowd, "It was a lovely event, Lady Wilkins, but we must be leaving now. Please let Bethanne know I'll call on her soon."

Mouth agape and utterly dumbstruck, the woman slowly nodded.

Chapter Eighteen

S carlett's thighs chafed under her damp gown as the three of them jogged towards the park entrance.

Tate instead led them to where all of the picnic guests had parked their barouches and carriages, stopping at the largest one. It had ornate gold trimmings and an *L* crest on the door.

"We will use Richard's carriage."

"But won't he need it soon and find it's missing?"

His irises twinkled golden in the sunlight as he smirked. "I didn't say it would be going anywhere."

"Then what need do we have with a carriage? And where are all the drivers?"

"When I arrived, I saw them all run over to the pub across the street. Since the event lasts all afternoon, I imagine they won't return to their posts for at least another hour. That should leave us with plenty of time and *privacy*."

Tate tied Brissot's lead to the front bar of the carriage and lifted his dripping form onto the driver's bench where the wet pup promptly flopped down, basking in the warmth of the sun.

"Tate, what are we doing here?"

"Let us say we are waiting for the driver to return. You could not have very well walked home in your state." Tate opened the carriage door and held out a hand for Scarlett.

She took it and stepped inside. "Well, no I couldn't have. My legs . . ."

The implication of his words dawned on her. Her heart fluttered against her ribcage. She settled it with a hand pressed to her bosom. "You did say we needed to get out of these wet clothes, did you not?"

"Yes. Immediately. Otherwise, we may catch cold." He stepped in after her and shut the door. His large fingers nimbly untied the bows which held open the window curtains.

With the heat radiating off Scarlett's skin, she certainly wouldn't be catching cold. But she was not about to inform Tate of this fact, not when she believed she was about to get what she'd hoped for since their moment hidden in the laurels.

Tate's muscular chest was almost entirely visible under his wet garments, the linen clinging to the curves of his pectorals. Her hands twitched with the desire to rip away his shirt and feel the man underneath without any fabric in between. Water droplets dripped down his neck, and she imagined licking them off one at a time.

Tate caught her staring. He lifted one of her feet from the carriage floor and removed her slipper. His fingers brushed underneath the hem of her skirt, searching her skin for the top of her stocking. With touch as light as a feather, he rolled the fabric down her calf, stopping at her ankle.

"So when is our wedding?"

Did her heart just freeze or was it her whole body? She wiggled her toes on his lap. No, it was only her heart.

"Yes, I lied in order to show everyone how serious our courtship is, and how unserious my engagement to Richard is. I'm sorry."

"Oh. It was no lie. You proposed to me." He finished pulling off the stocking. His knuckles grazed the arch of her foot, sending shivers up her legs.

"I did not."

He got to work on her other foot, throwing off her slipper and yanking down the stocking. "I believe, in your own logically illogical way, you did. And I accept." He punctuated his words by plucking the clothing off her other foot, leaning towards her, and planting a lingering kiss on her lips.

Scarlett came up for air bleary-eyed and dizzy.

"Now as your fiancé, I need you to tell me you love me."

Well, that cleared her vision.

She slumped. The cushion of her carriage bench squished like a sponge beneath her wet form. The off-putting sound echoed in her silence.

"Scarlett?" Tate's tone was tinged with concern.

"I've never said that word to anyone before, besides Brissot. But, come now, you have seen him. He's adorable."

"Neither had I until you. And don't think I have forgotten you avoided hearing it by seducing me." The suspicious squint of his eyes didn't match his smile.

She half-smiled in return. "Love is supposed to be certain."

"And your feelings for me are not?" The corners of his mouth fell. His eyes looked like Brissot's when she didn't share the chicken from her dinner plate. Heartbreaking yet winsome.

"I picked you out of a crowd on impulse. I hadn't been searching for anything so emotional." She rubbed his knee to recapture his lowered gaze. "But I met you, and now I yearn for you. Every moment of the day, I haven't been able to think, to read, to eat without thoughts of you. I don't know what love is—I don't think I ever truly will—but I have known since our first dance you are the only man worth marrying." She paused to consider how to repair this rift in their intimate moment.

Being in love had never been something she imagined for herself, too busy with her purpose, her desire to make a place for herself amongst the greater thinkers of society.

To prove she was not some ridiculous girl.

If she'd fallen head over heels in love, she would have made herself to be as ridiculous as the rest of her peers.

But now, with how important Tate had become to her, with how much she'd missed him these past few days and how heartbroken she'd felt over the idea he cared for someone else, it was clear being a *little* ridiculous for a man was worth it if it kept him by her side.

Because what was the point of fighting with sabres or

philosophical moralities if there was no one willing to witness her cause? She could wield words and swords until her mouth dried and arms failed, but there was no purpose to the crusade if no one cared to listen.

Tate listened. And he understood. And he supported.

Even now, he was listening while she was silent. His comforting, earthen eyes watched her through a softly lidded gaze, like wrapping her in a fire-warmed dressing gown. She wanted to sink into that warmth and never escape.

She wanted forever to feel this excited contentment that coursed through her chest whenever he was near. She desired him to always be *there* next to her, laughing with her when Brissot broke wind in his sleep or ready to spar over tea and chocolate about a theory from a book. He may not have known as much about philosophy as she did, but he'd learn with practice.

A jolt like the electrical phenomena she felt every time she donned her wool redingote struck her, shocking her spine straight.

Perhaps she was not incapable of love. She was only unpracticed.

He need only give her time to learn.

As if time is not already short in supply for our future.

Luckily, she was a quick study. She would learn, and it was fine if it scared her because love was something all-consuming. She very much wanted someday to be consumed by him.

While someday would come, Tate needed reassurance now.

Before he decided she was too much work and cried off.

She sank to her knees in front of him and used his declaration from the park the morning after they first met to make her point. "Tate, with me, there's no sport, no ambiguous repartee, no guessing, no waiting games. No bouts—*fine*, some bouts." She giggled when he looked at her with doubt scrolled into his eyebrows. "But there is one thing." She grabbed his hands and splayed them over her chest. "The knowledge I will give you everything you want. Someday. Only now, I want to *dance.*"

By the shocked slant of his grin, he picked up on her meaning and thankfully dropped the subject she'd yet to master. "I believe our courtship is less of a waltz and more of a *demand for satisfaction.*"

He trailed his hands to her waist and hoisted her up onto his lap. His body's demand was evident in his trousers, pressing into her backside.

"Would you prefer to meet me on the field at dawn?"

"No, here will do."

At that, their mouths collided into a hot, wet melding of lips and tongue.

Scarlett didn't notice Tate had been unbuttoning her bodice and unlacing her stays until a rush of air blew down her spine. She stood, holding the front of her gown up against her body.

Her breathing came in shallow, rapid gulps as he pulled his shirt overhead. His chest was broad and muscularly rounded like a barrel. The lines in his neck which seemed sculpted by the masters continued down to his collarbones, down between pectorals, down the side of his stomach, and ended in the shape of a V above the waistband of his trousers.

"I'm sorry I'm probably not what you expected," he murmured.

She was taken aback. "What would that have been?"

"Trimmer. I'm strong, physically. Stronger than anyone I know, but it doesn't appear so. I grow thick, but my muscles never seem to come to the surface as others do."

"Don't be ridiculous. I see how strong you are. I've been dreaming of what you look like under your clothing since we met, and you're even better than I'd imagined." Her gaze raked over his half-nude form.

A lopsided grin dimpled one of his cheeks. Then his hands moved to his trousers and halted. "One last thing." He paused to take a deep breath. "Against my basest judgment, I feel the need to warn you. I'm large."

"Yes. Like I said, I could see that from the moment we met."

Tate's eyebrows rose into his hairline. Then he chuckled and reiterated, "No, I am *large*."

"Oh." The sound coming from her mouth never seemed to stop trailing off.

"But I promise to be careful."

"I know. You always are." Scarlett cupped his stubbled cheek. Although short and prickly-looking, his whiskers were shockingly soft against her skin.

With her reassurance, he nodded and shimmied out of his trousers. Free, his manhood rose like a stone column, rounded, thick, and pointing to the sky. Nothing like what she'd seen on the sculptures at the museums. She now understood what he had meant by a column being both structural yet a thing of beauty.

His hand gripped it, slowly stroking up and down as he watched her, waiting for her to undress.

This was the first time he would see her bare in the light. Starlight counted for very little when it came to judgment of the human form. She'd studied her reflection in the mirror enough to know she found herself beautiful, but would he?

All of the pretty little things her other suitors had previously professed to her in her drawing room were meaningless. "You are the sun." "You are a flower amongst a field of thorns." "You are a rainbow, rare and rapturous." She hadn't read enough poetry to know whether or not these men had been quoting Byron, but it was all tea dregs to her.

What would matter more than any other man's carefully crafted metaphors was the comfort Tate inspired within her. She would undress for him because she knew, undoubtedly, that if she didn't wish to, he would redress himself, help her with her stays, and simply hold her. However, she was too curious about the stirrings he'd enlivened inside her to let that happen.

One after another, her arms slid from the sleeves of her gown. Closing her eyes, she let go of her grasp on the fabric over her chest. The clothing pooled around her ankles.

She waited. And waited. And—

Melted. His hands held up her heavy breasts, taking the

weight from the strain on her back she'd assumed only a corset was capable of doing. With much less caressing, of course. The heft of her bosom spilled over his sizable palms. His thumbs stroked the sensitive peaks.

"They're even better than I remembered," he murmured. "And I remembered vividly." He pinched her nipples and rolled them between his thumbs and forefingers as the rest of his fingers kneaded the roundness.

A current of pleasure swept through her base. Her eyelids snapped open as her knees wobbled beneath her. He caught her and grabbed her hips, seating her straddled on his thighs.

His mouth found hers. Like silk, their lips glided along one another. His tongue slid along her bottom lip. At his touch, she opened to him. The thrill of his exploration inside her was only a mere taste of what she expected was to come.

His mouth left hers as quickly as it came, snaking down her neck and chest. His fingertips traced the curve of her back from her neck down her buttocks, rubbing the fullness of her backside.

She leaned in involuntarily at his artistry of touch, pushing her hips closer to him. His shaft pressed against her stomach, rigid yet smooth. Unfamiliar yet thrilling.

"Tate."

"There's no rush. You need to be ready for me," he whispered into her breast, mouth beckoning her nipple.

She pressed into him, moaning from the vibration of sensation traveling from the nipple under his toying tongue down to her core.

"Tate. Please."

Maybe if she dared to touch him, he then would do something which would resolve this wave of tension building inside her. Her fingers grazed the tip. The skin was a feather-soft covering over a brick-solid structure.

He growled. His hands grabbed her arse, fingers digging roughly into the muscle and lifting her off his thighs.

She inhaled tightly between her teeth and knelt above him. With one hand, he aligned his cock with the space between her legs. With the other, he led her hips down until he met her opening.

"Hurry. I need—I need—" She wasn't sure what it was she needed. Whatever it was, it would have to drag her over this mountain of tensity.

She dug her fingernails into his shoulders, bearing down tightly. "I need you."

With a groan, he slid himself into her.

She gasped from the quick snap of pain which undulated into—fullness. Pressure. Rich, satiating pressure. Tate's hands rocked her hips in a rhythm against his. Now the pressure was . . . pleasure. Syrupy dripping pleasure. Each rock back and forth like a drip of honey into a teacup.

She caught on to the rhythm, gripping his neck as a support. Her fingers weaved themselves into the short hair at the back of his head. Her breasts pressed to his chest. Her nipples grazed the soft, curly hair between his pectorals, the light touch sending another wave of tension deep inside her.

With him pushing and pulling and pushing inside, the pressure lifted her higher, closer to her peak. Like when she'd taken in thin air at the top of the ledges in the Peak District on holiday.

How could it build anymore than it had already? There couldn't be many steps until she passed whatever was at the highest point. Right now, she was in the clouds. Teetering with the crumbling edges of the cliff. Lightheaded and giddy. If she looked up at the exact moment, would she see stars as she had in his arms amongst the laurels?

T ate could tell she was close, possibly closer than him, and that was saying something since he nearly blew it from the second he entered her tautness. By some miracle, she'd been ready enough to bury himself deep.

Is she really that attracted to me? She must be, yet she's still incapable of admitting she loves me.

Courtship was confounding. At least he got to reap the benefits of her further avoidance. And reap he did.

Honestly, he could have burst his load the moment he witnessed her bosom fall out of her dress. Even now, her perky, rose-pink nipples taunted him as her breasts bounced with her rhythm riding his cock.

Ugh, he needed to get her now and good before it was too late for him. She needed him to take her over the top.

Holding her up against him still buried inside her wetness, he stood. The carriage roof was too short for him to stand upright, so he bent his knees.

Now, from this position, he could do the moving. Gliding himself in and out, he pounded into her up to his hilt. The tip of him felt the end of her press back every time he sheathed himself.

The carriage rocked from side to side, sweeping back and forth in time with his thrusts.

Her arms stretched over head, hands planting on the roof. "Oh! Oh, Tate. Oh . . . " she cried, her delicious lips spread wide in a rounded shape.

There it was. Her tightness rippled, closing like a vise around him. Her breast shook with the force of her release.

She was so good. Such a grip pulsating around his cock. Holding himself back, he bit down on his lip so hard he drew blood.

Her eyes rolled into her head as her body relaxed into his arms. When she was finished rolling over him, he walked them towards the carriage wall and pressed her back against it.

"What are you doing?" she asked, her voice distant like through a fog.

Wanting another taste of her spice, he kissed her, nipping her lip as he pulled his mouth away. "I'm not done with you."

"But I thought—" She protested.

"We are making love," he paused at that word to survey her unreadable expression, "in a carriage in the park during daylight. Evidently, this is not the time for thinking."

His mouth caught hers before she could respond. He plunged himself into her the deepest yet. Her breath caught into his lips.

Using the carriage wall as leverage, he stroked through the waters of her. At the veracity of their exertions which rocked the entire carriage, the door flew open. Sunlight poured into the small space and over their naked bodies.

Scarlett's eyes went from heavy-lidded with the cloud of arousal to wide open. Her hands fluttered against his chest, her moaning mouth incapable of speech.

Tate reached out, yanked the handle, and slammed the door shut. With a cracking split, the door handle shirred off into his palm. He threw it across the carriage, then continued his thrusting.

Her hair spilled from its pins as it rubbed against the fabric-covered wall. One pin pierced the fabric and ripped a gash downwards.

Thrust after thrust, she only grew tighter for him. Her lips spread in the beginnings of a scream, but he held a hand over it to capture the cry of passion. Her voice muffled a string of expletives against his palm. Her hands gripped his head and pulled on his hair.

She was there again, coming for him. This time he wouldn't be able to stop himself. She gripped around his cock, making it impossible for him to unsheath himself in time.

He shivered in his crash of release as he spilled inside her, a first experience for him. And, possibly, quite a complication.

Damn, she was such the irresistible force. How else could she have convinced him to tup her without any confession of her feelings? He was a supplicant to her commanding undeniability.

Both entirely spent, they melted into a puddle of bare limbs onto the carriage floor. Tate nestled his head into her lap.

"I'm sure this is not how you planned to lose your maidenhood," Tate stated between pants, gesturing to the jacquard silk-lined confines of the carriage. "And I'm sorry I did not—could not—I was not able to—"

"Extricate yourself?" she offered with a sly smile. "We are soon to be married, are we not? So, should the need arise, we'll claim a honeymoon miracle and premature delivery. But, I'd asked my lady's maid recently for assistance on fertility matters, and according to her calculations, it's unlikely at this stage."

He raised a brow at her salacious foresight, and she planted a kiss on it. Of course she would know to do such things.

"When did you ask?" He couldn't help his curiosity.

Had she been wanting this as much as him? Enough to plan for it? The thought made his cock twitch. And his heart ache. She was willing to plan for fornication, but not love.

Was he not worth the emotional risk?

She was at least willing to marry him. That and his career would have to suffice because there was no way he was letting her go now. He may not be enough to inspire love, but she and all of herself that she would be willing to give him would be enough for him. It would have to be. She had ingrained herself into his thoughts too thoroughly to extricate. If he tried, his work, his life, his very vision would suffer.

They had friendship and attraction, which was more than most couples of the Ton could claim. Once Scarlett married him, if they got that far, he would only need to throw himself into his work on the days his heart beat hardest for her.

"Not long after we met," she answered, pulling him from his grim resolution. There, on her cheeks, a blush briefly slid across her skin. It was quickly replaced by an upturned chin and steely gaze, Scarlett's expression of defiant glee. "As for maidenhood, I had no plan. It is an unfair concept meant to control women." *Ah*, his Scarlett. So admirably dedicated to justice. "The only reason I'd yet to lose mine is I didn't wish to see any man naked until you."

Then why won't you admit you hold a torch for me? He pushed the thought away and forced a chuckle, rolling over to drop a kiss on the soft flesh of her stomach.

She was at least dedicated to him. Her love could someday come exactly as she was known to do. Like a force. He hoped. And he would be waiting there for her when it did.

Her fingers brushed through his hair. "Not that it matters anymore now that we've declared our intentions, but why exactly were you unavailable when I called?"

In their—*ahem*—distractions, he had somehow, not really surprisingly considering she'd been naked before him, forgotten to tell her the most exciting news of his life.

"I was interviewing at an architectural firm, Asher Alexander & Co."

Scarlett sat up abruptly, jostling his head in her lap. "And?"

From this angle, her bare breasts were terribly distracting. "How about we dress and then I tell you? If you don't put some clothes on, I will tup you again. There's no time for that. The picnic will most certainly be ending soon."

As Tate laced her stays, he told her about his success at the interview, how they had raved over his designs, and how it'd ended with a potential job offer if he could manage to bring in a few new clients with him.

"I just don't know how to go about finding people who need new properties. I'm not charming enough to garner the required attention."

"You are plenty charming. How else do you think you would have gotten me naked in Richard's carriage?"

She thinks I'm charming. At least I now know that much. Every bit of feeling she showed him was a meal of breadcrumbs to a starving man.

He smirked. "I don't think showing potential clients what's in my trousers would be as effective as it was with you."

She gasped, lightly smacked his chest, then helped him tug his shirt over his shoulders. "How long do you have?"

"However long until Richard forces me to sign the commission, which is sure to be soon if I cannot find solid income and he threatens to cut me off." He donned and undonned his boots, distractedly forgetting clothing to cover his bare arse. "He already does not appreciate me staying at Langley House. He will likely kick me out on the street after hearing we're engaged this afternoon."

"Why don't we go to Gretna green?"

"What?" His head snapped up to look at Scarlett as he jumped into his trousers.

Scarlett's dress floated over her. Her head popped out. "I am serious. Why do we not go to Scotland, elope, and return to lease a small place here in London together? With the small funds I make from tutoring Ava and the money from selling your old commission, we can surely find somewhere cheap to stay until you earn enough." She shook him by the shoulders.

"Because I want to marry you properly." Tate tamped down the surge of unrequited love in his chest, spun her around, and buttoned her bodice. "You've been given the opportunity to tutor a duchess, and I have a prospective job. Neither of us can afford to be shunned." He couldn't afford to lose his chance at a near perfect future at the hands of such a rash decision, no matter how tempting it was.

As she nodded, more hair fell from her coiffure, resulting in a fawn-colored waterfall over her face. She brushed it away in a huff. She was radiant even when she was irritated and rumpled from love-making. And she was all his.

Mostly his. Her heart remained her own.

Damn him, he would earn it. Even if it took him years into marriage to convince her he was enough. He would work himself to the bone to gain her love.

He straightened her slumped posture with hands on both of her shoulders and dropped his voice to a low, quiet rumble. "We will fight until we get what we want."

"But how? This time, I kept my hands and feet to myself, and where did I end up? In the river." A single tear rolled down her pinked cheek.

"At least it resulted in our engagement." Tate's mouth tilted in a crooked smile.

"Our wet engagement." Her voice caught in a tearful hiccuping giggle. Then she ran the pad of her thumb across the short stubble on his chin. "I see you have kept this here for me."

"Since the day we walked in the park." His lips tingled and his body ached to be nearer her again, naked skin to naked skin. The closest he could be to her.

However, outside Brissot began barking, alerting them to the oncoming voices of the picnic-goers approaching the carriages. They rushed to finish dressing, tiptoed out of the carriage, untied Brissot, and scurried through a nearby patch of trees to remain hidden.

Chapter Nineteen

ould you perhaps make the neckline less revealing?"

"Yes, Lady Halloway." The dressmaker inched the fabric covering Scarlett's bust higher.

Her mother apparently had no qualms with spending Scarlett's dowry money. Per the verbal agreement for Scarlett's impending union to Marquess Langley, her parents were permitted to keep the fund and were already using it with abandon. Lady Halloway insisted they see London's most fashionable dressmaker to create Scarlett's wedding dress and trousseau. Apparently, she couldn't have her daughter becoming a marchioness in dusty old designs and cheap fabric. Although, those would have been more within their budget.

Scarlett's back ached, a cry for the desire to slouch as she stood on the pedestal. However, any one of the hundreds of pins holding together what would become her wedding gown kept her rigidly still. If she hadn't thought to use this same dress for her wedding to Tate instead of its intended use, she would have been happy to let all the pins fall or even prick her. Then again, she wouldn't have even let her mother drag her here in the first place.

As it would be the gown in which Tate would see her walk down the aisle and also likely be the last custom gown she'd have designed for a while, she was determined for it to be done right. Tate would someday achieve great success with his career and be able to afford to dress her plenty well for her lack of fashion standards. She was sure of it, and, quite frankly, she was also sure she'd enjoy any life he could afford them.

However, they couldn't wait for his success to marry, especially not after how their post-picnic dalliance had ended. Memorably. She didn't plan to wait long for a repeat of the events either. Which meant they very much needed to wed soon. Her monthly calendar was helpful, but she couldn't promise herself she wouldn't completely forget about it should she find herself alone with Tate again.

Chances were they would have very little time after they somehow managed to make Richard dissolve the contract before her parents sold her to someone worse anyhow. Possibly some octogenarian on his fourth wife. In a month, she could be married to the heirless eighty-five-year-old Earl of Dewchester and his eyebrows with hairs longer than those on his head. Nausea gurgled in her stomach.

That was if they still were able to fight Richard. After their splashing end to the picnic, she was unsure anyone would believe she and Tate were the better match. They had caused a literal, slopping mess, and she'd brought embarrassment upon herself once again.

"Scarlett, stand still. You're moving too much."

"I *am* standing still, mother. I believe it's you who is moving too much."

"I want to ensure this all is perfect." Her mother stopped pacing to approach the pedestal when the dressmaker stepped away to grab yet another handful of pins. She dropped her voice to a barely audible volume. "Your father really needs this to happen. We've spent too much trying to make you look as eligible as possible over the years."

Offended, Scarlett prickled. Her body jerked and was stabbed by at least five pins at once. She winced and ground out, "It's not just me who has been expensively clothed and bejeweled to please the Ton. Most of the expenses are for both your pursuits, the club, your jewelry, his drinks, your expensive tastes in perfumes . . . " She paused, pursed her lips, then continued, "In fact, the only things I've ever bought were books and cinnamon tea. You both are the ones who have made us poor, and you're trying to force me to pay the price."

Her mother pretended to be fussing with the unfinished sleeve hem and glared at Scarlett. "Shhhh, girl."

The dressmaker walked back into the dressing room. "Would the lady like silk or lace?"

"Which is more à la mode? My daughter is to be a marchioness you see, so she will need to be setting the height of style."

"The lace trimmed silk it is," the dressmaker practically squealed. "I will have the gown and your trousseau ready in plenty of time before your big day, miss. Just over two weeks. Your fiancé will not be able to take his eyes off you."

"Which fiancé?" Scarlett asked under her breath.

Neither of the women heard her as they were distracted by a commotion that was coming from the direction of the shop front.

"I must speak with her at once."

"But ma'am, she's busy with a client," the shop girl protested.

The fuschia velvet curtains that formed the door to the dressing room flung open. Scarlett scrambled to cover herself even though she was dressed in a half-formed garment with a corset and slip underneath. Her flurry resulted in prickings all over her torso and arms.

The dressmaker politely brushed past the intrusion. "Lady Grovington, I don't believe we have an appointment today. Are you here to pick up your dress for Lady Wordsworth's ball? Sarah can help you with that at the front."

"I'm not here to speak with you, Jill," Lady Grovington addressed the dressmaker, then turned to Scarlett's mother. "I came to speak with Lady Halloway."

"Lady Grovington, May, this is my daughter's wedding dress fitting. Would it be acceptable if I called on you tomorrow instead of speaking here now?"

"No, Rose, I must share my thoughts before you have the

poor girl dressed for the wedding and sent down the aisle. I think it is positively horrid what you're doing to her." Rage emanated from Lady Grovington's typically sunny demeanor, like the scorch of summer.

Both Scarlett's and her mother's jaws fell at once.

Her mother regained her composure before her. "Whatever do you mean?"

"I mean this sham of a marriage you are forcing her into." Lady Grovington stomped one foot.

Scarlett's mother laughed nervously. "The pair is far from a sham. Scarlett loves the Marquess and is excited to become his wife. Are you not, Scarlett?"

Scarlett took her chance to speak her mind. "Actually, I am no–"

She needn't complete her much-rehearsed monologue because Lady Grovington responded for her. "I've seen your girl around both men who claim to be her intended. Why just this last Friday, it was obvious to all with eyes and ears with whom this girl belongs, and it's clearly not the Marquess."

Scarlett's mother shot her a withering glare. When Scarlett had told her she had attended the Wilkins' picnic with Tate and announced their engagement, she hadn't believed her. As with any other time she'd tried to plead her case, it hadn't helped.

What was apparently helping, and even better than she'd imagined, was how when a few of the right people truly listened to her, they chose to support her. Fight for her. Fight with her.

Those few saw she wasn't just some silly girl waving a sabre around. She was a woman fighting to maintain control of her life. Fighting to not marry a man who would dictate her choices and believed her incapable of achieving her desires.

She was striving to marry his brother, the man who wordlessly lent her a hand out of a river without demanding veneration and cheered her on after she kicked a ratbag's bollocks. The man who was conscious of the strengths of everyone but himself and who hadn't used his power to push her into admitting her feelings before she was ready.

And that man happened to be quite well-endowed and knew how to properly . . . wield his sword. Just thinking about it made her dizzy enough to steady herself on the pedestal.

Her mother reached to touch Lady Grovington's arm and was shooed away. "May, you must understand. My daughter has the opportunity to become a marchioness. Surely that's reason enough to accept the offer on her behalf?"

Lady Grovington's thickly rouged mouth pursed.

Scarlett winced, yet no pins had poked her. Because of what her mother said, her family would now be labeled as social climbers. It was something everyone did, but no one spoke aloud, and yet another unwritten rule Scarlett had had to learn when she became a lady.

"How dare you separate such love? How can you not be proud of your daughter for finding a perfectly suitable love match?" Lady Grovington spat. When she turned to Scarlett, who was actively trying to keep herself from twitching at the word *love*, her whole demeanor shifted to a sweet tone and dimpled cheeks. "Dear, I will be sure to ask Lady Wordsworth to double check that she's invited Lord Tate Langley to her ball for you."

"Thank you. Would you please ask her to invite Miss Camilla Bertram as well?"

Scarlett owed her newest friend an apology. She'd believed her to be an obstacle between herself and Tate and had behaved coldly when she encountered her at Langley House. All along, Camilla had only been a good friend and a part of Scarlett's inspiration in discovering her devotion to Tate.

"A friend of yours? Without the support of your family, you've surely had to rely on them more frequently." Lady Grovington stuck her chin out as she gave a sidelong glance at Lady Halloway. "She will be there, dear."

Scarlett gave the deepest curtsy she could in her unfinished gown without spewing pins in every direction. Lady Grovington spun around and swished the curtains back to leave.

Lady Halloway called after her, "May, I will see you at your charity meeting on Wednesday."

"I wouldn't be so sure," Lady Grovington grumbled.

When the shop door whooshed closed, Jill returned to her work. She pulled the half-gown over Scarlett's head.

While Scarlett's face was encompassed by fabric, her mother ranted at her. "What have you done, Scarlett? See how much chaos you've caused? The match we had made for you was most suitable for everyone."

Scarlett's response tumbled as a mumble into the fabric.

Her mother was not finished. "When you announced your relationship with Lord Tate Langley, I didn't take you seriously. You never showed any signs of being capable of loving a man. I'm convinced that the only thing you love is being obstinate." She massaged her temples. "I'd thought you would flirt with him until you grew bored. It would have been good practice for your marriage to the Marquess. But you went and mucked it all up."

She did not know just how much Scarlett had mucked it up.

Jill broke Scarlett free from the linen prison and fled to the back room.

"I know before Lord Tate I'd never even liked any suitor. But I—I—" Scarlett stuttered, incapable of using The Word when it still felt so foreign. "I feel strongly for him, mother. I will marry him. At this point, I must," Scarlett whispered, staring pointedly at Lady Halloway.

If it would help to imply to her mother she had been intimate with Tate, then it was worth the try despite whatever nausea of embarrassment it brought to her stomach.

Her mother planted her hands on her hips. "No. You will marry his brother. Plenty of people carry on with someone else while married. Why, just ask your father—"

"Mother!"

"Fine. Fine." Lady Halloway held up both hands. "Here's what we will do. You will attend the ball with the Marquess. At which, we will show the Ton how we as a family support your union to Lord *Richard* Langley, and soon after your wedding, the Ton will forget about your immature . . . friendship with his brother."

Scarlett quietly redressed into her morning gown. The familiar muslin was a thousand times more comfortable.

If she said anything to refute her mother's plan, there was no way she'd be allowed to attend the Wordsworth Ball. And when she attended, she was determined to ensure a very different outcome.

"Ma'am, where do I send the bill?" Jill sheepishly interrupted.

Scarlett observed her mother's thin-lipped expression, so she answered. "Send it to the Marquess Richard Langley." She spoke to her mother this time, "I'm sure he will cover the amount. After all, he has already paid for me."

Her mother turned to the mirror to fuss with her hair. "Yes, do as the girl says."

Chapter Twenty

Tate was so close to having everything. Which meant everything was just as close to coming crumbling down in a pile of rubble.

He had a profession. Well, he would if he could find a project to bring in with him. A glass of scotch at the club surrounded by the men of the beau monde would be sure to provide the right environment for client-prospecting. Perhaps if he could drum up enough business, he'd even be able to afford a ring for Scarlett.

Scarlett . . . He also had Scarlett. He had really *had* her, in the most delectable sense of the word. As much as her wild spirit could be had given her heart was still on the run.

It was more she had him, was it not? He was wrapped around her little finger, hanging on by her promise that she'd someday give him everything he wanted.

She'd started with the betrothal. She hadn't intended to

propose, but why waste the opportunity? She'd asked him to dance when they first met, so it only made sense she would also ask him for his hand in marriage. Up until the picnic, they'd unspokenly decided that was where their courtship was headed.

In a match such as theirs, both parties usually confessed their love before that part, but he'd be worth it enough to earn hers eventually, especially if he could get his act together in time to be offered the position. It wasn't as if they were performing the typical decorous mating ritual of London's marriage mart anyhow. Intellectually, they couldn't be more suitable, and, as they recently discovered, somehow their physical relationship was even more natural than their intellectual one.

He couldn't allow himself to think of that at the moment. It was incredibly uncomfortable to ride with an erection. Under the hooves of his chestnut stallion, the uneven cobblestones of the lane on the way to the club induced acute agony.

Besides, it wouldn't matter unless he could get her to an altar without Richard having something to say about it and shipping him across the world.

He distracted himself with the clop of his horse and the shouts of the hired hacks' drivers maneuvering down the street. A woman selling cut flowers from a wicker basket waved at him as he passed, shouting about her low prices. A newsboy wearing tattered pants behind her tripped on his run to sell to a gentleman across the lane. Tate's gaze trailed behind as his horse continued forward, waiting to see if someone helped the lad back up on his feet.

As he looked back, he spotted a lanky man on a horse who was staring at him fixedly, the same man from the picnic. He was two carriage lengths behind Tate, but every step Tate's horse took, his horse copied.

He's probably a thief mistaking me for a gentleman richer than I am and hoping to catch me alone, Tate reasoned in an attempt to calm his nerves.

Cracking his reins, he sped up. He'd be safe in front of the club. No thief, no matter how brave, would steal from a gentleman in broad daylight outside of the most illustrious hub for London's upper crust. He reached the club's building and waited for the man's passing to dismount and hand a groom the reins.

The man's gaze traveled away from Tate as he rode along down the lane.

Tate sighed with relief. This was not the continent. This was England. There was nothing to make him a target now that he was simply a citizen in his own country.

Or perhaps that was exactly what made him a target. Twice now that man had followed him in only a few days' time. Was this something of Richard's doing? The worst he'd ever done to Tate before—other than convincing him to join the military once already in the past—had been pushing him in a lake, but a lot more was at stake now than being upset over who ate the last slice of pie. Had he hired someone to ensure he took the commission?

That was a problem for another time. If he didn't focus on his goal at the club, there'd be nothing preventing his professionless self from rejoining the military.

He'd sent out an advertisement for his architectural services through the paper, but that could take weeks to pay out. And he didn't have that long to prove himself for Scarlett.

The club wasn't his favorite place to drink. It only allowed members of the peerage, leaving most of his friends from the military to find somewhere else to imbibe. This meant it was stuffy and quiet. Light chattering was about the most noise one would hear while the men drank their brandies and discussed their affairs, business and others. Sadly, this was what made it the perfect place to find clients.

However, with its vaulted ceilings, columns, and arched door frames, he found enough there worth visiting, at least for the sake of his career. That was without even a mention of the bow window.

Tate took a deep breath before entering through the double doors. Hopefully Scarlett was right about his charm. Otherwise, he'd have to say farewell to his career and his love.

Once inside, there was one friendly face, Roberts. He beckoned for Tate to join his table. Tate held up a hand with splayed fingers, indicating he'd join him in five minutes. Settling his shaking hand back against his thigh, he approached a table of older gentlemen, some he recognized to have been friends of his late father. Though difficult to keep his voice steady during his pitch, the conversation went well, and they promised to keep him in mind should their wives ever decide their homes needed fresh faces. Kinder rejections were never before heard.

He bid them goodday and slumped in the seat across from Roberts. One drink between liaising couldn't hurt. With every nerve-settling sip he savored, he gained more confidence to speak to the next set of likely rejections. That was until his brother entered with Lord Cullen hobbling behind him. Tate's liquid-derived bravery flew out the beautiful bow window.

Richard directed a single acknowledging nod towards Tate. He was just the audience Tate needed while wrestling with the precarity of his future. He required a few more sips in the company of his friend to rebuild some semblance of poise.

Roberts smacked Tate's arm. "I hear congratulations are in order. Why did you not tell me when we saw each other? I had to hear about it from Mrs. Riverston's parents after the event was over."

"It only just happened." Tate sipped his scotch. The liquid burned the cut on his lip. A wonderful little reminder of his time in the carriage with Scarlett.

"Ah, so it was settled privately then?"

Tate gave in. "Actually, yes. But it's a complicated matter."

"What a rake you've become. I always knew it was possible if you met the right woman." Roberts exclaimed a little too loudly for the club environment. He murmured his apologies to the surrounding gentlemen.

Tate cracked a smile. Roberts always had a way of doing that.

"I am no rake. Just a man in love." Tate's stomach twisted at the confession. He set his glass down. He had no desire to speak on his unrequited feelings when his brother was within spitting distance.

"Well, that much was obvious with the way you were fawning over her at the picnic. I thought you were going to have my head just for speaking with her." Roberts tugged at his collar. "I take it that means you two are in quite the rush to the altar?"

"That's none of your business." Tate chucked him on the shoulder. "Enough on me. How did you meet Mrs. Riverston?"

"At the Grovington's. I tried making eye contact with her, but she kept looking away. You know I love the chase." Roberts wagged his eyebrows wolfishly and tapped his fingers on his glass. "Luckily, her parents were more than willing to provide the introduction."

Before Tate could respond, Richard approached their table. Without asking to join them, he swung a chair around and sat on it backwards. Lord Cullen limped over after him, tossed a chair back, and slumped into it with a groan.

Richard took a gulp of Tate's drink and smacked his lips. "Brother, do you happen to know why my carriage was wet after the picnic?"

"No," Tate lied.

"Then I can assume you also don't know why the handle is broken and the fabric ripped?"

"I have no idea how that could have happened. You ought to keep a better eye on your property next time." Tate bit his lip to keep from laughing and winced when pain shot through him.

Lord Cullen pointed to Tate's face. "Did Miss Halloway do

that to you?"

"Yes, Tate, has Scarlett finally given up on you? Is that how you busted your face? Did she hit you?" Richard taunted. "Or is civilian life proving a little difficult for you and you have taken to boxing for money? You can sign the papers at any time."

"No. " Tate glared at them both. "She and I are very much happily engaged."

"For now. Lord Cullen and I know what that's like. Putting up with Miss Halloway's flighty whims is nearly more work than it's worth." Richard and Lord Cullen raised their almost empty glasses in a toast.

Lord Cullen swished his sip between his teeth and sighed loudly as he swallowed. "Even worse when the chit refuses to choose the best of us."

Richard elbowed Lord Cullen. "What are mistresses for if not to always feel chosen?"

Did Richard have a mistress? Tate shouldn't be as surprised as he was. Why was Richard insisting on marrying Scarlett if he was already involved elsewhere? Was it because he just enjoyed stripping all of the joy and choice from Tate's life? Most likely.

"Besides, Julian, we wouldn't have become friends had it not been for the long waits we shared in Miss Halloway's foyer. And I have already found our friendship to be quite useful." Richard downed the rest of his drink.

"Miss Halloway does seem to inspire more than just injuries. She is Mayfair's Helen." Roberts chuckled and glanced at Lord Cullen.

"She is a bitch who is much too proud of herself," Lord Cullen mumbled.

Tate slammed his glass down on the table. "What did you just call her?"

It was enough this man had tried hurting Scarlett not long ago. Now he was smearing her reputation. While Scarlett was fully capable of standing up for herself, he wouldn't stand for this. This man would never touch or speak to her thusly again.

"A bitch." Lord Cullen crossed his arms and smirked.

"You do not speak of my betrothed that way in my presence." Tate sprang from his chair. His large, muscular thighs jostled the table in his ascent.

"Your betrothed?" Richard rolled his eyes. "Calm down, Tate. Cullen is out of line, but we wouldn't want your apish body breaking anything around here. It's not as if you can pay for repairs."

Lord Cullen stood, swaying with the overconsumption of alcohol. His fists rolled through the air.

Roberts joined Tate at his side and leaned in to whisper, "He's not worth it. The women have hurt him enough for how he speaks of them. You needn't add to his misery and risk a duel."

Tate inhaled sharply and squeezed his eyes shut. What was it Scarlett always said? It was better to wield a sharp wit? But what if one was too angry to find the right words? That was probably the sign to remove oneself.

After a few calming breaths, he opened his eyes and turned

to leave. Richard was right. He couldn't afford to damage anything, especially after this entirely unsuccessful attempt at finding business. He should have known better than to visit anywhere his brother frequents. For there lies priggish arseholes who were incapable of taking anything, including a lady's good name, seriously.

As Tate stepped away, Lord Cullen burst out laughing uncontrollably. "Yes, do leave, you untamed beast."

Maybe Tate shouldn't punch the man. However, he could still shake him up a little. Lord Cullen was too dumb to understand words of reason anyways.

Tate whipped around to face him. Gripping him by his woolen coat, he heaved him off the ground. The tips of Lord Cullen's shoes grazed the floor. His throat gurgled against the fabric bunching under his neck.

Tate shook him in the air. His growling breath rushed like a violent wind over the man's face. "If I catch you using such language to describe a lady again, I will not be so gentle." He dropped him suddenly.

Lord Cullen stumbled into the table. His mouth opened, but no sound came out. His hands rubbed the pink lines around his throat.

Before he could be asked to leave for such an outburst of anger, Tate shoved the club door open and walked out.

Roberts trailed behind him. "What did Richard mean about your pay? I thought he was supporting you."

"With Richard, support means control. He expects me to

take another commission."

"Will you?"

Tate kicked the pebbles under his boots. "I hope not to, but I'm almost certain he's having me followed. I wouldn't put it past him to force my hand."

"Would another commission really be so bad?"

"Yes. This one is in India. Scarlett certainly could not join me there. I'm this," Tate pinched his fingers together, "close to becoming an architect. I have a position lined up."

"It appears a second congratulations is owed." Roberts slapped Tate on the back as they waited for the club's groom on the edge of the street. "Why don't you tell your brother to bugger off then?"

Tate scratched his whiskers. "I've tried. This is the most persistent Richard's ever been for anything in his life. It's the first time he hasn't been given exactly what he wants. Richard wants Scarlett, and he wants me gone. And in two weeks, he may get exactly that unless I can prove I'm capable of caring for her."

"Always with the self-sacrificing." Roberts rolled his eyes and shoved his hands in his pockets. "I think if she can stand up to that lobcock Lord Cullen by herself, then she can also manage to ward off Richard."

"Oh, I know she can. But it won't make a difference. The monies are not on our side."

With a swift flick of the wrist, Roberts thumped the back of Tate's head. "Since when does money matter to you?"

Tate rubbed his sore scalp. "Since Richard bribed her parents for her hand."

"Oof." Roberts winced, then smiled lopsidedly. "And of her dowry?"

A groom approached them with Tate's horse.

Tate adjusted the saddle and mounted. "Her dowry is hers, not mine, and certainly not enough to financially support a marriage, no matter the sum." He said goodbye to Roberts and rode away.

As Richard left the club minutes after Tate, he spied Post unsuccessfully hiding behind a lamppost in front of an alley across the street. The man dipped his head back and forth from either side of the metal pole, peeking around it.

Richard stomped through traffic, bringing a few horses and a carriage to a halt. "It is broad daylight, you dunder. If you're to take a man away without anyone noticing, you must do so at night."

"I wasn't planning on taking 'im today. I was just doing a bit of research. Seeing 'ow he acts, where 'e goes," Post explained.

"And yet somehow you did not notice he has already left?"

Post scratched his head full of scraggly hair. "'As 'e left? I didn't see 'im."

"How?" Richard seethed. "He's huge."

Post shrugged.

Richard inhaled sharply. "Take me to your boss. I must speak with him."

Along the way, Richard lost sight of Post in the throngs of the busy street, so he went to the seedy butcher shop again. He walked to the back room and jiggled the doorknob, but the door didn't budge.

"This week, they're at the brothel across the street," the butcher in the next room announced.

Richard stopped in his tracks. His mouth opened to deny for whom he was searching, but the *whack* of the butcher's cleaver on the chopping board sewed his lips tightly shut and sent his legs into a flurry for the door.

When he entered the brothel, the eyes of a few men at the bar peered at him over their ales. The crunch of his boots shuffling against the sticky floor woke a slumped man from his slumber at a table.

The man snorted and sat up with wide eyes. "Richard? What are you doing here?"

"Lord Halloway? I could ask the same of you."

"I came here for some solace away from all the wedding preparations. My wife is unbearable. I assume the same goes for you?"

Richard laughed. "Luckily, I haven't had to handle much of that." *Besides the enormous bill from the dressmaker.* He gritted his teeth. "No, I'm here to handle some business. Have you seen a gentleman with a scar?"

"He's likely in the madam's office." Lord Halloway pointed to a door behind the bar, downed the foamy dregs of his flat ale, and slumped back onto the table.

Richard mumbled his gratitude and marched over to the bar. The busty barmaid shouted at him to get back and pushed him by the shoulders, but he trudged past her and knocked on the door. Someone cracked it open, asked who was knocking, and shut the door firmly. After a minute, the door swung wide open.

Inside, there was a makeshift desk formed of crate wood and mismatched table legs near the back wall at which the scarred man sat. A woman with an overly-powdered face and a massive pile of curls pinned to her head, presumably the brothel's madam, propped herself against the desk with her skirts rucked up and her legs crossed. Two statued guards stood behind the scarred man against the back wall.

"Nice to see you again, dandy man." The scarred man slapped his hand down on the desk.

The madam twitched, evidently startled.

"I couldn't agree less." Richard stamped the ground and yanked on his lapels. "I gave your men ample coin to take care of my little problem. Why haven't the papers been signed yet? Why is my brother still roaming around unemployed, causing me chaos?"

"We've been busy here making sure we don't lose out on more of our money from men running out on their bills." The scarred man glowered at the madam. "Besides, Post did warn you he may need help, did he not?"

"Yes, and I gave him extra in that case."

"I think I could light a fire under their arses if you give me a little more tinder," the man crossed his arms behind his head and leaned back in his chair.

Exasperated, Richard rubbed his forehead. "Have I not given you enough already?"

"I guess your lady isn't worth more than one measly bag of coins . . . "

The madam sauntered up to Richard and ran her hand down his arm. "For that much, you can get more than your money's worth from my girls."

He shook her off and mumbled, "I have enough women on my hands as is."

The door behind Richard squeaked opened and shut again. Someone's fingers ran over his shoulders and squeezed. A cold itch crawled over his skin.

"Are you 'ere to tell the boss 'ow 'appy you are with my work?" Post stood next to Richard and nudged him.

"Are you late because you were wasting the money I gave you to wet your dick?" Richard spat.

He brushed the man off, then readjusted his waistcoat. It was loose. Reynolds tailoring had been sloppy since Tate's return.

"No. I wouldn't do that. The boss owns this lovely 'stablishment," Post declared.

The madam nodded with a strained smile plastered on her face. The light streaming in from the filmy window revealed her yellowed, gapped teeth.

"This dandy man is here to give us another generous donation in exchange for a completed contract." The scarred man pulled a cigar from his front jacket pocket. He waited for Post to acknowledge that he'd heard his statement with a nod before he lit it.

"Frankly, I was not."

The madam's eyes widened. She squeaked and fled out of the room like a mouse from a cat, slamming the door shut behind her. Post backed himself up against a wall.

The scarred man straightened in his seat. The legs of his chair came crashing down onto the wood floor. "I believe you were."

The two men glared at each other without a single flinch. Half a room and a desk separated them, but Richard swore he could feel the hot air blowing through the man's flared nostrils.

In their silent feud, Post wheezed through his hand covering his mouth.

The scarred man broke the tension. "Post, grab the example from the bar."

Post scrambled out of the room and returned a minute later, gripping Lord Halloway by the collar. The man hiccuped.

"You know this man, do you not?" the scarred man asked.

"He is my intended's father, yes," Richard replied, utterly perplexed.

"Then I'm sure you are acquainted with the fact that he's teetering on bankruptcy as we speak."

Richard turned to Scarlett's father. "You're bankrupt?" He'd known the Halloways were not as comfortable as him, had used that fact to his advantage, but he didn't know their situation was dire.

"No, I am only *teetering*." Lord Halloway's words slurred, and Post had to keep him standing with an arm under his armpit.

The scarred man stood, shuffled some papers on the desk and approached Lord Halloway. "He came to me asking for help with paying his bills. Wanted me to loan him a couple thousand pounds." He brushed the ash of his cigar off on Lord Halloway's tailcoat, leaving a little, round burn mark on the lapel. "When he decided he did not need to pay the interest–"

"Because you increased it by the day," Lord Halloway interjected.

The scarred man backhanded Lord Halloway, knocking him to his knees, then continued, "When he didn't pay, I had my ladies here take a little visit to his home." He turned to Richard and leaned in close. "Of course, they made sure he was out cold before taking the deed to his country property."

Lord Halloway struggled to pull himself up from the dusty floorboards. A scratch streaked across his cheek.

Despite the fact the window appeared to be painted shut, a chill, frigid and slippery, ran up Richard's spine. He tried shaking it off, but the sensation only ceased when he vowed to himself he would never be there, down on his knees before a criminal.

He was wrong to take this this far to begin with, but he needed the job finished. He could afford to complete the contract the right way. It wasn't worth risking it all for one stupid mistake. A little more coin, and it'd all be over.

If he paid however much they asked for, he could ensure Tate wouldn't be injured in the process. His brother would be safely out of his way before the boat even set sail, he'd be married to Scarlett, and his private life would remain private.

The Langley estate, and thus the Langley name, would remain untarnished.

"How much?"

Chapter Twenty-one

N ow lunge." Scarlett's feet slid over the dew-slick grass in the park, demonstrating for her student. "Perfect, Ava."

Lady Ava Halfurst copied along with the movement. Her arm thrust a lightweight foil into the open air, which was abundant given the entire lawn's worth of space every passerby gave them.

What did they fear? It was not as if sword-wielding women could catch like the plague. People wouldn't suddenly have all the women in their households stabbing them with butter knives and embroidery needles.

During their practice bout against one another, a gentleman had whistled at them as he strolled down the walkway. However, when they'd turned towards the noise, flashing the swords in their hands, he'd taken off running. The cloud of dust he'd left behind still floated in the air.

"Perhaps we should conduct our lessons in your gardens?"

Scarlett blocked Ava's wobbly stab.

Ava disengaged, pivoted, and stabbed again, making contact with Scarlett's foil. "To do so would entirely contradict our purpose."

Scarlett swiped her blade along Ava's, knocking it from her grip. "The purpose of teaching you how to protect yourself?"

"No, the purpose is for others to know *I know* how to protect myself." Ava retrieved one of the weapons from the grass, one of which she'd purchased and provided for these lessons. "You underestimate the power of collective knowledge. I find it to be most useful, but, then again, I do have a penchant for scandal." She winked and reengaged. "A 'notorious gossip' is what I hear your friends refer to me as, correct?"

As Scarlett was directing a strong swipe with her foil, a voice spoke behind her, "May we join you ladies?"

Scarlett turned and immediately wiped her damp forehead with the back of her hand. "Lady Grovington? Lady Irving? This is a private tutoring session."

"Did I forget to mention I had invited them?" Ava stabbed her foil into the dirt. It sprung back and forth with a twang.

Ava had said some of her friends shared her appreciation for Scarlett's bollock-bursting, arse-arbitrating abilities, but that had never translated to a group lesson. Although, it'd mean more funds to save for her and Tate's future home. It'd also be beneficial for Ava to practice with someone other than Scarlett for once.

This was Ava's third lesson, and she was already lasting twice as long in a bout than she had from the start. She'd also managed to bruise Scarlett's arms and step on more than a few toes. Definitely on purpose.

"You're welcome to join. I could use a break from The Hellacious Duchess of Halfurst here." Scarlett handed Lady Grovington her foil.

"Oh, hellacious. I much prefer that to notorious gossip." Ava beamed.

At the head of the group, Scarlett marked each movement in half-time while describing the motions for the newcomers. The three women followed along, the two newest practicing for the first time with swords.

"This is most diverting. I can see why my husband spends hours doing this." Lady Irving giggled. She swiped at a flitting butterfly, only managing to jostle the breeze underneath its wings.

"You hope that's what he's doing instead of spending his time at the brothels," Ava murmured while stretching out her calloused hands.

"Ava!" Lady Grovington gasped.

Ava shrugged. "What? Now she can show him what for next time he returns home smelling of cheap perfume."

"Ladies." Scarlett's heel stamped into the ground, digging into the dirt. "We do not learn to fence in order to terrorize people. Even if they deserve it." She squinted at Ava to suggest she keep her likely interjections to herself. "We learn to protect ourselves, which hopefully never has to happen."

"But Ava is right. My husband cheats at more than just cards. He thinks there's nothing I can do to stop him." Lady Irving pointed the foil to the clouds. "Now he's wrong."

Scarlett stepped in, taking the two weapons from the women's hands. "The only way I will promise to continue teaching you is if you promise to wield your earned power wisely. I wasn't allowed to train because I was foolish and reckless. I won't have you facing the same treatment I did."

Ava laughed, clutching the sides of her purple silk dress. "No, it was because you are a woman. I was there. I would know."

"As was I," Lady Grovington admitted.

Both women had been there? It was so long ago. Scarlett hardly remembered all of the faces which had stared down at her. She'd been a mere child, but it came as no surprise her champions now were ladies who'd witnessed the maltreatment.

Scarlett sighed. "Nevertheless, when you fight, you are representing the ability of not just yourself but all women. We mustn't make our sex appear vengeful and dangerous."

"And if we're fighting for something unjust?" Ava rested a hand on Scarlett's shoulder. "Say a woman has been forced into an unwanted engagement. And say this woman is expected, by law, to walk down the aisle in a week and a half to marry said man. What then, Scarlett?"

Scarlett clutched the foils to her chest. Was what Ava was suggesting vengeful? Or was it righteous? If a woman defended more than just herself, if she defended what was right and good, was that wrong? Or was it exactly what Scarlett had once tried to do and failed? Was it exactly what she was doing with Richard?

Who said men and their wars could be the only defenders of justice? These women right here wielding weapons in Mayfair were proof that was not the case. And that would not be the case for Scarlett.

What then, Scarlett? Ava's question remained unanswered.

"Then . . . " Scarlett flipped the handles of the foils in her hands, pointing them outwards. "Then she fights."

The three ladies had varying reactions to Scarlett's armament. Ava's lips stretched into a wide, cat-like smile. Lady Grovington offered a single, dignified nod. And Lady Irving squealed and clapped her hands. Scarlett would have to keep her eye on that one.

"Lady Wordsworth has an interest in medieval artifacts, does she not?" Scarlett asked.

Lady Grovington's brows quirked. "Yes, in fact, she does."

"Wouldn't it be smashing if she displayed them during her ball?" Ava posited.

"Indeed. It would."

A thrill effervesced in Scarlett's sternum at the idea of picking up her sword again. And, just as a man would on a battlefield, she would dedicate her efforts to her beau. To Tate. It would be an effort in the same vein as love and her first step in romantic education.

"Scarlett?" Ava whispered in her ear. "Do you know why I had my gardeners plant laurels?"

Wanting to keep her response to the mention of her and

Tate's secret tryst just that, secret, Scarlett simply shook her head.

"They represent triumph."

Chapter Twenty-two

Tate didn't need to remind himself the Wordsworth Ball was his last chance at finding anyone interested in his designs, anyone willing to save his career and his dreams for his future. He didn't need to because Richard already had.

"Did you hear me?" Richard's fingers snapped inches from Tate's face.

"What?" Tate dipped around his brother's arm, retrieving his top hat from its place on the mahogany dresser in his bedchamber.

He brushed dust off the brim. The last time he'd worn it was before his service, but tonight he must look as presentable as possible if he was going to show the Ton that he was an architect worth their money and prove to Scarlett that he was a man worth her love. Even though it always squeezed his scalp.

"I asked if you will be attending my wedding? It's in less than a week now, and I'd like to know if I will need to reserve two seats for your wide buttocks. I hope you do. It'll be the last time I see you before I depart for my honeymoon. You see, we will be heading to Walden Manor right away, so I certainly won't see you before you leave for India." Richard used his years of practice daggering Tate's weakest points with that one.

Perhaps he does so because he knows I am close to thwarting his plans. Or he's just a prig.

Tate squared his shoulders. "Shouldn't you be on your way to Halloway House to escort Scarlett?"

Richard blinked. "How did you know that?"

"As I am the fiancé she actually wants, we discuss such things. I know this is a foreign concept to you." Tate glared at Richard through his mirror as he straightened his hat. "That's how I know about you, about how the Duchess of Halfurt has convinced Lady Wordsworth to change the theme of tonight's event, and about how Scarlett managed to have Camilla added to the guest list."

"Camilla will be there tonight?" Richard's voice squeaked in a crack.

Tate shrugged. "I assume so."

Shuffling through the papers on his desk, he obtained his best designs and folded them neatly into his pocket to use as examples should someone ask to see the quality of his work.

When he looked up, Richard was gone, no longer a hovering ghoul. He left to instead haunt Scarlett. Tate hurried after him, not wanting to leave her alone to deal with Richard longer than necessary.

His long legs took the steps down the front of Langley House two at a time. When Callows shut the front door behind him, two men rounded the corners on either side of the stone steps. One was the thin man Tate recognized as having followed him at the picnic and club. The other was a stubby, bald man who was rolling up his sleeves.

Tate thumbed the papers in his pocket. "Bollocks."

While seated at her vanity, Scarlett squinted at the dress hung up for the night's ball.

"What do you think, Brissot?" She reached around her neck and clasped her necklace. "Will it do?"

Brissot yipped and rolled onto his back, rubbing his fur into the frayed Persian rug.

"No, I didn't ask if it's pretty. I asked if it will allow me to move well enough," Scarlett argued with her dog.

Brissot's mouth opened wide in a squeaking yawn. His tongue flopped out from behind his teeth and onto the rug.

"Oh, don't worry. Soon all this madness will be over and we'll be able to see Tate every day." Scarlett fiddled with the container of rouge on the vanity. "I only wish he was the one escorting me tonight. Being too near to Richard is only going to make my plans more difficult."

In a flurrious cloud of red fur, Brissot shook from top to tail. The flapping of his jowls against his teeth had her snorting with laughter.

A click resonated as Scarlett's bedchamber door unlatched. Lady Halloway entered the room, picked up her skirts high above her ankles, and stepped around Brissot. "I'm pleased to see you're in high spirits."

Scarlett rolled her eyes and swiveled in her seat back towards her mirror, fixing her baubles to her ears. "He's never bit you, mother."

"I won't let tonight be the first time. This evening is too important for our family."

"And all women," Scarlett mumbled.

"What a preposterous thing to say. You're attending with your fiancé, *the* Marquess Langley. Why should all women be excited for you as you take away the most eligible bachelor in England?" The mass of jewelry on her mother's wrists clattered as the woman shook her arms in the air.

While whipping around to face her mother, a curl fixed atop Scarlett's head loosened and boinged across her nose. "Because I will not be marrying Richard, and Tate and I will be showing everyone—"

Her mother interrupted her, "Yes, yes. Something about justice and good and other philosophical chatter. Now are you nearly ready?" Her hands untangled and reshaped the wily curl around Scarlett's face. "Your father is insistent we be on time tonight. He's already in the carriage. Do *not* ask him about the scratch on his face. I tried. It did not go well.

"Is that the dress you are wearing?" Her mother pointed to the frilly bluish purple thing hanging on the wall next to Scarlett's wardrobe. "It's perfect. Demure and definitely suitable for a future marchioness." She clapped with glee.

Scarlett strained to refrain from rolling her eyes. "Does father have to join us?"

Her mother leaned in front of Scarlett to check her visage in the mirror. "I had been clear we must have the appearance of a united front, had I not? My face is under-powdered. I'm beginning to glisten." She shooed Scarlett out of her vanity chair and sat, ready to preen.

In her best attempt to chastise as well as her mother, Scarlett wagged her finger. "Perhaps that is because you are exasperating yourself by carrying around all those bribery trophies on your arms."

"I do so for your best interest, dear. The Marquess is a perfectly honorable gentleman. Any other girl would be exceedingly happy with the offer. You're the most cantankerous young lady in all of London." Her mother pursed her lips, smearing on a fresh coat of lip rouge.

"Then any one of them can have him. He's not who I want. He's not who—who I could grow to love," she stammered, testing out the words on her tongue for the first time. A choke of something newly familiar, something she claimed as enduring adoration, caught in Scarlett's throat and wetted her words.

"For god's sake, Scarlett. The man you want is his brother.

How different can they be? Take the one with more money and the title, and your comfortable life will have you forgetting all about the other in no time."

Scarlett ripped her dress off the wall and stomped out of her bedchamber.

Tate was very different from Richard. And her plans for the night would prove to everyone just how much so.

"Where are you going?" Her mother shouted after her.

"I would rather dress in a broom closet than speak to you a moment longer."

The carriage ride with the Halloways was more than awkward, and not just because Richard hadn't spoken a word since leaving Tate behind with Post. The prospect of seeing Camilla at the ball dried any conversation from his mouth. Her likely presence was already becoming a distraction.

However, the Halloways stunning lack of communication with their long stretches of wordlessness and teeth-grinding set him even more on edge. Lady Halloway attempted to make conversation more than once, but Scarlett kept her lips sewed together.

"For having actually dressed in a broom closet, you look as impeccable as always, Scarlett."

Silence.

"Those trees in the square are enchanting, are they not?"

More silence.

Scarlett's father might as well have not been there at all because he made no attempt to interact with anyone. His face remained angled towards the window, presumably to hide the scratch the scarred man gave him, and he actively averted Richard's gaze.

The carriage squealed as it braked in front of Wordsworth House. Richard assisted Lady Halloway and Scarlett down.

Lady Halloway pulled Scarlett aside, but not far enough for Richard to help himself from overhearing, "Scarlett, one last thing. You will not, I repeat *not*, be disgracing our family tonight. When his lordship asks you to dance, you dance. When you are not dancing with him, you are quietly conversing with friends. *Female* friends. Do not make a scene."

Scarlett held her head up high and stared at their group with defiance oozing from her very being. Richard peered at her in expectation of her usual insolent reply. Instead, she offered them all a wickedly fake smile before brushing past her parents, taking his arm, and sauntering towards Wordsworth House.

"I'm surprised you're being so amiable tonight," he whispered in her ear as he assisted her in removing her pelisse in the Wordsworth's foyer.

"Just you wait."

Chapter Twenty-three

Must we do this now? I am indeed rather busy tonight. My lady expects me." Tate's breath circulated in the fabric sack over his head.

With everyone off to the ball, no one had been around to witness the two ruffians when they'd cornered him on the stairs. The large one had held his arms back, wrapped them with rope, and pushed him towards the carriage across the street while the lanky one had bagged his head.

Now they were riding down the darkened streets of London in a circuitous manner. The jostling of the carriage on the brick road wasn't nearly as diverting as the carriage jostling he'd done with Scarlett. Actually, it upset his stomach. Gurgling burps rumbled up his gut.

"The boss said tonight was the night, so yes. Now quiet." The thin man scooted over to the window seat and gazed out the window.

"You know I can see through this, right?" Tate asked.

"Boulder." The thin man smacked the back of the other's head. "You were supposed to grab the thicker one. This one's for the boss's apples."

"Don't trouble yourselves, boys. I know where you're taking me and why. My brother paid you to force me to sign another commission." Tate squirmed against his bindings. "Now can you remove this. I get carriage sick, and you've seated me backwards."

"'Ow do we know this isn't some ploy to break free?" The thin man squinted at him.

"Because I went with you willingly. Did you not see my size? I assume you know I'm strong. Otherwise, you wouldn't have brought Rock over here." Tate's jutting chin gestured at the man.

"His name is Boulder."

"My apologies, Boulder." Tate dipped his bagged head in the man's direction. "I could have broken free before you even pushed me in this carriage."

"Why would you go willin'ly?" Boulder spoke for the first time. His voice was as shockingly high-pitched as a meadowlark.

"Because I knew there was no other way out of this that did not involve injury, but perhaps I can reason with your boss."

If Scarlett was correct, if he was indeed as charming as she believed, then he might be able to charm himself out of signing. It hadn't worked at the club, but Richard hadn't left him with much opportunity to try. Or, at the very least, he could take a note from her book and kick them all in the groin. It was quite the provenly effective maneuver.

As his recent altercation with Lord Cullen demonstrated, he was still plenty strong enough to disarm a man. But three or more? Maybe not. All he'd need was a minute head start, and he'd be on his way to the ball, ready to steal Scarlett away for Gretna Green if he had to. Their life would have to be simple, but maybe they could start over on the continent or in the Americas. Surely people needed fine building there as enterprise flourished.

Post ripped the sack off of Tate's head. "Good luck with that."

The carriage stopped in front of a ramshackle, chipped stone building. As Tate stepped onto the steady ground, his upset stomach lurched three steps ahead of his feet. He whirled around, aiming for the gutter, and doubled over, casting up his accounts on both men's trousers.

"Bloody hell!" The thin man sneered and held out the fabric bag for Tate.

Tate coughed into it. "I warned you."

The men prodded Tate inside, up two flights of stairs, and through a set of rooms. In the final sat a wrinkled man at a desk.

"Mr. Bosworth?"

"Tate Langley! Nice to—*oof*—see you again." Mr. Bosworth trembled in his leather desk chair when a man with a scar that slashed from his wrist to the tip of his middle finger planted his hands on his shoulders. It seemed the regimental agent was just as unwilling of a player in Richard's scheme as Tate.

Boulder pushed Tate down into a seat and tied his bindings to the spindles of the chairback. Tate's wrist popped in the sockets at the force of the restraint.

"So, gentlemen, there's only one small matter which brings us here today," the man with the scar said. He had the cadence of a gentleman, but wore a tattered woolen tailcoat.

"You expect me to sign the commission," Tate stated matter-of-factly. Best not to show a criminal one's own fear.

"Exactly." The man cheered. "The regiment leaves when, Mr. Bosworth?"

"In a week," Mr. Bosworth squeaked.

The man sat on Mr. Bosworth's desk. "A week it is. Tonight you will sign the commission. Then we will so dutifully care for you until the ship leaves the dock. In the meantime, you'll help my boys out with whatever they need, of course. Can't have you wasting our resources while you wait. And after, you will enjoy a fulfilling life in India."

"No." Tate used all the charm he could muster with that one.

The man chuckled. His throat bobbed with the low, calculated rumblings. "You misunderstand. Allow me to clarify. You are accepting the commission whether you personally sign or Boulder here signs for you."

Boulder stepped forward and wrung his hands. "Sir, I can't write."

"Fine. Post will sign it. All Mr. Bosworth needs to hear is this man's verbal consent." Boulder's boss waved his hand in dismissal, then gagged. "What is that smell?"

"He puked on us," Post admitted.

"Disgusting. Leave the room so that I don't have to experience this wretched odor any longer." The fingers in the man's nose made his voice hum.

After the two men shuffled out, the man dipped a quill into the inkpot on the desk and held it up to a loose sheet of paper. "If you are ready to sign, I shall hold the paper behind your back so your bonds remain intact. The signature needn't be perfect. Ready?"

"No." Tate puffed his chest out, straining the buttons of his tailcoat.

It was risky, he now had the upper hand. Who would have imagined his little motion-related foible would benefit him in a hostage situation. With the lackeys out of the room, it was two to one. That was if Mr. Bosworth still had some of his power left in him from his glory days in the Royal Navy.

An echoing whack brought him back from his plotting as the man with the scar slapped the paper and quill onto the desk. "Tell me to sign the paper for you, and you will have a few years overseas and a few more thousand pounds in your wallet to show for it."

"Lord Tate, I would do as he says. He has ways," a shaky Mr. Bosworth leaned forward and whispered to Tate as if the man was not sitting between them. Remnants of snuff powdered his nostrils. "I had already locked up for the night, yet this man knew how to get into the building and hold me hostage.

Under the gazes of a leering criminal and a quivering coward, Tate was on his own. As with every other time in his life, he was left to face his brother's wishes by himself. Richard may not have thought him deserving of better, but Scarlett did.

If Scarlett were present, she would lecture these men on the injustice of the inability to choose one's own path in life with her fist planted on her hips and her cheeks burning an angry shade of red. She was the only person who believed him capable of achieving what he wanted. Without her, he wouldn't even be in this room; he would have signed the papers weeks ago when Richard first asked.

Instead, he was here, and he would fight for her just as he'd promised. To prove to her he was worth her future and her love.

He writhed in his bounds, rubbing his skin raw against the rope. "I cannot sign. I would lose everything."

The man with the scar scoffed, a bitter, livid sound. "You have nothing to lose. Your brother is the one with all the money to throw around. He's the one with the title. His name is on all of the deeds. What do you have?"

Tate had nothing yet. However, soon he could have everything or lose it all in one moment. Brute force wouldn't work. He'd just have to do what Scarlett always said. Time to use a little bit more of his wit.

L ady Wordsworth's ballroom, and her whole manor for that matter, was decorated exactly as Scarlett had hoped. Armoured statues stood along the walls, displays of antique weaponry were arranged on pedestals throughout the room, and imposing ring chandeliers hung above the dance floor like cages waiting to drop.

The story went that someone had once asked Lady Wordsworth why she didn't update her style to be more modern, and she flew into a rage, claiming she deserved to have a style of her own simply because she liked it, that she wouldn't be convinced to decorate her home with unpatriotic French furniture or fragile oriental pottery.

While her sentiment was arresting, the hazed, brooding affect the design style had on the atmosphere was even more so. The candles lit all around the ballroom cut through the dimness like the half-moon on a foggy night. The event was much better than the ice theme Ava had convinced Lady Wordsworth to switch from, and it came with the added benefit of extra cold drinks in order to waste not. Not to mention the swords of all shapes and sizes conveniently placed within reach.

Snaking past a group of mature matrons, an ogling set of repugnant rakes, and a flock of fanning debutantes, Scarlett broke free from her parents and Richard who had been following closely behind her since entering the ballroom.

She sought the refuge of the two women, one familiarly blonde and the other recognizably raven-haired, who were seated on a bench next to a footman with a tray of drinks. Both women's backs were slumped against the wall while they gazed at the whirling colors of the people on the dance floor.

Scarlett grabbed a drink from the footman. "Why are we not celebrating?"

"Celebrating what?" Bethanne asked.

"Celebrating your upcoming nuptials to Richard? Or celebrating the fact that I managed to receive an invite to this event despite my father's lack of title?" Camilla offered some bleak suggestions.

"Neither." Scarlett gestured to the footman to bring over two more drinks. She held up her glass and toasted, "To the downfall of Richard Langley and all people who believe they can dictate what a woman can and cannot do."

"What? Scarlett, a ball is not the place for you to share your philosophies." A squeaking Bethanne splashed her champagne onto her gown.

Camilla patted Bethanne's shoulder. "I believe what Bethanne means to say is, you obviously have lofty expectations for the evening. May we ask what they are?"

Scarlett downed her drink and set the glass with a *clink* on the footman's silver tray. "I'll be teaching Richard and everyone here a lesson."

"Before you do anything . . . " Camilla paused to drum her fingers on her chin, then continued, "permanently damaging, please allow me to try to reason with him first."

"By all means. I won't enact my plans until I have spoken with Tate. Have either of you seen him?" Scarlett asked.

Both women denied spotting Tate anywhere in the ballroom or the drive.

Scarlett's toes smashed against the boxes of her shoes as she rose to crane above the crowd in hopes of sighting her intended. His large stature was missing amongst the elaborate assortment of feathers and hats on the heads of the other guests.

If he was not yet in attendance, Scarlett would have to wait until he was and she could explain herself. She didn't want to blindside him with her actions. Without the chance to inform him of her plans, he may try to help, which would only undermine her point and risk his reputation for his career.

Until then, Scarlett would have to avoid Richard like the plague. Once she was ready for him to ask her to dance or some other face-to-face opportunity presented itself, then it'd be time to strike. Camilla could provide her with a good escape from him for at least a little while until she found Tate.

"Evening, ladies." Roberts sauntered towards their trio.

A few middle-aged widows with their bosoms pushed to their necks feigned swoons as he passed.

Bethanne leapt from her seat, knocking Camilla's hand and spilling more champagne onto her skirt. "Calvin! I—I had not thought you would make it. I'm glad to see you here tonight."

His gaze raked over her wet gown. "I can tell."

Bethanne's cheeks glowed. "That's just wine."

The pair stood close enough to touch but remained separated by what appeared to be Bethanne's greatest effort involving some seriously unbalanced swaying.

Camilla shared a knowing glance with Scarlett. "Do you think if we said something right now, they would hear?"

Scarlett snorted in a giggle. "Allow me to try. Roberts, have you seen Tate?"

His head turned towards Scarlett, but his gaze didn't follow, his eyes still trained on Bethanne. "No."

"He must have known better than to separate you from your true intended tonight," Richard's voice responded behind her. "Speaking of which, Scarlett, may I have the honor of a dance?"

Their group was silent, so silent one could clearly hear Lord Neels across the room complaining about dripping eclair cream on his waistcoat.

Richard raised his voice over the eight-piece orchestra beginning their next piece. "Miss Halloway, may I have this dance?"

"No. According to my dance card, I'm unavailable."

The slip of paper hanging by a ribbon around her wrist danced in front of his eyes in a flash.

"Don't lie. I know it's empty. We've not been here long enough for you to fill it, especially considering all you have done is speak to your friends." He avoided Camilla's probing gaze. "Besides, I am the one escorting you tonight, which implies at least two dances." He stamped his foot and held his hand out in expectation.

"But I have promised the first numbers to Tate and Roberts. Oh, and Lord Neels." She pointed to the man stumbling over his own feet on the other side of the dance floor.

"Speaking of which, shall we take to the floor now, Miss Halloway?" Roberts held out his arm.

The man must have seen the panic in her lying eyes and offered to play along. Why did this woman inspire such loyalty from her friends?

The din of Lady Halloway's bejeweled appendages cut through the noise of the chattering guests around their group. The woman barged past people on her way over, glaring at Scarlett. With bulging eyes, Scarlett weaved her arm with Roberts' and dragged him into a quadrille.

Richard stalked the edges of the room, following Scarlett's dance with his brother's friend. He stifled a yawn. This struggle wearied him. Before, his desire to marry had been an evenly-matched war with his chosen intended as his only combatant. Now, it included his brother, her friends, a contract with a criminal, and, from the amount of glares he'd already received tonight, what seemed like over half of the women of the Ton.

He should cut in. He'd allowed her antics to go on long enough. As he took one step towards a bouncing Scarlett, someone tapped between his shoulder blades.

Camilla's voice, as slick as silk, tickled his ear. "Richard, may we speak in private?"

His muscles shook, either from her light touch or his frustration over the inappropriate nature of their proximity. "I can't spare the time."

"Fine. You'll have plenty of time when the news gets out and your engagement is dissolved. I will speak to you then."

"You get five minutes," he seethed through gritted teeth.

"Funny. That's all it took last time," she mumbled. "I'll meet you at the end of the hall to our right."

Moments later, he found Camilla in an empty trophy room through the second to last door in the hall. She clicked the door shut behind them.

Richard paced, studying one gun cabinet then another. "I assume you haven't brought me here to discuss my interest in rifles. What do you want?"

"I could be pregnant Richard." With her back pressed to the closed door, her sigh creaked the wood in its frame.

"That is what tends to happen when one does what we have done as many times as we have done it." His tongue dragged over his lips before they stretched into a smirk.

Her hands smoothed the flat front of her gown. "Someone could find out it's yours."

"I know that. Why else do you think I'm trying to marry Miss Halloway?"

It was a shame. He'd hoped to enjoy a few more dalliances with this one after his marriage before the nature of her womb exempted her or he inevitably grew bored. Although, he had yet to after their three years of sporadic trysts. She'd been quite diverting and definitely more adventurous than his previous mistresses. And, having known each other for over two decades, she was a whole lot easier to converse with.

Disgust wrinkled the elegant, sharp point of her nose. "To cover up our affair? I wouldn't have believed you to be capable of such despicable behavior."

"It is not despicable. It's practical. So what's your plan?" He rubbed his palms together and blew into them. The room was chilled so far away from the party and its clouds of body heat.

"Why should you care? It's not as if you are offering to help me should our actions produce a babe." She swiveled and surveyed a trophy piece, speaking at the mounted deer's head. "Either way, I'm out of luck and options."

"I was never an option."

Tears stained her cheek. "Why not, Richard? I'm not a pauper. I know you know I love you. I told you so when we spoke before you left the country. I know you heard me, so why is that not enough for you?"

"Because . . . " he began.

Her steps brought her chest to chest with him. "Because what?"

Why was it not enough? He genuinely enjoyed his time with Camilla. Every time they met, without fail, they not only explored each other's bodies, but they explored each other's minds. Which meant they'd had enough discussions for her to guess the exact answer he'd rehearsed for her; he was not the marriageable type. Well, his upcoming nuptials ruined that excuse.

Now she was asking for the truth.

"Because you are not what my father told me to marry." The words tumbled from his brain to his mouth. Camilla's knack for undressing him, both literally and verbally, was unnerving and irresistible.

Her blue eyes slitted like a crack in ice, and her nostrils flared. "What your father told you to marry or who your father *suggested* you should marry? I know how deeply you respected his opinion, Richard, but those are two very different things."

"I'm trying, Camilla." He ran his hand over his face and released a shaky stream of air through his lips until his lungs nearly collapsed. "I'm trying to find a way you and I can be to each other what we have been without raising suspicion. Why else do you think I chose a woman who would ignore me if not to spend more time with you?"

"Who says we must remain what we have been? Could we not be something more?" Her fingertips traced the line of his jaw. "I thought after the last time I saw you, you might be changing your mind . . . "

He shut his eyes to the touch and leaned in ever so slightly. The fronts of his thighs grazed her skirts. She was warmth in its purest form, and he was drawn to her.

"I took a leap to follow you here to London despite how clear you'd been that our relationship must remain in the shadows of Northamptonshire. It was frightening, but it was also the most fulfilling decision I've ever made because . . . " She paused, her gaze searching his face. "Because I was honest with myself about my love for you. I chose to live for myself, not the notions of others. Maybe you should start there."

The warmth of her slender palms against his cheeks had carried him into a trance. A trance which was broken by her selfish words.

His eyelids snapped open. He took a jerky step back from her, leaving her hand to float midair.

"I am living for more than myself. I am living for the Langley legacy. I must do what is best for it."

Her hands came down in a skirt-dampened slap to her thighs. "I may be carrying the Langley legacy in my womb. What will be best if that's true?" she asked, her tone colder than the draft in the room. "Surely you don't expect we will carry on while you're married to another woman? You certainly can't marry Scarlett when another woman is carrying your heir."

His throat crackled in a bitter laugh. "I wouldn't be the first gentleman to do so."

After a moment of weighted silence, she stammered, hesitated, then continued, "And nothing Scarlett or Tate could do will stop you?"

Richard propped himself on a leather armchair out of range from her shaking form. Good. There would be no pleading, no cries for affection or demands for assistance.

Camilla was a smart woman. She'd spent enough nights sharing his bed and enough mornings walking herself home to know there was no room for sentiment between them.

Educated by her extensive experience with him, she should know that he couldn't be tricked by her supposed love. Once he'd decided what was best for himself and the title, which was his *duty* to bear, he would never allow himself to stray. Even if that meant never seeing her again. Never again laughing together when their ankles twisted in the sheets. Never again running into each other in the woods between their families' properties and using the fallen leaves as their bed. Never again sneaking into the barn during the day when his staff were cleaning his bedchamber.

No, she knew him better than that. She knew the only way his plan could fail was if he were physically forced to quit. Since his brother was likely signing the papers right this moment, defeat was nearly impossible.

"I suspect, at this point, Tate is incapable of doing anything to stop me."

Her lips rounded in a gasp. "What have you done?"

"Nothing. His failure to appear at the ball tonight is of no consequence to you. And Scarlett is a young lady—a selfish one at that. No one will listen to her long enough to stop our wedding in only a matter of days." He approached the door, twisted the knob, and added, "Be sure to wait a few minutes after I leave. We wouldn't want anyone thinking anything untoward about us."

"Of course, *my lord*."

As he shut the door behind him, her icy expression of

determination froze in his mind, leaving him with no hope they should continue as they once had.

Chapter Twenty-four

W hat do you have?" The words rang in Tate's ears louder than the ticking clock on Mr. Bosworth's desk.

What did Tate have? The man was right; he had no property to manage or responsibilities to maintain which deemed him an invaluable asset to crown and country. All he could claim to his name were the relatively measly sum left over from his commission, a vocational dream, and a fantasy of love. Scarlett was his intended, but she was not his in full while her heart remained undeclared.

But his love for her was the most he had on his person at all times, especially while he was bound to a chair with only his wits to shield him.

"A woman," he spoke into the silence.

The man with the scar hooked his thumbs in his pockets. "I have fifty. And?"

When it became clear there would be no appealing to this

man's romantic side, Tate scrutinized him with focused eyes.

The scarred man's jacket, although torn and patched in a few places, was crisply pressed. He held a rigid posture and appeared to be well-groomed with a shaven face and bluntly cut hair. The man clearly carried himself with dignity and commanded respect.

In a calculated tone, Tate admitted, "And I have a profession I can't leave behind."

The man doubled over with laughter. "What profession? Professional gentleman? Professional brandy drinker? Professional card player? Professional horse racing gambler? I would wager you have no clue what it takes to be a man of business."

"I am an architect."

One of the man's eyebrows quirked. "You are an architect? Prove it. What buildings have you made?"

"None . . . Yet! But I have designed hundreds. Check my pocket," Tate said, remembering his love for Scarlett was not in fact the only thing he had on him.

"Let me see these *designs*." The man's scarred hand dug into Tate's pocket and came up with a few sheets of folded parchment.

Mr. Bosworth's chair creaked as he leaned, peering over the man's shoulder. "Tate, I didn't know you had such the eye. My partners and I were looking for a new office space." Mr. Bosworth wrestled the paper from the man's grip and tossed him a sidelong glance. "Needless to say, Clipton Street is no longer ideal for our Mayfair clients. Would you be available to take us on?"

Tate instinctually went to shake Mr. Bosworth's hand to seal the deal and came up short, pulling on his bindings. He settled for a, "Most definitely."

Had he just found his first client while being held hostage? Perhaps Scarlett was right. A charmless person could not achieve such a feat.

The man with the scar stole the design back from Mr. Bosworth. "Your brother did not tell me you are a man of business." He paused, squinting at Tate. He was silent as he approached, striking his hands on Tate's shoulders and clawing his grip into the muscles. "I respect that. I, too, am a professional and a misunderstood second son."

"Does this mean you respect me enough to let me go?" Tate couldn't keep the false hope from tainting his tone.

"Not quite. As a fellow professional, you must understand that I cannot allow for a change in contract without a fee. I have learned through your brother that you have a sum from your previous commission . . . "

If Tate could smack his forehead right now, he would. He would also wish to strangle Richard for being so foolish with this whole ordeal. Involving himself with criminals? Who did he think he was? Someone who lost their family a considerable amount of money for a petty competition, that's who.

What was better? A future spent scraping by with Scarlett or one wasted not by her side? As if Tate even needed to ask this of himself.

Hopefully Scarlett earned well from her tutoring because their coffers would be near empty without his commission fund. Of course, Mr. Bosworth would pay, but it would take months to see that money, months in which they would have to wait for a wedding. During that time, Richard could convince her *he* was worth enduring for the security . . .

Tate needed to get out of these bloody bindings and to her side now before it was too late and his absence left her wondering about his true intentions, his bankrupting love for her.

"You drive a hard bargain, but I dare say my freedom is worth parting with a couple thousand pounds."

"Deal. I will send my boys to collect within the week. And believe you me, they *will* collect," the man threatened with a pointed look, then untied Tate's bindings and jutted out a hand. "I don't think I have properly introduced myself. Name's Mr. Michaels, founder of The Spare Boys."

"Nice to meet you." Tate shook the man's scarred hand, then rubbed his own numb wrists.

"Your dandy of a brother will not be happy to hear we have wasted his money," Mr. Michaels warned.

"His accounts will survive the blow." Tate chuckled dryly, then made for the door with wide, galloping strides.

The floorboards creaked under Mr. Michaels' shifting weight as he stood in Tate's way. "Wait. I can't very well let you go without a struggle, or at least the appearance of one. I would lose my boy's respect. They adore me, you see, and they don't need to know I have a weakness for men of business."

"Of course," Tate's voice took a sharp, quizzical turn.

With a wink, Mr. Michaels picked up the chair with Tate's bindings still hanging from the spindles and threw it across the room. It crashed into a wall, splintering in five different directions and puncturing a hole in the plaster.

"No!" Mr. Bosworth cried.

"Perfect show," Mr. Michaels whispered through a toothy smile.

Mr. Bosworth's face fell into his hands. "This isn't for show. I just had those polished."

Tate consoled Mr. Bosworth by pouring them both glasses of scotch from atop the cabinet at the side of the room. Meanwhile, Mr. Michaels ripped the curtain rod off the wall, swung it around, the teal curtains acting as two flowing sails, and rammed it into a glass window pane.

The glass in Mr. Bosworth's hand nearly emptied with his shake. Tate swished the liquid along his tongue, swallowed the burn of success, then poured the rest of the bottle onto the unsigned commission papers.

S carlett nicked the edge of Roberts' toes during one of her steps. To be fair, her gaze was by no means focused on the lively dancing around her. It was centered on the doors, awaiting Tate's entrance. They didn't budge. There was no squeak of the hinges nor were there liveried footmen guiding him from the foyer.

Sweat beaded on her forehead. Why hadn't he arrived yet? He was late. That was all. He would make an appearance soon and be present to witness her take down Richard. He would witness the moment she achieved what they'd been fighting for to finally be together freely. Then he'd be able to tell how deeply she felt for him without her having to say so in so many unexercised words. He would be here soon.

Soon.

"Do you suppose Tate is merely late?" She couldn't help herself. Her common sense was numbing from the fog of anxiety inside her.

Roberts shrugged as he hopped to his next step. "He isn't usually the sort."

Well, that was less than comforting. If Tate was not late, then he was missing. And if he was missing, Scarlett knew exactly which devil was to blame. Could Richard have forced Tate to sign the commission tonight? Could he have somehow already sent him away?

No, Tate had promised her. He'd find a way to her. He was just late. That was all.

At the final twang of the violin, the quadrille ended. As she stepped away to make room for the next dance, Scarlett swayed to and fro, struck by dizziness. The flickers of the candlelight shot across her whirling vision like shooting stars.

"Need a lemonade, Scarlett? I have an extra. Just be careful not to *make a splash*." Lucy Bell glided to Scarlett's side and snickered.

The chilled glass, slick with condensation, wetted Scarlett's palms. The coldness slowed the swirling in her head, but it didn't diminish the speed of the pulse beating in her veins.

It wasn't worth asking Lucy if she'd seen Tate yet, was it? The girl probably wouldn't have registered if she had, let alone cared to remember.

Scarlett rolled her eyes. "Ah, so you saw me at the Wilkins' picnic. Yes, I fell into the river. How droll."

"You have made quite the splash in the society set as well. Everyone is saying what a darling couple you make with Lord Tate Langley. I personally do not see it." Lucy toyed with the necklace resting against her clavicle and sipped her lemonade. "But, by all means, save the more eligible men for the rest of your friends."

"Eligibility is not always determined by title. Most frequently, intelligence matters more. Let me guess . . . " Scarlett mockingly stroked her chin in thought. "That's why you remain unmarried on your third year despite being the daughter of a duke."

Lucy gasped so hard the tips of her auburn curls darted into her mouth. She spat them out. "I see you have dropped your pious philosophist act in place of a bitch's bite."

Scarlett blew out an exasperated huff. It was not this girl's fault she'd been taught to value the more tangible aspects of a person. However, if Scarlett was successful with her objectives for the evening, Lucy would soon receive a memorable lesson on this exact subject.

"Lucy." Scarlett's hand grabbed Lucy's in a grip so tight color drained from the girl's skin. "All I mean to say is not everything revolves around which man chooses you. *You* get to choose who you marry, or if you wish to marry at all. Don't allow a man's title to dictate your life."

Before Lucy could respond, the people around them interrupted by crowding closer. One gentleman elbowed Scarlett in the ribs. Another bumped into Lucy's shoulder. Everyone in the mass was murmuring into each other's ear as they all pivoted towards the hallway behind them.

A wide gap in the crowd formed, leaving two figures displayed in the middle. The couple stood a foot apart, the man in front of the woman. Given their frozen stances and the mumblings of the crowd, they presumably had just been caught leaving the darkened hall together. For one's reputation, a fate worse than death.

Scarlett squinted. Who were they? One, the man, stood a fair height above others. His brown hair waved across his temples. The bitingly sharp, ice-blue eyes underneath were all too familiar to her. Richard. Which would mean the blonde woman who was cowering behind him was none other than

Camilla.

Why had the two of them been speaking anywhere but the ballroom? Poor Camilla must not know town is nothing like the country. The fragility of a lady's reputation in Mayfair knows no bounds.

Someone tugged on Scarlett's elbow. Ava's head popped between Scarlett and Lucy.

"Excuse me, Lady Lucy, but Miss Halloway needs attendance from a maid. Her hem was ripped while dancing."

Lucy nodded, still open-mouthedly dumbstruck by the newly compromised pair.

While Ava pulled her aside, Scarlett twisted, trying to see the back of her gown. "Is my dress really torn? I didn't feel a thing."

"No, but whoever buttoned the back needs to have their eyesight examined. They're missing a few." Ava grimaced.

"That was me, thank you. I think I did a passable job for having dressed in a broom closet."

Ava ignored her comment, perhaps because the buttons were far less than passable, and shook Scarlett by the shoulders. "Now's your moment. All eyes are on him. The Ton is treating the Marquess and that woman as if they've contracted leprosy."

Scarlett winced. "Socially, they may as well have."

Camilla didn't deserve the judgment. She'd only pulled Richard aside to help Scarlett's case. However, the Ton didn't know that. They only saw a couple leaving a dark hall together, which inevitably meant Camilla was now tainted by whatever unspeakable things Richard was believed to have done.

Ava was right. It was the perfect moment. All attentions were fixed on Richard, and, even better than Scarlett had hoped, he'd just shown the Ton exactly how undignified and arse-ish he actually was. This was her moment to expose him. She could show everyone the truth and the full, unbridled extent of her skills. And hopefully recoup Camilla's honor in the meantime.

"But I can't. Tate is still not here," Scarlett thought aloud.

Ava rubbed her forehead with the back of her wrist. "Do you need him?"

"I want him." Wetness pooled in the corners of Scarlett's eyes. "He needs to see me defeat his brother."

What was the point of her stopping others from dictating their lives if it could be that he was away signing the papers right this moment exactly as Richard wanted?

At the time a week ago, writing to Tate about her mother's demand for Richard to escort her to the ball against her will had seemed like a good idea. If not a smart idea, at least an honest one. And what was a courtship without honesty? But had it driven him into believing Richard would win despite their measures? Had it steered him into signing the commission?

Scarlett's freedom alone should be of enough value to go through with her plans, even if Tate had given up on her. But something about it didn't feel right. If she couldn't be with him, why did it feel so much less worth the effort?

"You and I both know you will never have a time better than this." Ava stared at Scarlett expectantly, awaiting her next move.

Scarlett squeezed her eyes shut to think, blocking out the

jumble of the crowd around her.

A future without Tate was a future not worth saving because her future *with* him would be so much more than she ever could have imagined. Because of him, she could see a life beyond one like her parents expected of her, a marriage like theirs. She could dream of a future in which she held aspirations she could achieve and would find support from her husband. She would have a life spent enjoying herself outside of the shadows of her bedchamber tucked into a book.

Although, she and Tate would likely be spending a lot of time in their bedchamber.

Beyond that, for the very first time, she was capable of experiencing hope.

If her outlook for her future was that exciting, why did she feel she couldn't make the leap without him here to witness its fruition? Should it be that he was simply late, she knew he would be happy to listen to a retelling after the fact, but why did that not feel like enough? Why must he watch firsthand her battle devoted in his name?

Realization struck her across the temple.

Damn it all, because I love him!

Defeating Richard wouldn't merely be a sign of her devotion to Tate. It was a declaration of love.

And it—this—love *was* perfectly logical. Not an impossibility or an improbability or a farce. It was the feeling of rightness inside her that had begun to blossom since the very first moment they met. A vine with thorns of thoughts of him wrapping around her very being and pricking her until she felt something. She was thoroughly ensnared now. There was no desire to escape the lush bramble their entanglement had become.

Of course she would realize so when he wasn't present for her to proclaim herself. It was that newly recognised love, a sunrise cresting in the distance, which she must put her trust in and continue on with her plans whether or not he appeared in time to witness.

With a gloved hand, Ava swiped away tears Scarlett hadn't known were running down her cheeks. It was the sweetest gesture a friend had offered Scarlett during her turmoil this season, but she couldn't blame Bethanne for her lack of support. It was only within the last minute that she truly understood how devastating it must be to leave one love behind for another in widowhood.

"Why are you helping me so much?" Scarlett sniffled.

"You aren't the only woman who's been forced into an unwanted engagement. My parents sold me away to the Duke when he met my family during his travels. I was then only sixteen and had to leave my country, my people, behind. Let us hope you are successful tonight or you will end up as I did." Ava's bony fingers twirled Scarlett around and prodded her in the spine towards an array of medieval memorabilia.

Scarlett straightened her shoulders. Now was not the time for tears. Now was the time for retribution. On behalf of herself, Tate, and every woman and man whose lives were controlled by those who deemed themselves too powerful to be stopped.

Ripping the cold, sharpened steel from the lifeless hands of an armored statue, she squeezed the hilt of a sword in her palm. The short, lightweight blade cut through the air with a *whoosh*.

"Henceforth, you shall be named Plato," she whispered against the flat side of the weapon, her breath fogging the shine. "For justice. For myself, for my friends, and for my *enemies*."

Chapter Twenty-five

S carlett, what on earth are you doing?" Lady Halloway shrieked, clasping her hands to her chest.

If there were a few stragglers at the ball who had yet to notice Scarlett was pointing a sword at Richard's neck, then they were all sure to have turned at her mother's gold-bracelet-orchestrated outburst. What they saw when they did, however, was by no means unwarranting of said sparkling cacophony.

The tip of Scarlett's blade danced back and forth through the air as it followed Richard's ducks and weaves. He held his palms up in the air and cried for assistance. Camilla scurried away somewhere destined to be safer than behind the bobbing man's back.

"I think they are about to duel," Roberts suggested in response to Scarlett's mother.

Bethanne thumped his arm. "They cannot duel. They're

technically betrothed. And she is a lady."

"Bethanne, you have been my friend my entire life. You should know by now the fact I am a woman does not make me a stranger to a sword," Scarlett chastised as the edge of her blade inched closer to Richard with each gliding step.

"Spare me the lecture on the capabilities of women," Bethanne huffed.

Lord Neels put a finger to his lips and shushed. "Would you all be quiet? Of course they aren't dueling. This must be a game they're introducing to us."

"This is not a game nor a duel," Richard answered, chuckling.

"Of course it isn't," Roberts called out. "Because you know she would win . . . "

Rage flashed across Richard's face. At his request, Lord Cullen tossed him a blade from another statue. He bounced it between his palms. When he found a sturdy grip on the groove of the handle, he stilled and poised the weapon at Scarlett.

She settled into a readied stance and smiled until her lips cracked. "En garde!"

Lord Neels coughed. "Nevermind. They are, in fact, dueling."

"We are not," Richard claimed while lifting his arms in the air in mock surrender. Sweat stains pooled under his armpits. "Scarlett merely has a headache from all of our wedding planning and is confused at the moment."

"No, she's likely upset you fondled that country lass and has gone mad," someone in the crowd shouted.

Scarlett faltered at the insult. Mad? Had she gone mad? Had Richard driven her to blistering rage? Yes. It would, however, do no good for her to fly into a fury in front of all these people who were expecting such from her. No, instead this was her moment to show them who truly controlled her life. Not Anger or Petulance. Not her mother or father or Richard.

She did.

"I have not lost my wits. In fact, I have never felt better." Scarlett planted her feet on the parquet floor. "While I am entirely clearheaded, I am quite furious." She shuffled her lunge closer to Richard. "You see, everyone, this man has not only ruined the reputation of an innocent friend of mine, but he has also bribed my parents."

Her sword swung to point at Lord and Lady Halloway. Lord Halloway hid his scratched face in his hands. Lady Halloway let out a breathy laugh and twisted her bracelets.

Turning her sword back to Richard, Scarlett continued, "The Marquess paid for my hand against my will. No matter how many times I have asked to be released from our engagement to marry the man I truly love," she paused, allowing that newfound passion to throb in her heart, "this man has decided I have no mind of my own. He has also tried to pay his way into removing the competition. Where is Tate tonight?"

Richard twisted his head to the side while glaring at her. "I don't know."

"Let us be honest for once!" Scarlett's blade swiped at his

waist.

He leapt sideways and blocked her move with a clash from his weapon, only just barely. A large slash in his shirt revealed the pale skin underneath.

He grabbed at the fabric, examining the tear with shaking hands and wide eyes. "Fine! Fine. I paid criminals to hold him in their custody until the regiment leaves."

The crowd gasped. Lady Grovington clutched her bosom. Lucy swooned into a clump of men who caught her under the arms.

Richard had Tate kidnapped. That was the second worst outcome Scarlett could have imagined. The worst would have been Tate had chosen to leave on his own accord. That he didn't love her enough to defy Richard.

But he did love her. So much so he ended up heaved away by hooligans, likely strong ones if they were able to take him away presumably conscious.

Scarlett's breathing rasped at the constricting sensation in her lungs. If only she could use this sword to slice her corset laces. Thinking about the stakes before her would be more tolerable if she could breathe. Now more than ever someone needed to take this beast Richard down so that both Tate and their future could be rescued.

"Admit you have treated me, Tate, and, frankly, everyone around you," she swung her sword in a circle, gesturing to every person in the ballroom, "as if we were cows for sale at market. You are not the only one to do so, but you're perhaps the worst."

Scarlett swiped at him again, this time from the left.

His eyes bulged. He jerked his blade up, nearly missing his block in time.

Scarlett spun around his back, swimming in the sticky, humid air, and swept the sword around him. It cut the tails off his coat. "Admit you believed you could bend me to your will simply because I am a woman. Simply because I don't hold a title. Simply because I don't have the power you were born with."

Richard twirled around to face Scarlett and stumbled a step on the sliced fabric.

"Renounce our engagement. Do as I ask, and you will remain unscathed." Scarlett dove in. Her blade hovered inches from his jugular.

A woman deep into the crowd screamed, shaking the crystal glasses on the footmens' trays.

If the Ton had seemed scandalized by Richard and Camilla's unsavory reentrance, they were positively raving with lunacy over Scarlett's swordswomanship. Men gasped. Women hollered. Debutantes blasphemed. Elderly ladies tapped their canes and clapped.

"Ha!" Richard balked. His Adam's apple grazed the knife edge of her weapon as it bobbed. A single drop of blood beaded on his skin. "You're just as you were when you were a girl. Silly. Foolish. Erratic." He snaked his blade up between her weapon and his torso and shoved.

Scarlett stumbled, her knees nearly giving way. But she caught her balance with her toes digging into her slippers, finding purchase on the polished wood. Her chest muscles ached at the sheer force of his retaliation. He was a tall man, and his size packed power into his movements. She couldn't match it. But she could use it to her advantage.

This was it. This was the end. It had to be. She had to put a stop to this now. To deliver the final blow. The past was not something anyone could use to haunt her anymore.

She was not a girl, nor had she ever been a fool. She had been a child with dreams. Now she was a woman with goals. With steadfast beliefs and promising opportunities. With love.

And that love needed her.

A screech avalanched from the peak of her lungs to the very base of her being. The chandeliers overhead quaked on their chains from the force of her bellow.

"No one can tell me I cannot fight because I am a woman." She paused to shake her unraveling chignon free. Her hair spilled down her upper back, melding to her wet skin. "No one can tell me who I must marry because I am a woman."

She jabbed at his stomach. Then again, lower this time.

He averted both, stepped aside, and swiped at her blade. The scratch of metal on metal stung the air. A cascading shower of sparks flew in all directions.

Richard paced the edges of their sparring ring, a wide circle in the center of the dance floor whose boundaries were defined by their assembled audience. "Did you not learn the last time you pulled this stunt how ridiculous you were being?"

Scarlett matched his steps. Her palm slicked with sweat in its grip on the hilt. She dared not wipe it on her skirt. To do so would signal weakness. The liquid dripped down her wrist, trailing down her forearm. She gripped tighter. The veins between each knuckle pulsed at the surface.

"I was a mere child then. I did not yet know there was nothing you could actually do to stop me. That you found me ridiculous because . . . " She paused to assess Richard's expression.

His brows wiggled, mocking her speech. His lips held a tilted smirk. Masks for arrogance and entitlement. Everything about this man was a mask hiding whoever he truly was.

She and Tate were incapable of utilizing masks. With Tate too large to hide behind anything, and herself full of opinions and snorts too loud to be contained, they only ever chose to be themselves.

"You find both Tate and me ridiculous because we are something you could never imagine being." Like a conductor's wand, she waved her sword with each word she spoke. "We are brave enough to be ourselves."

A flash of lightning crossed over the raging ocean of Richard's eyes. His feet pounded towards her in wide, lurching steps. His soggy hair fanned over his forehead. His blade swayed with each step, side to side.

Scarlett stood still. Her blade angled out from her waist as he grew closer. With the most incremental of twitches, she looped the tip of her weapon around the hand Richard used to hold his sword.

His steel crashed to the ground in a series of rattles until it settled flat. Louder still, he screamed. His free hand clutched the injured one to his chest. Blood stained his shirt's crisp cotton.

"Richard, *I* release *you* from our engagement," Scarlett declared between pants.

As much as she had dreamed the entire crowd would cheer for her when she'd planned her confrontation, she'd expected perhaps half actually would. The true count? Four or five, all of whom were already her students or who, by the vigor of their admiration, perhaps wanted to become one.

Nevertheless, she bowed.

For them. For Lady Irving and the other women who were stuck in controlling marriages. For herself and the other children whose parents manipulated their lives. For Tate while he was captive somewhere, refusing to sign away his life, and the other people who had ever allowed the judgments of others to control their actions. For anyone in the crowd who believed someone could hold them back from following their desires.

When she straightened, the first person to focus through her blurred vision . . .

Was him.

Chapter Twenty-six

At the front of the crowd, Tate stood with tears streaming down his cheeks and around his quivering smile. The salty liquid burned the cracks in his lips.

Scarlett's sword fell from her hands. She sprinted at him, her feet springing off the ballroom floor. Her full force collided with his chest. Her arms looped his neck as she hung from him in an embrace.

If there was any air left in his lungs, he would have laughed. He squeezed her, tighter than what might be safe and tighter than what was proper around all the onlookers.

It didn't matter, for he was here with her in his arms, holding her, smelling her, touching her. He made it to her. And she did this—all this—show of loyalty for him.

Because she had found him worth the risk.

He hadn't needed to be more or do more for her. She hadn't even known he was there, yet she still fought for him.

Her forehead fell against his neck. Her whispering breath tickled his ear. "Carry me out of here. I can't feel my muscles anymore. Real swords are heavier than one imagines."

With her pressed to him, he marched away from all the slack-jawed members of the Ton, down the front steps of Wordsworth House, and out onto the graveled lane.

The night's breeze was crisp, but their embrace shielded them from the chill. The air was laden with the revivifying scents of the boxwoods and roses lining the building and paper and toasted cinnamon from Scarlett's hair which brushed his cheek. The fragrance of home, for he was truly home now. For good. The aroma of future and promises and freedom.

The stars above glistened brighter than any night sky Tate had ever seen. Brighter than the nights he'd sat at his desk in his childhood bedchamber and looked out the window. Brighter than any night in the battlefields of France. Brighter still than the night over the Duchess's gardens.

"Look up," he murmured.

Scarlett's chin tilted. "They are stunning."

Her green eyes shimmered, stars of their own. She dropped her gaze to his face.

"Tate?"

His breath hitched. "Yes?"

"I love you."

"I figured. One does not often duel over ambivalence," he joked, but inside his heart beat harder than his chest could keep time. "I love you too."

She laughed, ended it with a snort, and shook her head. "But I *more* than love you. I understand you. You crave to work your mind, work your hands. To engage with someone worth the challenge and be worth the match. You are everything to me, and I love you because I understand you." She touched her palm to his whiskered cheek.

Awestruck, Tate's blinked rapidly due to the weight of tears in his eyes. How could he ever have the chance of gathering words that could rival hers?

"Must you always be so precise?"

"It's in my nature. Blame is on the butter knives and books." The slant of her smile dared him to counter, a form of flirtation unique to her.

"Touché." His use of a fencing term earned him a quirked brow. He continued, "You may understand me, but you misunderstand one thing." He angled his face towards her, leaving less than an inch between them. "What I crave . . . " His lips brushed hers. "Is you."

She pressed fully into him and moaned into his mouth. Their tongues met slowly, languidly at the seams of their lips. On hers was the heady taste of champagne and her potent spice.

She pulled away from the kiss with a crease folded between her brows. "What do we do now? This is uncharted ground."

He pressed his lips to her worried furrows. What did they do now?

His Scarlett, the bravest woman, the bravest person he'd ever known, had dueled for their love and won. All while he set his career in stone—or brick, whatever Mr. Bosworth would prefer—and argued his way out of captivity. Nothing could stop them.

Richard was bound to be livid. He would likely kick Tate out of his house. And Scarlett's parents must surely be disappointed she was no longer making such a lucrative match.

Together, they'd stood up for what was fair, and together they would be homeless and without family for doing so. Well, not entirely without family. They had each other. And Brissot. The beginnings of a family.

"Marry me," he blurted.

She snorted in a giggle. "We are already engaged. Remember how I accidentally proposed?"

He unraveled his grasp on her waist and traced his hand along the side of her face. His large palm engulfed the suppleness of her cheek. "Marry me this week."

Her arms released their cling on his neck. She slid down his front like water along a mountainside. The delicious friction pumped blood into his cock.

"How? That is much too soon unless you plan to steal me away to Scotland."

"There is a wedding we can use. I received an invitation to it, and, if I'm not mistaken, it is no longer happening." He jestfully stroked his stubble.

After the public mess Richard made of his own reputation, the vicar would surely understand the need to change the groom's name on the license at the last minute. He would likely shove the special license in Tate's hands and skip with them down the aisle in a week without any need for the three-week reading of the banns.

She laughed, her lips sputtering together before the guffaw. A more indecorous sound Tate had never heard. A melody to his ears, definitely no one else's. Certainly not to the carriage horses in the lane who whinnied.

"I believe I, too, heard it was cancelled," she mumbled between giggles.

This woman, covered in sweat and—were those marks on her bodice the spatterings of his brother's blood?

This woman, snorting, wearing a blood-stained ballgown, would soon be his wife.

Scarlett had treated him as the handsomest man, the drollest comedian, and the greatest architect in the world. And she had encouraged him to believe he truly was all those things. And the results of her designs? He was left with a profession, a home country which would stay his home and felt as such, and a love.

She deserved everything he could give her and everything he could not yet afford to give her, including, eventually, a ring. However, he would start with something better. Something which would surely deliver a glimmer to her eyes. And relief to his pulsing cockstand.

With a maddening gasp from her mouth, he scooped her into his arms and marched towards the carriages.

Scarlett nestled in Tate's arms as he carried her past elaborately lacquered coach after coach in front of Wordsworth House. His chest muscles flexed against her cheek and hardened with every small movement he made. The scent of the night's efforts—salt, musk, and a hint of whiskey—was woven into his shirt fabric, intoxicating her into a dream state of drifting eyelids and soothed spirits. He lifted her into a crestless, paint-chipped carriage.

"Tate, where are we going? Whose carriage is this?" She settled herself on the bench.

Tate returned from directing the driver and scooted in close to her side. "Mr. Bosworth's. Given he believed it was stolen this evening, he lent it to me after I freed myself."

"You freed yourself? I told you you were strong enough." She squeezed his arm.

At her touch, the muscles in his jaw tensed. Drool pooled under her tongue at the memory of his muscles flexing around her, and within her, the last time they were this alone.

He turned his heated gaze to her, tilted her face to meet his, and whispered, "Oh, you don't know just how strong I am."

A movement in his lap caught her attention. His manhood, a solid pillar, jumped in his trousers.

Her lips tingled, wanting to plant a kiss on his jawline, on the beat of his neck, on the ridges of his chest muscles. Perhaps even somewhere more . . . columnous.

He smirked when he saw where her eyes wandered. "I wanted to take you right on the steps of Wordsworth House. But I have something better planned."

"Which is?" Her voice was lighter than air.

"Your much-deserved ravishment."

The wheels rolled to a stop outside of Langley House, but Scarlett didn't notice. Eyes closed and lips melted to Tate's, she only realized they'd arrived when he murmured, "Come with me," into her mouth.

With a strong grip on her hips, Tate led her out of the carriage and up the steps. The veins in his arms pumped underneath the surface of his skin like the roots of a tree sprawling across grass. His stiff member rubbed against her buttocks as they walked, leaving her hot and breathless. Pressing himself to her, he used the tip of his boot to knock on the door.

"Lord Tate, how was—Oh! Evening, Miss Halloway. May I be of any service to you both?" The butler answered, his expression somehow markedly less shocked than when she'd tried calling on Tate not long ago.

"No, thank you. The only thing we need is a locked door, a set of clean sheets tomorrow morning, and some privacy please, Callows." Tate instructed over his shoulder as he prodded her upstairs.

"Understood. What shall I tell his lordship?" The butler inquired after them.

"Tell him you have prepared his bandages," Tate yelled from the doorway before kicking the door shut and clicking the lock in place.

In the dim lighting of a few lit oil lamps along the wall, Scarlett could just make out the mess of papers on his desk and the scuffed boots he often wore next to the wardrobe. A washbasin sat filled next to his dresser with a cloth hanging from the small stand. An array of charcoal pencils and measuring devices littered the dresser top.

Her heart thumped between her ribs, shaking her bosom. Somehow, the presence of a bed, one draped in crimson brocade silks, made this all the more real than it had in the midst of their hunger in the carriage. It made her wantonness all the more thrilling. Their times in the garden and the carriage had been all about passionate need. Craving. Rushed desire. This was different. There was a weight to it which lingered in the air. The presence of the future laying itself out before them.

Behind her, Tate ran his fingers through the long waves of her hair, pushing her locks to the side.

"Close your eyes," he demanded, his breath breezing across her spine.

His gliding hands worked to remove her ballgown, popping open buttons and sliding down fabric. The incremental release of her lungs from her corset opened her from the inside. Left to all senses but sight, every graze and caress he made was like scalding water poured over her limbs in a bath. The rough touch of him cupping her buttocks. The heft of her breast in his palms. The rolling pinch of her nipples.

Tate's footfalls stepped away for a moment, abandoning her nude form to the draft in the room. When he returned, she was soothed by his warmth so close to her naked skin.

Then, damp cloth dragged across her body. Down her arms, along her neck, around her breasts, trailing across her stomach. Liquid dripped down her legs. It was just warm enough to feel the slow beading of droplets running down her skin.

"What are you doing?" She asked, her voice sounding far away. The gentle pressure of the cloth swiping along her back left her too delirious to open her eyes even if she wanted to.

"I'm bathing you," he murmured, running the cloth along her inner thighs. "After all you have done, you deserve to be treated as a warrior goddess, and this," he grazed his lips on her stomach, just above her curls, "is my worship."

"Mmmm."

Her moan was a catalyst. He groaned, threw the cloth against the wall with a *splat*, and walked her until her knees hit the edge of his bed. She collapsed onto the mattress. He towered over her, broad and sturdy. A statue with a member as stone-like as marble poking out beneath his trousers.

He caught her staring again. Rabidly, he ripped off his clothing. His cravat, tails, waistcoat, shirt, then trousers all went flying through air and spread throughout the room like seeds cast by a farmer's hand onto a field. Nude, his muscles were sculpted by shadows and dim, carving light. A divine being with a seriously plump arse.

Planting hands on either side of her face, he hovered over her and brushed his lips to hers. His mouth stole hers, his tongue dancing with hers in a luscious waltz until he sucked her lower lips and bit down.

She gasped, feeling a torrid rapture of pleasure dart through her. Pain could inspire such sensations? A greater discovery she had never before made.

Tate lowered himself closer to her, ravishing the bare skin of her chest. The touch of his mouth on her nipples made her writhe, but his firm grip on her forearms held her in place. She crumpled the bedcovers in her tightly clasped hands. He released her arms, and she flew to lift her mouth to his.

"I need you," she whispered against his lips.

"Not yet." His breath brushed her neck.

From his position above her, she could feel his member pressing against her core, taunting her. "Tate, please."

"No. I plan to worship you." He nibbled at her earlobe.

She could not wait any longer. She reached down between their bodies and wrapped her fingers around him, raising her hips up to meet his.

"You are terrible at listening," he choked out with a smirk and wide eyes. He rose from the bed, forcing her to release her grasp. The calloused pads of his fingers grabbed her hips and slid her to the edge of the bed.

She propped herself up on her elbows. "What are you doing?"

He kneeled before her.

"Tate—"

"Shhhh." He hissed against the side of her knee, his whiskers tickling the sensitive skin there. "Let my design speak for itself."

As his kisses rose up her thigh, a flutter of nervous anticipation filled her stomach. She dared not say another word. The flames in the lamps flicked at the same rhythm as her heartbeat.

When his lips grazed the soft skin of her inner thighs, her legs instinctively closed shut against his head. One of his dark chocolate eyes winked as he rubbed his hands against her legs, slowly pushing them back apart.

His gaze stayed entwined with hers when his mouth touched her core. His tongue flatly lapped her sex, undulating back and forth. Then he sucked on her pearl, and she wanted to scream. She bucked, but he held her down by the hip bones. Her arms gave out at the sensation of his mouth against her. With her legs dangling over his shoulders, she would have laughed at how odd she must have looked if she had been capable of feeling any emotion other than ecstacy.

Like sipping tea, or rather, for Tate hot chocolate, he inhaled her, swallowing her sex, swirling her core with his tongue. Her useless hands flew to his hair, entangling her fingers in his locks and pulling. Her legs shook and her arched back cramped as she felt the same sensation she had twice in the carriage. The exhilaration of pure bliss cascading into contentment.

A ragged breath escaped her mouth. If it weren't for the presence of the bed underneath her, she would have thought she was floating. After she came off her peak, she collapsed into a puddle of sheets.

Raising from his genuflection on the floorboards, Tate rejoined Scarlett on the bed. He peppered kisses along her hand, her arm, and her neck until she regained her senses.

"I think, given an entire lifetime, I will never get tired of that," she admitted with eyelashes fluttering and lips barely moving.

"Luckily, I have an entire lifetime with you to test that theory over and over again."

Laying beside him, the curve of her waist to her rounded bottom to her lush thighs made his cockstand pulse painfully. He ran his hand down from her shoulder to calves, feeling every dip and swell of her body.

"Is this what you meant by liking to work with your hands?"

"I had never dreamed I would be so lucky."

He truly had not. Never in all his lonely nights would he have predicted he would someday share his bed with a companion who understood him as Scarlett did. As their limbs entwined, so did their spirits and minds. To be able to touch her like he did, kiss her here on her bosom, and know she felt it in more ways than one, that she never wanted him to stop, was healing. She'd healed him. He was no longer the repulsive behemoth of insults past. He was as strong and beautiful in her eyes as she was in his. But together, locked in each other's embrace, they could soften.

Maybe not too much. He was certainly still undeniably hard, and he had to do something about that.

Her eyes widened as he pounced on her, hovering above her on bent elbows. His knees slipped on the cotton coverlet, landing him flat on top of her with hastened apology. Her bare breasts quaked with her breathy, snorting giggle.

He pressed his forehead to hers. "As much as I love your laugh, I want to hear other sounds escape those," he brushed his lips along hers, "alluring lips of yours."

In a crash, his mouth returned to hers and did not part as he gently pushed into her. She expelled a breathy, beautiful moan.

After the evening away from her he'd had, he yearned to be as close to her as possible. If he could have it his way, he would devise a plan to never leave her side again.

With his slow strokes, he drew himself closer and closer to her, bringing her nearer to climax. Her hips rolled beneath his, begging him to increase his speed, but he refused. The luxurious intimacy of the future before them left him in no rush. The pleasure was in the unreachable end. The stasis of forever. Love was found and given in those moments of patient desire.

The problem resided in the fact he loved her too much, and if she did not find her end first soon, he would. He strained, holding himself back for her, to give her the ending she deserved. She was too tight. The aroma of her sex too sweetly intoxicating.

Her wetness too deliciously slick. He was damned.

When her muscles tightened in orgasm around him, her rose lips bloomed in a crying part, and her emerald eyes rolled back, he was lost in her. Delivered from her pleasure a starlit flash of ecstasy of his own.

Both breathless and incapable of speech, Tate tore himself from Scarlett, tumbling next to her on the mattress and curling her against his chest. He held her tightly as her eyes fluttered closed. Contentment swelled within him. This moment, with Scarlett resting in his arms in this quiet room while only a few days out from calling her his wife, was the most fulfilling time of his life. He drifted to sleep lulled by her quick, slumbering breaths and the smell of cinnamon.

Chapter Twenty-seven

After picking up his wedding attire from the tailor's, Tate thrust open the front doors to Langley House, practically humming with joy, and immediately wished he had not. The putrid odor wafting through the hall punched him square in the face.

"Holy hell! What is that stench?" Tate cried with a muffled voice, his hand covering his nose and mouth.

"I believe–*hiccup*–that is me." Yards away, Richard laughed from his seat on the floor slumped against the wall.

"You need a bath."

"No, what I need is a bath," Richard drunkenly corrected.

"That is what I said." Tate sighed. "Where have you been?"

"Let me see." Richard held up his hand. "Since the Wordsworth Ball, I have been to the club." He put down one finger. "Then I went to play cards at Lord Drafton's." He put down another finger. "Then I visited a brothel." He accidentally put down two fingers. "Then I visited a gambling hell with Lord Cullen." He lifted a finger up. "So that makes two places, correct?"

Careful not to bump his brother's bandaged hand, Tate lifted Richard by the armpits. They were damp. He gagged.

"You need—to get—some rest," he said between gasps of fresh air over his shoulder.

"She is gone," Richard whispered.

"Who?"

"Camilla. She has left town. After the ball." Richard turned his face towards Tate's.

"I'm sorry if this sounds insensitive, but why do you care?" Tate spoke to the floor to avoid Richard's hot, rancid breath.

"I—We were—" Richard stuttered.

A realization dawned on Tate. All those times Richard had pestered him about Camilla. All the times he had said obscene things about her body over the years. How he secretly had a mistress. Richard had feelings for Camilla. And if Tate encouraged him to follow her, it was possible he wouldn't show up for the wedding. A luckier hand than this had never before been dealt.

"I believe I understand." Tate paused, arranging his next words carefully. "Richard, had you hoped to spend your life with Camilla?"

"I had. It is father who does not."

"Did not," Tate emphasized. "Father did not want you to marry a gentry woman. He's long dead." Tate dragged Richard into his bedchamber and dumped him on the bed.

Richard rolled to his back and stared at the ceiling. "She is gone. She has left, and I cannot even blame her." He wiped his tears and snot on his jacket sleeve. "I have been awful. I wanted them both, brother. I wanted Scarlett to keep Camilla, and I have lost her in the process."

Tate grabbed a fringed pillow from the head of the bed and nudged it under Richard's neck. "That was your dumbest idea yet. Dumber than your drunken tree climbing at Oxford. Why had you thought that would work?"

Per usual, Richard ignored his question. "Any hope I had of maintaining a relationship with Camilla was reliant upon my marrying a woman who was too distracted to notice my affairs. You wouldn't understand this. You were allowed to live for yourself. I," Richard paused to jab a finger to his chest, "have never been allowed to do so."

Tate rolled his eyes and yanked Richard's boots off of his feet. While his brother was an arse who deserved all that Scarlett had done to him, he was still his brother. And if Richard had the chance to experience even half of the love Tate shared with Scarlett, he would be a fortunate man. Maybe then he would be less of a prig.

"Richard, I'm your only living relative, and thus the only other person who cares about the reputation of our family name. If you feel the need to have permission to follow your heart, then here it is." Tate threw his hands up in exasperation. "I, Tate Langley, second in line to the Marquessate, give you permission to marry the woman you love."

"I do not love her." Richard huffed. "My days are just better when I'm around her. She makes me laugh. When we spend time together, we have the most riveting conversations. And, sometimes we don't talk at all." Even drunk, Richard and his wiggling eyebrows could be suggestive.

"That is love you utter knobcock. Don't let Scarlett do all of the fighting around here. Go fetch your lady. Of course, wait until you're sober. Wouldn't want you breaking another arm like you did falling from the willow." Tate shook his brother's elbow.

Richard sat up abruptly and glared at Tate with half-closed eyelids. "Speaking of your woman, she cut me. I'll be scarred for life."

"Like your friend Mr. Michaels. I wonder which woman he enraged to earn his scar," Tate mused, stroking his overly-whiskered chin.

He would need to ask Reynolds for a trim before the big event tomorrow. Scarlett loved his scruff, but she deserved to see him at least cleanly lined without hairs trailing down his neck.

"Who is Mr. Michaels?" Richard slurred, then crumpled back onto the bedspread.

Did Richard seriously not know the name of the man he'd hired to kidnap him? The nerve. Tate shoved his fists in his pockets, fighting the urge to poke Richard's bandaged hand to provide a reminder.

"Do you want the family ring?" Richard mumbled, his

mouth barely moving as he drifted from this plane of consciousness.

"No. I think it is meant for Camilla's hand. Besides, Scarlett does not like pearls. She finds it unfair to steal from oysters." Tate chuckled over the memory of her pontificating about jewelry during one of their promenades.

"But mother and father would have wanted you to have it. They always preferred you, you know."

"Richard, if that was truly the case, I don't think he would have been so critical of me."

"At least he gave you attention. I tried. I tried so hard," Richard blubbered, sounding on the verge of tears. "They always prefer you. You're the more sympathetic sort. The *smart one*. 'Ts why I sent you away the first time. I don't really think all those things I say about you. I just didn't want you around so that I could be favorite for once."

"I know, brother," Tate lied for the sake of ending this uncomfortable argument. "But you were once my favorite if it makes any difference." It was long ago as boys that Tate worshipped the ground Richard walked on, but stubborn affection lingered enough to not extricate his brother from his life completely.

He waited a few moments for a reply from Richard. When instead he heard an ear-splitting snore, he flipped his brother onto his side and clicked the door shut.

When footsteps halted outside her bedchamber door, Scarlett slammed her book shut and tucked it under her pillow.

Since the Wordsworth Ball and her duel, her parents had the habit of stopping by on an hourly basis to admonish her. They expected her full attention for these lectures. The last time she had a book nearby while they were yelling had ended in a shattered window pane in the library and a tear in the cover fabric of her coveted copy of Plato's dialogues. Poor Forbush had to patch the broken glass with a plank of wood, and the man hardly knew how to use a hammer.

Her parents could say nothing which would hurt her or stop her wedding to Tate. She continually opted to allow their rants and only occasionally spoke for the sake of reason. The only argument which had worked in her favor was that at least the money they'd spent for her wedding to Richard would not go to waste. However, it hadn't taken them long to remember she would be marrying a man who had yet to earn a pence from his profession.

When the footsteps rounded the corner of her door frame and did not belong to either Lord or Lady Halloway, both she and Brissot let out breaths of relief then subsequent squeals of excitement.

"Tate, how did you get in here? Did you let yourself in? Is Forbush napping again?"

She'd become quite accustomed to opening the door on her own. She didn't wish to wake the elderly man. This annoyed her father. As he often snarled, *what else are we paying him for?*

"I'm an architect. I know the secrets of a building well enough to get in." Tate tiptoed into her bedchamber.

"So Forbush let you up?"

"Yes." He quietly clicked the door shut. "And he called me Mr. Radley again. Despite that, I think he likes me."

As he crossed the room, Brissot's tail wagged so hard his whole backend wiggled. Tate scratched the puddle of fur's belly, then joined Scarlett at her seat on the edge of her bed.

"I wanted to see how you were doing."

"I'm doing well. My dress was delivered yesterday. How are you? Not thinking about fleeing for India, are you?" She pressed a fist to her mouth to keep from chortling.

"Of course not," he cried incredulously until he noticed her smile. His lips cracked a shaky grin in return. "It's only that—Well, I was worried you would—I know telling me you love me was difficult. I did not want you to feel as if—"

She interrupted him. "Tate. I love you. And I will tell you I love you in front of the entire Ton tomorrow. I'm not afraid to say it anymore. If I can say it with a sword in my hands, I can say it on an altar." Her fingers floated to his face, brushing over the scruff on his cheeks.

"I also came to give you this." He dug around in his pocket

and produced a small, wooden box.

She glanced at the object but was distracted by something still poking out from his pocket.

"What is that?" She pointed to the piece of parchment.

"This," he unfolded the paper, "is my design for Bosworth. I was working on it this morning."

She plucked it from his fingers. It was a drawing of a three-story building. The details were intricate. Each stone, each brick was sketched as if actually carved into the paper.

And he'd said he was not a man of the arts. Frankly, this was far more beautiful than anything she had seen in a museum as of late. It had depth and soul. It felt honest and crafted with intention. And, on the corner of the page in miniscule script read, *Designed by Architect Lord Tate Langley.*

An ache, so deep it was almost painful, grabbed hold of her heart. The seemingly insignificant paper in her hands was the first piece of proof that Tate was free to do whatever he pleased.

"This is beautiful. They will love it," she choked.

He blushed and smiled lopsidedly. "Do you not wish to see the ring?"

"Of course I do. Although, I doubt it could be more beautiful than this." She thumbed his sketch with the care one applies to a babe's cheek, then held out her palm for the box.

Instead, he flipped the lid and slid the jewelry onto her outstretched finger. The center stone was an emerald, small but with a magnificent *jardin* of cracks and swirls within the gem. It was debatable which was more eye-catching. Her gaze certainly didn't know on which work of art to focus, his sketch laying on the bed or the ring.

He squeezed her hand in his. The cut gems bit into her skin.

"I bought it to match your eyes. This way, everywhere you will go, you will carry around a memento of our moment in the *jardin*." He ran his hand through his hair and sighed. "I know the diamonds around it are hardly visible, but I figure they will still shine like stars."

She sniffled and wiped her eyes with the back of her wrist. "You are the most thoughtful man."

"I wouldn't be if not for you. You have inspired me, Scarlett. In my body, in my mind, in the trace of my charcoal, and in the throb of my heart, I carry you. Throughout my days. You are with me here." He grabbed her hand and tapped his head, then splayed her fingers over the finely knit shirt on his chest. "And here."

The view of his darling face was indiscernible as her eyes were drowning in thick, sloppy tears.

"And to think it is possible none of this would have happened if you hadn't been such a terrible dancer," she jested through her crying.

"I doubt that would have stopped you from falling in love with me." He smirked. "At least I know how to keep rhythm in other ways."

"You do?" Scarlett played coy, batting her eyelashes. "I believe I require a demonstration."

With a swoop, he rolled on top of her and dotted kisses along her neck.

She ran her touch up his arms, but pulled away from the damp fabric. "Why is your sleeve wet?"

"Brissot pulled at it when I pet him. I believe he thought it needed a few less stitches. What a thoughtful lad he is."

They both snorted with laughter.

Chapter Twenty-eight

Three Months Later

L ady Tate, to repeat, our deliberation requires you to explain how it was you came to the idea to create said," the magistrate paused to push his spectacles up his sharp nose and read the paper on the bench in front of him, "*School for Scandalous Women.*"

This would be difficult. Scarlett looked back to Tate and his nervous smile in the gallery.

The idea and its fruition hadn't happened at their wedding. Although, the event had been exactly as perfect as it could have been given their courtship had never been prone to smooth operations, fraught with many odd trials from kneed bollocks to river drenchings to criminals about as intelligent as the objects after which they were named.

Brissot had walked Scarlett down the aisle, not so much in a straight line, needing to stop to lick a few shoes. The ceremony had not been interrupted by her sulking parents or Richard as they had all been absent. To Scarlett's dismay, Camilla had also not attended.

There were, however, a few other unexpected interruptions. Lucy Bell had burst out crying when Scarlett had stood at the altar, and she was a singer with a serious set of lungs. Forbush had requested they speak their vows louder. And Lord Neels' sneeze had echoed through the chapel exactly as the vicar pronounced their marriage.

No, the idea hadn't happened then. It had happened less than an hour afterwards at the wedding breakfast. Actually, it'd happened when Scarlett called for a toast in which she announced to the world that she and Ava were starting a business. Thus, The School for Scandalous Women was founded, and Scarlett's reputation amongst the Ton was never more sparkling than when associated with the Duchess. Minutes later, their school had obtained twenty-two new students.

Scarlett had used her raised glass to hide her whispering lips. "Again, I must ask why we decided upon 'Scandalous Women?'"

To which, Ava had replied, "Because it's a whole lot more fun that way. Is it not?"

They'd even received a glowing review from Lord Grovington who had imbibed upon too much of the celebratory champagne. "I have noticed benefits in the bedroom as a result of the lessons May has taken," he'd hiccuped.

"Phillip Grovington, shut your mouth," Lady Grovington had shrieked.

His statement had brought them seven more students via eager married couples.

"So, to clarify, it was initially your idea to open the school?" the magistrate asked. His spectacles slid down his nose as he stared at Scarlett over the rims.

Scarlett slumped in exasperation. A stray curl slipped from her coiffure for the sixth time. She looped it behind her ear, then glanced at the clock behind the magistrate. It was no wonder even her hair was growing tired of this. They'd been here deliberating the case for three hours now.

Tate leaned over the wooden railing and stroked her arm. His gentle, centering touch settled the whirling wind of justifiable rage within her.

There'd been no end to the exhaustion. Just when it'd seemed as if they would have the time to squeeze in a honeymoon, albeit a short one in the countryside at one of Ava's cottages, between running her school and his busy schedule of contracts from the businesses fleeing Clipton Street, they'd been requested to appear in The Court of Chancery.

At least the small townhouse they'd leased had a miniature courtyard big enough for two. Well, three with Brissot. This had proved to be plenty of space for them to take their breakfast together every morning the weather allowed. Sometimes,

Forbush would squeeze in to join them as he had finally saved enough to retire from her parents' employ and now lived with his sister's family in Cheapside.

During these breakfasts, Scarlett would sip her cinnamon tea and Tate his chocolate while they discussed topics such as the preferred sources of building materials for brick and the effects on the people who gathered them or the ethics of redeveloping property in an area where people couldn't afford to pay for the updates. With that one, he'd relented that she was correct no matter how much he believed everyone deserved a beautiful home. They'd agreed he would provide affordable updates for safety purposes to neighborhoods in need.

Luckily, their courtyard also had more than enough space for the regular stargazing dalliance, which was better than any honeymoon. She'd definitely seen her fair share of stars. Her legs shook at the memories.

She pinched herself through her dress, regaining enough righteous anger to continue arguing in this mud-sloppingly slow battle. If someone handed her a sabre, she would have this resolved in minutes.

"Why does it matter whose idea it was?" she shouted. "Either way, we will not be forced to stop conducting business. Our students require the lesson we provide. It affords them the ability to walk freely and confidently through London's streets."

And I require it. It's the only place where I am seen for the greatness I possess. The only time when people value the knowledge

I am so keen to impart. Without it . . . She didn't wish to imagine what life would be like without it. At least she would still have Tate to listen to her ramblings.

Beside her, Ava slammed her fist into her palm. The fleshy noise reverberated through the high ceilings of the courtroom. "Exactly. Lord Cullen here has wasted your time with this case simply because he is distraught over his lack of prospects now he can't force a woman's attentions."

"Please, be civil." The magistrate raised a silencing hand to the air. "His lordship's true concern was the disruption your lessons have caused to the peace of the park."

Scarlett's forehead ached from scrunching too tightly. "And yet men are permitted to shoot there when it so pleases them?"

"That is precisely correct." Lord Cullen at the opposite table proclaimed. He thrust out his arms to gesture and winced.

One arm was in a linen sling and evidently hadn't healed much by the twist of agony in his expression. His ruddy-faced barrister patted him on the back but was swatted away.

According to Ava, rumor was he had demanded a kiss from a woman at a soiree. The woman was apparently a student of theirs. The encounter had supposedly broken his arm and put a hole in a wall.

The magistrate examined the papers silently, then set them down, placing his spectacles atop as a magnifying paperweight. "Lord Cullen, what these ladies are doing is not by my knowledge breaking any laws."

"How can it not?" Lord Cullen cried. "These two and their

absurd beliefs have caused utter mayhem. Just look at my arm!"

"Was your arm injured in the park during one of their lessons?" The magistrate asked.

"Well, no, but it is a direct result of—"

The magistrate cut him off. "My lord, if your injury was not performed by either of these women or did not happen during their teachings, then it is not a part of this case. May we move on?"

So Ava's rumors were true. Scarlett peeked at Tate whose earthy eyes danced with hers in an unspoken jest. While shaking from his silent laughter, a drafting pencil slipped from behind his ear and fell with a *clink* to the oak floor. Everyone swiveled their heads over in his direction.

He never remembered to take those out. Every night before bed, Scarlett found herself pulling them from his hair after he fell asleep with her reading in his arms on the settee in their drawing room. She would pluck them out and jostle him awake, and he would scoop her up, carrying her to bed with him.

She covered her mouth with a paper to hide her twitching cheeks. She mustn't laugh, or snort, in a room full of twenty or more men wearing ridiculously over-powdered wigs.

Besides, who was she fooling? Ava's rumors were always true. Including the one about Bethanne . . . Poor Bethanne. Roberts had proved to be a right arse, leaving Bethanne unexpectedly so soon after their nuptials. If only Bethanne would answer her countless missives. Scarlett's best friend hadn't been the least bit thrilled when Scarlett had opened, how Bethanne had put it, "an indecorous school with an even more indecorous woman." Scarlett wouldn't have guessed how difficult it'd be to keep friends after one finds oneself married and running a business. At least she still had Tate and Ava and Camilla, who was in the habit of sending the occasional letter from the country. And hopefully someday Bethanne would reach out again to mend their friendship.

"To recap, this hearing is to discuss the case of the operations of a women's fencing school in the park." The Magistrate readjusted his wig over his sweating, freckled forehead, then glared at Lord Cullen. "Not to gripe about your qualms with particular women. Even if the women are the founders."

"Frankly, sir, nothing they are doing is inherently illegal," Lord Cullen's barrister stepped from their table and into the well of the court and pulled his drooping trousers up his hips. "It is, however, immoral. Women ought not be burdening themselves with physical labor. If our wives suddenly decide they wish to fight, who's to stay home to care for the children should we return to battle?"

"Counselor, Napoleon is defeated. The chances of us returning to war soon are slim." The barrister Ava had hired, a young man with long, black hair trailing down his neck underneath his wig, leaned on the clerk's station beneath the magistrate's bench.

Lord Cullen's barrister followed suit, leaning against the clerk's station and crowding the poor mousy man behind the desk. "Exactly. Therefore, why should our women be readying themselves for war if there is none on the horizon?"

Both Scarlett and Ava sighed simultaneously.

The magistrate dug his fingertips into his temples, rubbing in a circular motion. "I demand a brief recess to consider both sides. I ask that everyone reconvene in one hour."

One hour. Scarlett had only one hour to find a way to save her livelihood.

She turned to whisper to Tate, "Someone hand me my foil."

Once in the hall outside of the courtroom, Tate wrapped Scarlett in his arms, steadying his jittery wife.

"We cannot lose the business. Without my dowry, we rely on both our incomes," her voice muffled into his chest.

Her warm breath filtered through his shirt's linen. He shivered. Pulling out from their embrace to capture her gaze, he brushed her stray curl from her face. "You will not be made to stop."

"How do you know that?"

He laughed, a hardy, stomach-shaking laugh. When she frowned, he quickly explained his outburst, which was warranted, but thoughtless nonetheless, "Because I know you. You didn't stop fighting for me until you scarred my brother. Should the court rule to cease the school's operations, I imagine some people will be wounded, either in ego or body, but you *will* change their minds. I have no doubt."

"There is always the fact that I'm absurdly wealthy," the Duchess interjected from where she stood examining the portraits of previous magistrates.

Some were slim, some stout. Some tanned, some as pale as clouds. All framed in gilt.

"I believe it is declassée to state your monetary status," Tate retorted. "And quite illegal to bribe a court."

"Not a bribe, dear, a donation," the Duchess clasped her hands behind her back and beamed.

"How about we keep our reticules closed until we hear the verdict," Scarlett suggested, then slid into a chair beneath the portraits.

Scarlett was right. Money would not solve this dilemma. Although comfortable with his salary, Tate had no extra funds to give, and Scarlett's parents had spent what remained of her dowry on themselves when they'd learned she was marrying him.

Even if they had the funds, money wouldn't fix the core issue; some of the Ton found what she and the Duchess did honorable while others found it detestable, that they were blurring the lines of propriety.

No matter how much Tate wished, nothing he could do would bridge that divide.

The magistrate ordered everyone into the courtroom exactly at the one hour mark. Scarlett was certain. The clock in the hall had ticked 3,600 times. She'd counted. Well, she'd asked Tate to count.

The magistrate cleared his throat, and Ava reached for Scarlett's hand, her nails biting into flesh. Scarlett winced at the pain, but didn't release herself, too nervous to move.

After surveying the room from his bench, the magistrate took a deep breath. "The court rules the following verdict. The School for Scandalous Women is no longer allowed to conduct business—"

"Yes!" Lord Cullen interrupted.

"Sir, allow me to finish," The magistrate raised his voice, glaring at Lord Cullen. "The School for Scandalous Women is no longer allowed to conduct their business *in the park*. They are, however, permitted to continue their lessons within the confines of a private structure."

Ava let go of Scarlett's hands, clapping so hard a few wigged men covered their ears and so loudly Lord Cullen's stomping tantrum was deafened.

Relief, a cold wash, flowed from the crown of Scarlett's head and over her face. She nearly collapsed onto the table in front of her. Her hands caught her fall with a *whack* against the wood.

Their school was saved. Their students would still have the lessons they loved, the teachings they needed to protect themselves. And she would still have her very reasons for being. Besides her husband, of course.

She glanced at Tate who was busy pumping his fists in the air.

She, however, did not join the rejoicing, instead gathering her things and filing out of the room after everyone else. The time for celebration was later, after she found a private structure to continue operations. Where could one find a building which was safe enough for women to frequent often unaccompanied? Certainly not Clipton Street.

Deep in thought, she took one step out onto the street full of carriages before Tate yanked her back into his arms away from the traffic.

Shaking Tate's shoulders, she cried, "Clipton Street."

He and Ava shared a set of raised brows.

Indeed, Clipton Street was the key. Many businesses were leaving the neighborhood as crime flourished under the rule of The Spare Boys, and who were they turning to? Her husband.

"Ava, it is time to open your reticule." Scarlett winked at her friend, then wrapped her arms around her husband's neck. "Dear?"

"Yes, my love?" Tate warily questioned.

"Tell your boss Asher Alexander your apprenticeship is over. I need a building."

Scarlett planted a kiss on Tate's cheek and marched away down the cobbled streets of London, armed for her school's next chapter.

Epilogue

Notice: Until the completion of the new School for Scandalous Women by Asher Alexander & Co, led by Architect Lord Tate Langley, all classes will be conducted in the gardens of Her Grace, The Dowager Duchess Halfurst's London property, read the flyer nailed to every tree in the park and pasted to every lamppost in Mayfair.

While instructing, Scarlett could not help herself from stealing the occasional glance at her husband hard at work. The crew constructing the school on Ava's land was comprised of many work-hardened men, but her husband was the only one she saw.

With his shirt sleeves rolled over his muscular forearms and sweat beading down the back of his neck, she wanted to bathe him in herself, drenching him with her body as she turned to liquid. She craved for him to pick her up, throw her over his shoulder, carry her into the laurels, and take her.

There she would tell him, with nothing and no one between them, how much she was proud of him for building himself into the man he always wanted to be. How, without his support, nothing she called her own would be hers. How, if she'd never met him, she would never have returned to who she was at her core.

She would say all of her devotions to him with just three words.

"I love you."

Tate leaned against a half-finished brick wall. He caught his breath, contentedly exhausted from his day's work running around the site to monitor the construction of his wife's school. This was his life now. Tiring, but with such rewarding outcomes.

Across the lawn, Scarlett conducted the final steps of a lesson. He snuck up on her, hiding behind the trunk of a beech tree while awaiting her class's traditional conclusion with a bow.

She glowed under the late-afternoon sun. Bliss radiated from her. She was the brightest star. The strongest gale. The heat of a hot chocolate in cold palms, and the invigorating chill of a night's breeze. A man with very little talent in all arts not involving drafting charcoal, he obviously had no sufficient ballad or verse to describe his ardency for his wife's presence. What he did have, however, was the knowledge that she was a force. One with which he would always wish to reckon.

Observing her in secret, he had the clearest picture of her vigor and spirit. Pride swelled in his chest. Every one of her pupils so clearly admired her compassion and acceptance as well.

Among those in attendance were a number of bluestockings, some society matrons, and even a few men. These fellows had been banned from men's fencing clubs due to their romantic preferences—Scarlett had chosen to keep the word *women* in the school's name as it helped to deflect the attention of law enforcement away from these men who attended in secret. All of her students were all smiling, laughing when they accidentally dropped their swords or completed the wrong strike, and complimenting each other.

"Have a good evening. Don't forget to practice your steps at home." She waved her students away, then pointed to one in particular. "Lady Irving, I see you. The sword stays with me."

Lady Irving giggled and returned the weapon to the pile on the lawn, skipping away.

With grass-muffled steps, Tate ran up behind Scarlett, slid his arms around her waist, and spun her around. Her arousing aroma of cinnamon and heat misted into his nose. He buried his head in the curls around her neck, breathing her in.

"*Oof!* Hello, my love." She exhaled a snort, breathily laughing.

"Come with me." He set her down and walked her with hands to her hips into the hedges.

Together, they nestled chest to chest into a laurel bush, hidden from the world. Leaves caught in her hair as a sort of viridescent crown.

With a seductive slip of her lips, she wound her arms around his neck. "How did you know I wanted this?"

"Because I know you." He planted a kiss on each of her flushed cheeks, then met in the middle, brushing his lips to her luscious mouth. "And because I've caught you setting your sights on me all morning."

The Marquess is due for his redemption in autumn 2026. Don't miss out!

Author's Note

While many of the historical romance novels I love have plots which are rooted in history, I felt a pull to create a story that was highly unlikely. Not impossible, but improbable. I felt like a swindler for a while, peddling a story based on the history of possibility.

How likely was it that a young woman in Regency London could have become a fencing coach and open a self-defense school? As you may suspect, not very. According to historical accounts, the first notable women's fencing educations of the Western world were run by men, Colonel Thomas Monstery of the United States and Hans Hartl of Austria, in the late 19th century. While touring the United States, Hartl placed his female students in the Amateur Athletics Union's fencing championship, marking the first time women competed in a prestigious fencing event. Monstery taught famed swordswoman Ella Hattan, also known as Jaguarina. She was renowned for defeating scores of champion men in combat and was of the philosophy that her talent made her no less womanly than her fellow woman, believing that the nature of womanhood allows women to be both beautiful and strong. Similar to Scarlett's training, Ella's expertise had humble origins of knife-fighting practice in her mother's home.

Despite the absence of women's fencing in the Regency era, I hope I crafted a believable tale for the sake of all women throughout history who would have benefited from such knowledge.

Of course, there are still *some* tantalizing bits of history in this story.

In the 19th century, there was an influx of criminal organizations in England's restless working class. As these gangs gained power, influence, and money, their crimes worsened. They were start-ups of upstarts, if you will. The Spare Boys was inspired by such groups. As a collective of under-educated, under-employed men run by a second son, a spare, The Spare Boys were the remainders and the forgotten of society.

The firm that hired Tate, Asher Alexander & Co, was inspired by real-life Regency Architect Daniel Asher Alexander. Alexander was known for designing the colonnades which line the Queen's House in Greenwich.

Brissot is named after power couple Jacques-Pierre and Félicité Brissot de Warville. As a journalist and politician, Jacques-Pierre wrote philosophical and legislative works, including the *Théorie des lois criminelles* in 1781 which criticized the death penalty. He was an abolitionist and founded the anti-slavery group Société des amis des Noirs in 1788. In 1782, he and his wife moved to London where they associated with local philosophers and collaborated to form the *Journal du Lycée de Londres*, a publication which encouraged readers to question absolute power. This publication failed, but I like to believe Scarlett got her hands on a few of their early copies. Jacques-Pierre was inducted into the American Philosophical Society as a Frenchman in 1789. He went on to be a major figure in the French revolution, calling for the end of tyranny throughout all of Europe.

Félicité was also a force with which to be reckoned. When her husband was imprisoned for his radical ideas, she freed him using her connections with the Duke of Orléans. It is posited that she translated Mary Wollstonecraft's essay *Vindication of the Rights of Woman*, a work Scarlett was sure to have enjoyed, into French. She accomplished all of this while raising their children.

Even though Scarlett's pup cannot be compared to these two intelligent people, Scarlett named Brissot after them as a constant message that we, every one of us, deserve to be who we truly are not at the expense or gain of others.

I wrote this novel for myself, and I wrote it for you, whoever you are out there who chose to take a chance on Scarlett's story and a no-name author. I look forward to engaging with you someday. En garde!

Acknowledgements

Writing is a lonelier profession than one would think. Very few people ask how your books are coming along, or how it is to be balancing two careers, or what it's like trying to ride the perilous sea of publishing. For me, that narrowed down to only a handful of people.

My mother, a teacher by trade and nature, accepted this novel as if it were her grandchild and midwifed it into existence. Mom, you were my first beta reader, then my second beta reader after I tossed my shitty first draft—what a mess that was, right?—and then my first-pass editor. I'll never second guess your keen eye because without you, my siblings and I would have had to suffer to achieve our degrees and careers. By proxy, you hold a Master's in Public Health and Infectious Diseases, a Master's in Higher Education, and my Bachelor's in English and Writing. You were always our editor, fact-checker, and loudest cheerleader. You were one of the few people who encouraged me without a doubt to pursue the arts, and look what I have to show for it now!

Teachers have a habit of doing that, don't they? Guiding the ones in their lives to be their best selves and produce their greatest work.

Another former teacher I have to thank is my friend and fellow historical romance author Addie Bealer. Whenever I question my work, I recall your beta reading feedback and all of the kind things you've said to support me. You were the first friend I made in the writing field and are still the best. I will forever be a fighter in your corner because I've never doubted whether you'd be in mine. Now let's dress up as Regency debs and go sell some books!

I would also like to thank author Andie James. Your beta reading helped me embrace my bonkers style of storytelling and give up trying to pretend to be something I am not: decorous, put-together, and well-mannered. And I am all the better off for it.

To my other beta readers, including author Meredith E. Phillips, thank you for generously giving your time and effort. You each challenged and encouraged me to kill my darlings, including lengthening Scarlett's declaration of love. It was a painful process, but I think it hits harder to the truth I hoped to convey that women can experience the over-cerebralization of romance (let's call it what it is, and now everyone say it with me: commitment issues) as frequently as men.

To the Discord girlies, thank you for sending me pictures of who you would cast as Richard because he is sooo not my type and for listening to me soapbox about the sexual power women wield in a hetero dynamic.

And finally, to my husband. As you well know, I know many words, speak a multitude of languages and dialects. I hold verbiage in my head and whip the correct phrase out for you whenever your words fail you—as you do with numbers for me. I give you three options to choose from, and two more in other languages even though you didn't ask. However, this time I don't know what to say. As Scarlett would proclaim, "It was ironic, truly, that when a man finally wanted to know her thoughts, her mind nearly wiped clear." It is better this way, my mind being clear. You are the only person who has ever been able to quiet the chaos of anxiety and Sprench (Spanish-French. ™ by yours truly. Not really, but I should) and the countless New Girl quotes rattling around in my skull. You helped me organize that chaos into a writing career. You unknowingly wrote my love story before I even picked up my pen again. It's you and me against the world, Babe.

About the Author

Rebekka DeReu is a romance author masquerading as a marketing executive. When she isn't at her desk, she's exploring South Carolina, where she lives with her husband and their English setter and German shorthaired pointer. Together, they enjoy testing gluten free recipes to recreate the dishes she loved before her celiac disease diagnosis. A true bluestocking, she is thoroughly unaccomplished in the pianoforte, singing, the arts (unless you count paint by numbers), and embroidery, with her only talent of exception being a knowledge of the modern languages. To stay up to date on her future novels, follow her on Instagram @rebekkadereuauthor.